Love Like Your Heart's On Fire

Sally-Anne Lomas

Story Mach\ne

Love Like Your Heart's On Fire, copyright © Sally-Anne Lomas, 2023

Print ISBN: 9781912665181
Ebook ISBN: 9781912665198
Published by Story Machine
130 Silver Road, Norwich, NR3 4TG;
www.storymachines.co.uk

Sally-Anne Lomas has asserted her right under Section 77 of the Copyright, Designs and Patents Act 1988 to be identified as the author of this work.

All rights reserved. No part of this publication may be reproduced, stored in a retrieval system, or transmitted in any form or by any means, graphic, electronic, recorded, mechanical, or otherwise, without the prior written permission of the publisher or copyright holder.

This publication is sold subject to the condition that it shall not, by way of trade or otherwise, be lent, re-sold, hired out or otherwise circulated without the publisher's prior consent in any form of binding or cover other than that in which it is published and without a similar condition including this condition being imposed on the subsequent purchaser.

Set in Garamond.

Printed and bound in the UK by Seacourt Ltd.

Story Machine is committed to planet positive publishing. Our world is better off for every single book we print.

Story Machine is committed to the environment.
This document is printed using processes that are:

 100% Net Carbon Negative

 100% Renewable Energy

 100% ISO14001

 100% eco-friendly simitri® toner

 100% Recyclable Stock

 Zer0% waste to landfill

Printed by **seacourt** – proud to be counted amongst the top environmental printers in the world

Advance praise for *Love Like Your Heart's On Fire*

'A marvellous heart-breaking, heart-warming rollercoaster ride. Pen is passionate, strong and vulnerable, I was cheering and crying for her.'
Iain B. MacDonald, director of *Shameless*, *Wayne* and *Mansfield Park*

'Very funny. *Love Like Your Heart's On Fire* is a beautiful novel full of warmth and compassion.'
Hannah, reader

'A celebration of universal love. The evocation of Extinction Rebellion is authentic and gives the reader a felt-sense of Earth-love too.'
Dr. Rupert Read, Director of the Climate Majority Project, and author of *Why Climate Breakdown Matters*

Praise for *Live Like Your Head's On Fire*

'A gripping story, full of honesty, energy, heartache and joy. I love this book. Sally-Anne Lomas is a new and powerful writer.'
Yvvette Edwards, MAN Booker Prize Longlisted author of *A Cupboard Full of Coats* and *The Mother*

'The likeable Pen Flowers is engaging and spirited throughout.'
Suzi Feay, Best New Books for Young Adults 2021, *The Financial Times*

'An exhilarating, funny, heartwarming debut that will inspire you to follow your dreams.'
C. J. Flood, author of *Infinite Sky* and *Nightwanderers*

'Amazingly accomplished and immensely readable. A brilliant debut.'
Vulpes Libris blog

'Shows how life changing and life affirming finding your 'thing' can be. In the case of Pen Flowers, her 'thing' is dancing. When Pen dances she feels alive and connected – although like in all good novels she has to go through a series of trials and tribulations to succeed.'
Amanda Addison, author of *Laura's Handmade Life* and *Boundless Sky*

'I absolutely loved this book. An excellent story, uplifting and comforting, with great warmth at its heart.'
Reader

'Written with buoyancy and wit, with a turn of phrase that had me chuckling and snorting with laughter, *Live Like Your Head's on Fire* is a wonderful coming-of-age novel about discovering and following your dreams. Pen's journey is full of comedy, pain, embarrassment, longing and passion but what Lomas captures so well are the uncertainties and shifting friendships of adolescence. And in Pen's new friends, the vulnerable but dangerous Melody and the irrepressible optimist Vivienne, Lomas has created two real-as-life characters whom you can't help but warm to. This is a moving, satisfying debut.'
Richard Lambert, poet, novelist, and author of *The Wolf Road*

'A terrific debut novel, that fizzes and pops with the energy of youth. A story of dreams and friendship – the writing is warm and witty, but never shies away from the more painful aspects of adolescence. There are many laugh out loud moments, however I was also deeply moved and ultimately found myself cheering for Pen Flowers and her indomitable spirit.'
Reader

Love Like Your Heart's On Fire

For Anthony Frank Wright with all my love

'Set your life on fire – seek those who fan the flames.'
Rumi

'We do anger. We do love. In this world
to love is to resist.'
George Monbiot

'We are living in unprecedented times,' Jock spoke softly into the silence. 'Not only for our species but for all species on this planet. We take from the planet, but we have forgotten to return our respect for it.'

I was standing in the large dance studio at Tartan Fling's headquarters. There was a wall of windows along one side, with mirrors down the other, so the sunlight fractured into circles of swirling silver sparks and made me squint.

'Imagine a creature, one you care about', Jock demanded. 'Don't overthink, the first idea that pops into your head.'

Birds. The blackbirds. They sang to me this morning. Even in London, in a strange house, the familiar liquid golden stream.

'Dance your care, find the feeling and let the feeling move you.'

I tried not to look at the other dancers. To stop worrying about whether I was getting this right. I pictured the blackbirds on our lawn at home in Birmingham. Imagined a world without their morning song. I tilted my head as the birds did, hopped, and pecked, copying their movements as a way of connecting.

Reaching inside to find the feeling, I dived into a well of fear. I must look like an idiot. Everyone else was professional and used to improvising. Dear blackbirds give me courage. You can do this, Pen Flowers. You're living the dream, dancing with Tartan Fling.

Mum and Dad had agreed I could do work experience with the choreographer Jock Briggs. Dad drove me down to London yesterday. I was staying with the company manager in a three-storey terrace house a short walk from their studio.

This morning I'd helped in the office, putting flyers in envelopes, and answering the phone. The company was starting a new piece called *Respect* about the climate crisis and I hoped I'd get to watch some of their rehearsals. But then Jock called me upstairs into the studio and said everyone was happy for me to join in the dancing.

'Now what makes you angry? What makes you boil?' I could barely hear Jock's voice he spoke so quietly. 'Reach into the feeling and move with the anger.' There was a strange whirring soundtrack, more noise than music. I visualised great sweeps of rainforest being hacked down. My rage spurted out in a gush of arm-waving fury.

'Don't demonstrate, feel.' Jock spoke to the whole room, but I was sure he was correcting me. 'Forget about abstract ideas, find something personal. Something that got your goat this morning. Did someone push you on the tube? Has a friend let you down? Be specific, dig in.'

Before he left last night, Dad had said, 'make sure you phone Mum. She'll be worrying.' That pissed me off! What about me being on my own and scared? Didn't he think about that? Why was it always about Mum? She should call to see if I was okay. Dad could call her. He was the one who'd walked out and left us. Mum's mental health wasn't my responsibility.

I was hunched over, eyes scrunched up and jaw rigid. My hands had turned into claws. I was making small jerky movements that were tight and pointed.

'Good Pen. Yeah, that's it. That's real.' Jock was smiling at me. 'Own your anger. Use it, move with it.'

Part 1

Dance of the Bewitched

1

The new English teacher, Mrs Mulligan, had been a professional actor before she started at the Kings School for Girls. She'd been on the telly in an episode of *Midsummer Murders*. If that wasn't exciting enough, she sent the sixth form into a frenzy by announcing that this year the school play would be a joint venture with the boys' School. Never had there been such enthusiasm to participate.

Vivienne Cooper, my best friend and drama diva, dragged me along to auditions.

'Come on Pen, it'll be loads more fun if we're in it together.' I had no interest in acting but I stumbled through the embarrassment of standing on stage in front of Mrs Mulligan and a teacher from the Boys' School mumbling my lines, and was rewarded with a minor part as one of the girls in the chorus.

When the cast list was posted on the notice board a crowd gathered eager to see who had nabbed the major roles. No one was surprised that Coco Dunn was playing the sexy temptress. She was tall and slender with a sheet of platinum blonde hair that shimmered down to her waist. Her Mum was a model. But there was general confusion to find that Vivienne had got the starring role. At Kings, Vivienne was dismissed as the fat girl with a bursary who sold rejected chocolate bars from the Cadbury's factory where her Mum worked. She was in a youth theatre group and had done loads of performing. But as she never mentioned this at school, I was the only one who wasn't amazed at her landing the female lead. I'd seen her act. She was awesome.

Walking away from the notice board I could tell Vivienne was thrilled, but she was careful not to show her feelings until we were alone together in the library. Viv had learned that at Kings it was best to keep a low-profile if you wanted an easy life. I was working on my low-profile skills.

The library was an L-shaped room on the first floor. Viv and I had a favourite spot in the far corner out of sight of the door. There was a small table underneath a window that looked out over the hockey pitches. We could talk here without being overheard.

'Oh my God Pen, it's such a difficult role. Elizabeth Proctor, she's the wronged wife, she's got to be uptight and angry but still sympathetic. I need the audience to side with me rather than Coco. How am I going to do that?'

'You'll find a way.'

Vivienne sighed, looking worried, but then brightened.

'And you got a part, that'll be fun.'

'I don't know why I let you bully me into it. I'd much rather be dancing.'

'You're always on about wanting a boyfriend – now's your opportunity.'

'As if any of the boys will be fit?'

'You never know, keep an open mind.'

Vivienne had met the man of her dreams when she was fourteen, whereas here was I, sixteen years old and barely been kissed. Seemed to me that loving someone was an open invitation to pain. Didn't stop me from craving it though. I was desperate to throw myself into the flames. Passion at any cost. But I wasn't convinced that the love of my life would be found in the Kings school play.

*

'Welcome everyone.' Mrs Mulligan stood at the front with Mr Andrews from the Boys' School next to her. We were in the hall, sitting in a circle of chairs, boys on one side, girls on the other. There were two empty chairs between the last of the girls and the first of the boys. No one had planned it that way, but it was early days for inter-sex mingling.

Mrs Mulligan certainly knew how to hold the stage. She was tiny but dressed in a red sheath dress with shiny shoulder-length caramel-coloured hair and bright red lipstick. Her movements were quick and energetic, like a little bright-eyed bird, all peck and flap. There was an intensity that made her unlike any of the other teachers.

'The play we're doing is *The Crucible* by Arthur Miller, about the witch hunt trials in Salem in the late 17th Century.' She handed a pile of play scripts to the boy on her left and he passed them around. 'It's a truly wonderful drama, the subject matter as shocking and relevant today as it was when Miller wrote it in 1952, and I'm confident we're going to make a marvellous production. To kick off I'll go through the cast list and can the actor playing the role stand up and I'll introduce their character.' And off she went.

Grant Barker was playing the leading man, John Proctor. He stood up and took a mock bow to much tittering from the girls' side of the room. Vivienne was playing his wife, Elizabeth Proctor, hurt, loyal, and strong. As Vivienne rose from her seat Mrs Mulligan said, 'Vivienne's a member of the prestigious National Youth Theatre. I saw her performance as Mother Courage and she was excellent.' Vivienne blushed deep puce and sat down. The other girls stared at her as if reassessing. This play was going to do wonders for her social standing. Coco was playing Abigail; the beautiful young girl whom John Proctor has an affair with.

I was playing one of the young servant girls who, egged on by Abigail, accuse the Proctors of witchcraft. 'Mercy Lewis – Pen Flowers,' Mrs Mulligan called out and I stood up, 'described by the playwright as a fat, sly servant girl who's been seen dancing naked in the forest.' I sat down quickly, glaring at Vivienne. I had not signed up for this! Some of the boys were sniggering and whispering to each other. There was no way I was staying for this. I started to get up, but Vivienne put her hand on my arm and pulled me down.

'Keep calm,' she whispered.

Mr Andrews drew a finger across his throat to tell the boys to cut it out and they stopped. Mrs Mulligan looked over to their side of the room and said, 'Sixth formers or six-year-olds? Obviously, Pen is lovely and slim, but,' she turned to look at me, 'I'm told you're a dancer and I've got an idea for the start of the show.' She moved on.

'See?' Vivienne whispered. 'She's great, isn't she? No-nonsense.'

'Reverend Hale – Mark Burrows,' Mrs Mulligan continued and a tall thin boy with a strangely small head stood up. He was the one who had come up with the name Giant Arse Movie to describe a film of me dancing that had been shared around the Boys' School last year. The video featured a zoomed-in shot of my school skirt tucked up and my bum cheeks filling the screen. Thinking about it still filled me with shame. I knew my face had gone red.

Once everyone had been introduced there was a read-through of the play. It went on forever and as I only had three lines, there was a lot of sitting still and listening which I wasn't good at. Vivienne was the only one who brought any of the words alive. Once we'd done my first scene I drifted off. I'd won a scholarship to Kings, one of the best schools in Birmingham, and Dad had insisted that I stay on into the sixth form to do A Levels. But because I was determined to be a dancer, there'd been much painful negotiation until both Kings and Dad had finally agreed that I could go to City College, one day a week, to do Dance A Level. I liked History and English, but dancing was my true passion.

Tomorrow, we had our first choreography assignment and I wanted to try out the impro exercises I'd learnt in the summer with Tartan Fling. I moved my feet on the floor, tapping out different rhythms.

'Ouch!' I cried out as Vivienne elbowed me viciously in the side. Mrs Mulligan was looking at me with a raptor's gaze. My third and final line had arrived.

'It's on the beam, behind the rafter,' I said with none of the drama the line deserved. The room's attention moved swiftly off me and back to Coco. This was the part where the girls go hysterical and see evil spirits attacking them. The room livened up. The end of the play was also good with Vivienne's voice quivering with emotion as she forgave Proctor for his infidelity and declared her love. Grant Barker came over as way too full of himself, but wasn't as bad as I'd expected. When he went to the scaffold, I felt tears gathering in my eyes. Vivienne got the last line of the play which she delivered with power and dignity.

As we got up to leave Mrs Mulligan came over to speak to Viv.

'Excellent start Vivienne, you'll have the audience in floods.'

Vivienne blushed from her chest to her parting.

'Thank you,' she mumbled.

'But it's actually Pen I wanted to talk to.' My head jerked up. With luck she'd been so appalled by my terrible acting that she was going to drop me from the play. 'This idea for the start of the play.'

'There's no way I'm dancing naked.' I said quickly. Vivienne might be mesmerized by Mrs Mulligan's wide bright smile, but I could see the arrows of determination in her eyes. This woman would stop at nothing to get what she wanted.

She dismissed my concerns with a flick of her wrist as if waving away an irritating fly.

'Totally inappropriate. But the girls are seen dancing in the forest, so I want you to choreograph a short primitive dance sequence. Shades of voodoo, led by Tabitha, the slave. I'm imagining dim, shadowy lighting, a backdrop creating the forest, and the girls in loose shifts. Can you do it?'

I could see it immediately. Green light on white cotton, rhythmical African dance moves, something raw and shocking.

'It would make a provocative opening to the play,' Mrs Mulligan continued. I was about to say I'd think about it when Viv could contain herself no longer and burst out.

'Oh, that would be sooo brilliant. Pen you'd be brilliant. What a brilliant idea.' Vivienne's enthusiasm sometimes had the opposite of its intended effect. I considered saying 'no' just to resist the pressure. They both faced me, so I was caught on the triangulated point of two demanding stares.

'Okay,' I said, giving in. 'Yes, I'd like to do that. Only I'm in college on Wednesdays and…'

'Fabulous.' Mrs Mulligan having got her way was already off to her next victim. 'I'll be in touch to set up your rehearsals.'

The sun was setting as I got on the bus to go home. The number eleven Outer Circle Bus route was the longest in Europe, a twenty-seven-mile loop around Birmingham.

Some days I felt as if I spent most of my life on the number eleven bus.

Vivienne who lived five minutes from Kings would already have changed into her sweatpants. But I had miles to go before I got home. From the front seat of the top deck, I watched the orange ball of the sun turn the sky damson and magenta, all the deep reds, as it sank over the roof tops. The trees were blazing copper and gold so for a moment the grey streets of Kings Heath were on fire.

The bus ride was my dream and drift time, when I unhooked myself from the world and floated into imaginary spaces. The movement of the bus gave me my best ideas.

But today my mind kept returning to the stupid Giant Arse video. I'd been so upset I'd run away to London and spent a hideous night by myself on the streets. But even though it was the most terrifying experience of my life I realised that surviving that night and then dancing for Jock the following morning had proved how much dancing meant to me. Without that, I wouldn't have won the battle to do Dance A Level. So maybe in a weird way the video had been a good thing.

But I hated thinking of that disgusting clip of me still out there on the internet. Supposing I did fancy one of the boys in the play? There was no way they'd be interested after seeing me looking so gross and ugly. I was destined to die lonely and unloved.

I was feeling sorry for myself as the bus pulled into Bournville Green. Looking down at the pavement I saw Grant Barker get off. He looked up and saw me watching him. He was the type that'd find the video hilarious. I pretended to look at my phone.

As the bus lurched off up the hill an idea leapt out of nowhere. My fingers curled into a fist, and I dug my elbow into my side.

'Yes!'

If boys like Grant were laughing at me for having a Giant Arse, well, I was going to give them arse! Arse with bells on! I'd choreograph a dance for the play that was dark and dirty with thrusting buttocks everywhere. Instead of running from my shame, I'd flaunt it.

2

'You're Penelope Flowers, right?'

A tall, boyish girl was towering over me. I smiled up at her.

'Most people call me Pen.'

'I'm Frieda. We're working together this afternoon. On the duets.'

'Oh.' I hadn't even realised we were doing duets.

'The list's up on the notice board.' The notice board was also news to me. I was inching my way into college life. So far, I'd come in, done the lessons, and left. That was as much as I could manage. At lunchtime, if the day was sunny, I sat outside on my own and ate in the courtyard where there were benches.

'You don't say much do you.' Frieda sat astride the bench opposite and gave me a huge grin. Of course, I knew who she was. I'd watched her in class, she magnetized attention. She had thick black hair that was shaved at the sides but with a big curly quiff tumbling over her forehead. She wore huge trainers and black ripped jeans with a hoody. Her dark brown eyes were bright and scrunched up as if she was about to laugh. 'Yeah,' she continued before I could answer. 'We're doing opposition, so I guess they put us together because I'm tall and you're short.'

'How do you know all this?' I asked wondering if I'd missed an email. I let the 'short' reference go for now.

'I was just chillin' with Joe.' Joe Thorne was one of our teachers, a former ballet dancer whom I found alarming.

The thought of being able to 'chill' with him made me look at Frieda with awe. 'Don't worry,' she gave me the full blast of her mega smile, 'I'm used to teeny weenies, my Mum's your height. We can put in some lifts if you're up for it – I should be able to throw you about.' She grinned again and I found myself smiling back.

'Just don't drop me,' I said.

In class that afternoon Frieda proved to be completely right. We had two hours to work on a duet that explored the idea of opposites. Frieda, I soon discovered, knew everything that was going on before anybody else. That was her superpower.

'Okay here's what I think we should do,' Frieda launched in straight away. We were standing around the large dance studio in pairs. 'We should do opposition not opposite – standing up to power – like with Me Too or Black Lives Matter or LGBTQ rights – resistance to oppression – that's opposites in a way that really means something.' Frieda spoke fiercely, stalking around me and making punching movements in the air. Dressed for dancing in leggings and a vest top I could see the muscles in her arms. She must work out at the gym to get biceps like that. I wasn't used to other people having strong opinions about dance. She was so forceful that I felt a bit steamrollered. I had ideas too.

'Yeah, that's true. But I was thinking we could undermine the obvious ways we think about opposites – like people say, 'Big and Strong', and 'Small and Weak', but why not small and powerful, big and vulnerable.'

Frieda stopped pacing and stared at me. 'That's good. I like that. Just because I'm tall I'm somehow not allowed to have feelings. It's bullshit.'

'And because I'm small people treat me like a child.'

'Let's do yours,' Frieda said, and I was surprised she'd

let go of her idea so easily.

'I think we could put both ideas together. Look at Greta Thunberg, she was younger than us - a school kid when she went on strike taking on the government over climate change.'

'Yeah, and like Stephen Lawrence, he was an athlete but he still got murdered.'

I didn't know who Steven Lawrence was, but I didn't like to admit it. Frieda read my blank expression correctly.

'He was an eighteen-year-old boy doing A Levels who wanted to be an architect. He was standing at a bus stop when a gang of white boys murdered him. Just because he was black. They didn't even know him.'

'My God, that's terrible.'

'Yeah, you could say that!' Frieda sounded angry. 'And the police didn't bother prosecuting. Said there wasn't enough evidence. His Mum campaigned for twenty years to get justice.'

I felt bad for not knowing. I hoped I hadn't offended her.

'Let's start with those two examples,' I said quickly, 'and improvise some moves. See what develops.'

'Right on.' Frieda punched me in the arm gently.

I'd never worked with anyone like this before, as equals sharing ideas, and creating together. There was no one at Kings who was passionate about dancing the way I was. To be making something new with someone as engaged as me felt weird and challenging, but in a good way. I tried out some moves and Frieda responded. We were riffing off each other. I had a genius thought.

'I know – why don't I lift you?'

Frieda burst out laughing. 'Get you Mrs Ambitious! You couldn't. Do you know how much I weigh?' She banged her thigh. 'I'm 100% muscle.'

'Let's find a way to make it work – we'll be doing the total opposite of what anyone would expect.'

'Yeah sister, I like you. The Mighty Pen. Let's do it.'

Lifting Frieda was hard, and I kept dropping her. We were laughing but we weren't mucking about, we were completely into it. Frieda was heavy, but she was also strong and graceful. I loved the way she moved. We made a great team.

Our final piece was a protest dance that used our different body shapes in unexpected ways. Joe seemed pleased when we showed our duet to the class.

'Well done Frieda and Pen. Original use of relative body weights, you worked as a unit, showed trust.'

'That's our first 'A' in the bag,' Frieda whispered to me. She was so confident. I admired that. 'Let's get a drink,' she suggested after we'd showered and changed.

I hesitated. Even if I left now, I wouldn't get home until after six, and I had loads of homework to do before school tomorrow. But this could be the start of a new friendship.

'Sure, let's.' I followed Frieda to the first-floor canteen where I'd been too shy to go on my own. Frieda, I hoped, was going to open doors into exciting new worlds. College was so different to Kings – for a start, there were boys everywhere. Not many doing dance A Level, but in the corridors and in the café, there were lads sitting in packs and watching as we walked by.

'Wednesdays you get the apprentices in, plumbers, decorators, and electricians,' Frieda nodded at the boys. 'I thought about doing plumbing – you can earn good money but imagine spending your life up to your elbows in shit! Urghhh!'

We got our drinks and sat down at a table for two near the window. I expected Frieda to do the talking but instead, she asked me loads of questions and I found myself telling her about Kings, about Mum and Dad splitting up, and me doing work experience in London. In about ten minutes she had my whole life story.

'Yeh well, at least your Dad's still around,' she said when I told her about Mum and Dad, 'I barely know my Dad. He buggered off when I was a baby. Mum brought me up by herself. His parents, my grandparents, they live in Handsworth, so I see them and they're alright. Mum says it's important that I know about my Jamaican heritage even though Dad was born in Birmingham. Mum comes from Portugal. You gotta meet her. She's an incredible artist. She teaches here at the college. I used to go to school in Handsworth, but I got grief from some of the other girls for being gay. Here I can do Art, Dance and Politics A Levels. Handsworth thought that was an odd combo but makes total sense to me.'

A pretty girl with short blonde hair walked past our table and Frieda stopped talking to give her a whole-body smile.

'She's in my art class.'

'Is she gay?' I wondered how Frieda could tell. She shrugged.

'Who knows but she's cute. I've got a weakness for blondes. What about you? Any love action?'

I laughed, there was something so buoyant and irrepressible about Frieda. She was like a giant puppy.

'There was this guy Mick who I was seeing. He was alright, but I was never sure about him. I guess I didn't fall in love and now he's finished his A Levels and gone off traveling with his mate.'

'I want to go to Brazil. We've got relatives out there that I've never met. You could come too. Hey, we should dance in the Carnival.'

Hanging out with Frieda was definitely going to take me places - even if we didn't get as far as Rio.

3

The streetlamps had come on and the sky was turning inky as I walked down Knightlow Road from the bus stop. The leaves on the trees had started falling, decorating the pavements in patterns of yellow, red, and copper. Pretty soon now I'd be leaving for school in the dark and coming home in the dark. The night was closing in around me.

I turned the corner and saw a small red car parked in our drive. Dad drove a green Volvo and the lady from the mental health team who was helping Mum came in the mornings. As I squeezed past, I peered inside the car but didn't get any clues. I unlocked the front door twitching with suspicion. What was Mum up to?

'Whose car is that?' I shouted from the hall, taking off my coat and dropping my bag on the floor. The bag weighed a ton filled to bursting with dance gear and schoolbooks. My spine was starting to curve from carrying it. Mum came bustling out of the living room her face flushed pink and her eyes dangerously bright.

'It's mine. Ours,' she said beaming. Mum had agoraphobia and for the last ten years she'd not been outside the house on her own. Until this summer when Dad left. Now, with help, she could sometimes get to the corner of the street, two hundred yards away – which was a big deal for her.

'You can't drive,' I pointed out.

'I've got my first lesson tomorrow.'

'Ok, wow. Well done Mum that's great.'

The thought of Mum driving with her shaky hands and monumental capacity for panic was disturbing. But I was supposed to be encouraging so I didn't voice my concerns.

'Where's Thomas?' I asked. Thomas had just started at the local High School. It took him ten minutes to get home from school.

'He's gone to get fish and chips for tea.' Mum said.

'Oh brill.' This was excellent news. Life was much better now that Thomas was old enough to do the fish and chip run. With Mum not able to go out and Dad leaving, usually I had to do all the shopping.

When Thomas got back with the fish and chips Mum wanted us to sit in the car to eat. We put our coats on and bundled out. Mum sat in the driver's seat with me next to her and Thomas in the back. We couldn't even have the radio or heating on because Mum was worried about the battery running down.

'It's a shame we're not facing the road, isn't it?' I said. We were staring at the garage door.

'Yes.' Mum sounded worried, 'I'll have to reverse out tomorrow.' But she rallied, obviously determined to remain positive. 'By Christmas I'll be able to drive us out to the Lickey Hills.'

We used to do that with Dad. The mental health lady wanted Mum to imagine herself doing these things by herself and feeling relaxed and happy.

'Maybe we could get a dog then,' I suggested. 'You'd love a dog, Mum.'

Thomas stopped eating. 'Please, let's get a dog. A Staffy.'

'We're not getting a Staffy,' Mum said. 'Your Dad is dead set against any kind of dog.'

'Well, he doesn't live here anymore,' I pointed out.

Mum looked at me then spoke slowly as if she'd just

discovered the solution to string theory. 'No, you're right. He doesn't have any say in it.'

I'd eaten as much as I wanted. Fish and chips tasted delicious to start with but the second I stopped eating a tsunami of grease hit me first in the mouth and then kicked me in the belly.

'Can we go back inside now?' I asked. 'Only I've got a load of homework to do.'

I don't know why Dad leaving had made such a difference. He worked away half of the time anyway. At least now they weren't screaming at each other when he came home. Mum still had her bad days but overall, surprisingly, she seemed to have more energy and cry less than she used to. But I hated Dad not being there. I missed him all the time. With him gone I felt as if I had to fill his place and look after Mum and Thomas. If only I had a boyfriend I could talk to. Someone who cared about me. Vivienne spoke to her boyfriend Louis every night.

One of the exercises Mum had to do was rate her well-being between one and ten every day. I'd been bumping along at a lonely four but after the duet with Frieda, I reckoned I'd jumped up to a six. At least I had dancing and a new friend.

I lugged my bag upstairs and got out my books. We were studying *Wuthering Heights* by Emily Brontë as one of our A Level texts. What I needed to take me up to a full ten out of ten was a grand passion like Cathy and Heathcliff's. I wanted to run wild over the moors with a dark handsome lover. Not that their love brought them much happiness. The moment Heathcliff returned from his travels everybody's well-being score plummeted to rock bottom. Maybe I should embrace my single state and put my passion into dance.

*

I hardly saw Vivienne anymore because she had so many rehearsals.

'Honestly Pen, Mrs Mulligan is amazing. You can tell she's been a professional actress – she pushes us sooo hard.' We were sitting in the kitchen of the sixth form extension where we could make drinks and heat up food in the microwave. We shared it with the boys' school, so the atmosphere was completely different from that in the main building.

Viv was tipping powder into a cup and adding water to make something vaguely resembling soup which was all she ate for lunch these days. She was dieting for the play. Evidently, Elizabeth Proctor needed to be scrawny. Mrs Mulligan and calories were her two topics of conversation.

'Grant's much better than I thought he'd be. I was worried he'd muck about, but he takes it seriously. Trouble is Louis's gone weird on me.'

Vivienne had met Louis at her Youth Theatre. He was older than her, studying drama at college. They were about as secure a couple as it was possible to be.

'In what way?'

'He goes grumpy and silent when I talk about Mrs Mulligan.'

'Well, you're always going on about her. Remember he's a director too. Maybe he feels threatened?'

Vivienne looked at me while she stirred her soup, attempting to dissolve the fizzing lumps of yellow powder.

'Maybe you're right. And he keeps asking me about Grant like he's jealous of him.'

'Should he be?'

'What do you mean?' Viv was at me in a second, full-on glaring. I squared up to her.

'Well, Grant's super good-looking and you get to do these heavy emotional scenes with him.'

'God no,' Vivienne swallowed a mouthful of soup, pulling a face as if it tasted as vile as it looked. 'Grant's better than I thought he'd be at acting, but I don't fancy him. Urgh no, he's all cheekbones and sharp angles, too wired for me. Absolutely not.'

Viv shuddered and I thought she was exaggerating her distaste but let it go.

'Louis doesn't know that unless you tell him.'

'When did you get so wise?' Vivienne grinned at me sipping her soup while I tucked into my cheese sandwich. She was watching every bite I took and any minute now she'd tell me how many calories I'd eaten just to be helpful.

One of the boys came into the kitchen invading our space with a tube of rolled-up paper carried in his fist like a lightsabre.

'Hi Viv.' He had big shoulders and a wide neck with very short hair and ears that stuck out slightly. He and Vivienne obviously knew each other.

'Oh, hi Ed. How are you?'

'Yeah, good. I need to talk to Pen.' As he faced me his whole head turned pink - even the tips of his ears - I felt sorry for him.

'How can I help?' I asked quickly to prevent him from any further embarrassment. Ed unrolled the drawings he carried and smoothed them out on the kitchen table.

'I'm making the set for the play. Mrs Mulligan says you're choreographing a dance for the opening, so I need to know how much space you'll need. Would you like different height levels? Have you, you know, got any special requirements?'

The three of us leaned over the drawings. Ed explained them to us.

'This is the empty central area – will that be big enough, it's about,' Ed looked around, 'yeah I'd say it'll be about the size of this kitchen.'

I mentally evicted the table and chairs and imagined six girls dancing. 'Yeah, I think so, it should feel intense and claustrophobic.'

'How about if I put a block in there? You'd have a raised section you could use.'

'That'd work. I could have Tituba up there and the other girls below.'

'Then I can fit out these frames with vertical slats of wood and if we angle light through them the stage will be mainly dark but with stripes of light like you get in a forest. What do you think?'

I was impressed. 'Sounds great Ed, really creative.'

'Ok let me know if you think of anything else.'

Vivienne was poring over the drawings. 'Where's the Proctors' house going to be.'

'I haven't got the drawings for your scene, but I can get them if you're interested.'

'Oh please. I love sets. They help me get a sense of how the play will look to the audience.'

'Ok, I'll bring yours over tomorrow.' He rolled up the paper, gave us a quick shy smile, and hurried away.

'So how do you know Ed?' I asked.

'Primary School. He lives on the estate up the road. He got a scholarship place like us. Got loads of brothers. One of them got into trouble with the police. But Ed's alright. He's sweet, a bit quiet.'

'His head's a funny shape, all neck and ears.'

Viv frowned at me. 'Don't be mean Pen. He's got a nice face. He plays rugby that's why he's got a big neck.'

I felt guilty. 'Sorry, you're right. I didn't mean to be rude about a friend of yours.'

Vivienne shook her head at me.
'Why do you want to be rude about anyone?'

As I walked back to the main school after lunch, I thought about how I'd criticized Ed for the way he looked. I went through life secretly labelling people as attractive, ugly, clever, stupid, cool, not cool, even when I didn't know anything about them. Look at how I'd judged Vivienne when I first knew her, totally on her appearance with no idea what a loving, funny, caring person she was. I didn't want to be this superficial. I wouldn't want a boyfriend who judged me on my looks – I'd want them to love me for who I was as a person. I needed to stop this judgy attitude and become a kinder, warmer, more caring person if I was ever going to find love.

4

The opportunity to develop my softer side came sooner than I'd expected. At my first play rehearsal, I realised that my former friend-turned-enemy, Tamasin Fox, had also been cast as a servant girl. We both came on at the end of the first scene, so were sitting next to each other in the hall waiting for our cue. This was the first time we'd been alone together since she'd filmed me dancing and posted it online. For a laugh – she'd said. There was nothing funny about the Giant Arse Movie and I hadn't forgiven her even though she'd apologised. We both focused intensely on the acting in front of us. She obviously felt as uncomfortable as I did.

The play began in the bedroom of Betty, another of the young girls. She was lying ill in bed, apparently bewitched after dancing in the woods. The ringleader, Abigail, was her cousin and several of the other girls, including Tamasin and I, came to visit the sick girl. There was only one male character in the scene - the young girl's father - played by Sandeep, a slightly chubby boy with straight black hair that looked like it had been stuck to his forehead with glue. He was rendered speechless by finding himself in a room with five girls. Coco, playing Abigail, he couldn't handle at all.

'Sandeep, you really need to look at Coco when you're speaking.' Mrs Mulligan reminded him.

'Still learning the words,' he mumbled into his text which he was clutching so tightly his knuckles showed white through his skin. This was good casting by Mrs Mulligan because you could see instantly that Sandeep was no match for Coco who dominated the scene. Coco didn't transform into Abigail, the way that Vivienne became the character she was playing, but she spoke with frosty arrogance, and being tall and beautiful with her sheet of white-blonde hair, you couldn't help but be awed by her.

I didn't know Coco because she was in another class, and we'd never had any lessons together. I vaguely remembered that she and Tamasin had been to the same posh prep school. With my newly formed resolution to be kind, I made a tentative peace offering.

'Coco's good, isn't she?'

Tamasin jumped as if hit by an electrical impulse but turned towards me.

'Yeah,' she said and gave me a weird little grimace that may have been an attempted smile. We both turned back to the play.

Tamasin and I had been close friends for the first four years at Kings but when I started dancing and spending time with Vivienne, she'd turned against me and ganged up with a major a-hole called Sadie Thompson to bully me. Sadie had left Kings and started a police apprenticeship - the thought of her as a policewoman was horrifying. Since Sadie left, even though Tamasin was still part of the cool gang, she seemed to be on her own a lot. She was doing History and English like me, but her other friends were doing sciences. The classroom dynamics had shifted and several times I'd noticed her looking like she wanted to talk to me. But our friendship had revolved around mocking other girls and I didn't want to go back to that. How could I trust she wouldn't turn on me again?

'How's college?' she asked me while Mrs Mulligan was manoeuvring Sandeep closer to Coco. 'Must be good to get out of Kings.'

'Yeah, it's great, I can wear jeans or trackies even.'

'Cool,' Tamasin said.

'Did you think of leaving?' I asked to keep the conversation going.

'The parents wouldn't let me.'

'No, mine neither.'

'So, we're here for another two years,' she said looking at me with a needy expression.

Maybe I could relax my guard. Maybe it was time to end the big freeze.

'Stuck with each other,' I smiled. This was the nicest I'd been to Tamasin for six months. A warm inner glow spread through my body. Being kind felt good. Keeping up hating someone was hard work even if they had behaved like a dickhead.

'Tamasin, Pen, where are you? You've missed your cue!' Mrs Mulligan glared at us, and we rushed onto the stage, apologising.

While we were running through our scene Grant Barker walked in through the back doors of the hall. Mrs Mulligan followed my eyes.

'Ah Grant,' she said. 'Good, we can block out Mercy's exit now.' At the end of the scene, as Grant entered, I had to curtsy and giggle, and then scuttle off. I was extremely unhappy about this. I was getting used to dancing in front of others but acting was way worse.

As Tamasin's character had already left the scene, she could have gone home but of course she didn't, instead she sat there watching me squirm. I wondered if she still had a thing for Grant. Back when we'd been friends, she'd been crazy about him.

'Coco, you're standing by the bed where Betty's sleeping.' Mrs Mulligan was up on her feet pacing out the scene.

She wore tight black jeans and a black funnel neck jumper and dashed about like a blackbird pecking for worms. 'When Mercy leaves, you're going to be on your own in a bedroom, by a bed,' Mrs Mulligan was getting herself revved up. How many times was she going to say the word bed? 'With Proctor. You want him and you know that he wants you. We should feel smouldering tension between you.'

Even Coco, who seemed like a cold fish, blushed at this. Grant was laughing. Mrs Mulligan took no notice, turning on me,

'Mercy, you're a bold girl, excited by the drama. Proctor's a handsome man so you're going to do everything you can to attract his attention.'

I mumbled my line, not looking at Grant, and hurried off the set.

'No, no, no,' Mrs Mulligan called me back. 'Like this - watch me.' She exaggerated the sway of her hips and slinked towards Grant with a leer on her face, passing so close she brushed against him, gazing up at his face as she bobbed a curtsy and said with a giggle, 'Morning Mr Proctor,' before wiggling her way off stage. Grant looked freaked at having Mrs Mulligan throw herself at him.

'I want you to pass so close to Proctor that you can feel his biceps.' Grant grinned at me. Vivienne was in big trouble the next time I saw her.

'Come on, we haven't got all night. This is one line. We've got a whole scene left to rehearse.' Mrs Mulligan was getting annoyed with me. The dictator lurking behind the gilded exterior was peeking through.

I hesitated, trying to find some courage when Grant leapt towards me. He lifted me up over his shoulder and carried me off the stage.

'What the…' I was kicking my legs and struggling as he

put me down. Everyone laughed, even Mrs Mulligan. I didn't know whether to laugh or get angry. I was shocked at being suddenly upside down with his arms around my legs. My nose pressed against his back I breathed in gulps of boy sweat and fabric conditioner.

'Well, that's one way of speeding things up.' Mrs Mulligan laughed. 'And Proctor does want her out of the way so he can be alone with Abigail. But I think Mercy needs to leave of her own volition.'

I marched back onto the stage glaring at Grant. Arrogant prick - I'd show him. I gritted my teeth, took a deep breath, and imitating Mrs Mulligan's sexy walk came in close so that my arm rubbed against his. I looked up at him from under my fringe and curtsied while delivering my line. Strutting off I glanced back over my shoulder. Grant was watching me.

'Better,' Mrs Mulligan moved on. 'But, Grant, don't look at Mercy. Your focus is on Abigail. Move towards her as if you can't stop yourself.'

My trauma over for the night, I collected my coat and bag from the chair next to Tamasin. We both stood for a moment watching Coco and Grant. Things looked pretty steamy between them. They were having no trouble raising the sexual temperature. Mrs Mulligan was full of praise.

'Very good, yes. Keep that tension. Excellent.'

Tamasin picked up her stuff and we walked out together.

'Grant's such an idiot! But sorry - that was hilarious. Your face, so shocked.'

'Didn't you and Grant have a thing last term?' I retaliated.

'No way,' she snapped. 'He's not exactly my type.' Clearly a sensitive issue. I was never any good at picking up on the strange movements of the in-crowd. Who was in and who was out seemed to change overnight. I thought Grant was way too pleased with himself, but he seemed extremely popular. Maybe that was it – he was too obvious a choice now. With Tamasin there was often a subtext I didn't understand. Luckily, a bus pulled up at my stop.

'Got to run,' I sprinted off down the drive. Whatever was going on in my head nearly always came out of my mouth. I couldn't seem to stop it. But other people had this secret inner stuff churning away. With Vivienne, I felt safe. If she had a problem, she'd tell me. After an encounter with Tamasin I felt anxious, with this disturbed, swirling sensation inside me and questions lingering. If I was going to trust her again it'd take time.

When I got home, I went straight upstairs to dump my homework and change out of my school uniform. I could hear a male voice talking to Mum in the kitchen. Dad must have come for tea. I ran down to see him. But the man at the kitchen table sitting in Dad's chair and looking like he'd been there a while, was a total stranger.

'Ahh Penny,' Mum laughed for no reason whatsoever. An irritating, nervous titter. 'This is Mike, my driving instructor.'

'Hello,' I said wondering why the hell her driving instructor was in our kitchen at teatime. 'I'm starving. What's for tea?'

He took the hint.

'I'd better be off Jenny. Thanks for the cuppa. See you tomorra' then.' He stood up. He was taller than Dad with a huge belly that sat on the front of his body like he'd strapped on a sandbag for protection. Probably needed it with Mum driving.

'Your Mum's done very well for her first lesson,' he said talking not to my face but to my breasts. What a creep.

Then I realised that in my rush to get changed I'd left an embarrassing button undone. I turned away quickly to sort myself out.

'Yes,' Mum chipped in all perky, 'I learnt how to change gear.'

Mum showed Mike to the door while I got pasta out of the cupboard. As she hadn't started cooking I'd have to make something quick and easy.

'How come you're seeing him tomorrow?' I asked when she came back into the kitchen.

'I'm doing an intensive course with Mike. I should be driving by Christmas.'

'You get lessons every day?'

'Not at weekends. You could have lessons; Mike does a special 17th birthday package.'

I shrugged. There was way too much 'Mike' mentioning going on.

'I've put the pasta on. Call me when it's ready - I need to get on with my homework.' I was determined to avoid a conversation about her driving lesson. A vision of Mike's meaty paw resting on Mum's knee had come into my mind and was making me feel ill.

5

The week after our duet Frieda asked me if I'd like to go with her to a Black Lives Matter demonstration as part of Black History Month. I'd never been on a protest march before, but I knew Vivienne and Louis were going and I was keen to show my support. Frieda had made me realise how privileged I was. We arranged to meet outside McDonald's.

Frieda was dressed in black as usual. A cardboard sign with BLM painted in big black letters was tucked under her arm. Standing next to her was a small slender woman with long black hair tied back off her face. She was wearing a brightly coloured embroidered jacket and a long skirt with heavy boots. They made a striking pair.

'Yo - Pen,' Frieda waved her sign at me, and I ran the last few steps towards them, 'this is my Mum.'

'I'm Anna,' Frieda's Mum said clasping my hands in hers and smiling into my face. She was beautiful in a totally different way to Frieda who must have received almost all her genetic material from her Dad. The only physical resemblance between mother and daughter was in their bright black eyes and whole-face smiles. The thought of giant Frieda emerging from the womb of tiny Anna was a miracle too eye-watering to contemplate.

The protest march finished in Centenary Square where I was supposed to meet Vivienne and Louis, but as we walked past the town hall towards the library there were so many people I doubted I'd find them. The crowd was fired up and vocal, dressed for the autumn chill in padded coats and woolly hats. Lots of people had hand-painted signs like Frieda's. There were also signs full of names I'd never heard of. Frieda said they were innocent black people killed by the police in America. People were angry but positive, chanting 'Black Lives Matter' as we walked along.

'Can you believe it, Mum. Pen's never been to a protest before!' Frieda had been incredulous. She was as shocked by this gap in my experience as if I'd told her I'd never brushed my teeth. Anna shook her head laughing, but not at me. 'Frieda's been going on marches since she was six weeks old so for her this is as much a part of life as going shopping would be for most people.'

Frieda bounced by Anna's side holding on to her arm in an affectionate way. With my Mum's agoraphobia we never even went shopping. But I didn't say anything. I'd never be so openly affectionate with my Mum at a cool event like this, but Frieda wasn't embarrassed. They chatted away, including me in their conversation, but with such clear intimacy between them that I felt like an intruder.

The sound of electric guitars broke through the chanting and shouting.

'The bands are starting.' Frieda sped up.

I hadn't realised there'd be music. There was a loud cheer and the crowd at the front of the square started applauding. A woman began singing. Friendly but insistent, Frieda bumped her way through the tightly packed mass of people. Anna and I followed in her wake until we were standing right in the middle near the front of the stage. This was a rough construction of scaffolding and planks erected in front of the Symphony Hall. A canvas canopy sheltered the stage from rain and a large Black Lives Matter banner was stretched across the front. Underneath the canopy a band was playing; four of them, a drummer, two guitarists, and a singer. My heart nearly leapt out of my body and ran off down Broad Street when I saw her. I realised that my mouth was open and shut it quickly.

'Do you know who this band is?' I turned to Frieda. She looked down at me from her great height.

'The Night Angels – they're a local band. Do you remember, Mum? We saw them at the Hare and Hounds in September. The lead singer's hot.'

I didn't know the band, but I knew the singer and one of the guitarists. I'd stayed the night in Melody Jones's flat in Bearwood just up the road from our house. I'd been to London with her and Yogi, the guitarist. And now she was up on stage at an anti-racism protest, looking as beautiful as ever with hundreds of people listening to her and applauding. She'd always said she was going to be famous.

The music was a mash-up of different sounds with a disco beat, outbreaks of rap from the bassist, and Melody's strange sexy voice floating a soulful tune over the top. Yogi was playing reggaeton riffs on the guitar. The sound was totally different from the punk style band they'd been in six months ago. Somehow the clashing thrown-together styles worked. The music was upbeat and made you want to move. Around me, people were holding their cardboard signs above their heads and dancing. Frieda and her Mum joined in. I started moving but my eyes were mesmerized by Melody on stage.

'Are they well-known then?' I asked Frieda.

'Getting to be - they're regulars at the Hare and Hounds. I think they're fine.'

Melody looked as if she'd been born to do this. She had her flame on and was blazing away. I remembered watching her in the basement of her boyfriend's house and being surprised that she could sing. But how had she transformed into this confident performer? I couldn't match the girl dominating the stage with the Melody I'd last seen drunk, sprawled on the floor, totally off her head. And why were they playing here? She'd never shown any interest in politics when I knew her.

She was getting the crowd to chant a call and response with the band.

'Together we,' she called out and the crowd answered, 'fly free.' She turned her back to the audience and raised her arms, revealing a huge pair of tattooed wings that spread across her shoulders and over the backs of her arms. The crowd cheered when she moved making the feathers ripple.

I looked up at Frieda who was waving her sign high above our heads and shouting, 'fly free.'

The tattoos were new. Melody hadn't had them when I'd known her. They must have hurt but they sure added to her allure. As the song faded to a close, she wrapped her arms around the shoulders of the bass player and they sang, 'together we, fly free.' As the music finished, they both came to the front of the stage and shouted, 'Black Lives Matter', and the crowd roared back 'Black Lives Matter'. There was huge applause as they walked off. A group of women came onto the stage and the speeches started. Frieda was waving her sign and cheering. I tried to concentrate on what they were saying but I kept thinking about Melody.

She'd let me down badly in London, but I couldn't help but admire her determination. She'd had a rough life but here she was making hundreds of people happy and supporting an important cause. I was impressed. She was so professional. I could see her now standing by the side of the stage and on impulse I moved closer.

'Back in a minute,' I shouted to Frieda, and pushed my way through the crowd until I was by the side of the stage where the band was packing up their gear. Melody was perched on an upturned wooden crate glugging back water. Yogi was talking to some girls who'd gathered nearby. He spotted me and I waved. He nodded back and I saw him say something to Melody who turned quickly in my direction and then came running towards me.

'Pen.' She flung herself onto me hugging tightly. I felt again the fragility of her bones sticking through her skin. It was weird the way there was no weight to her. She dragged me by the arm back towards the bright yellow van where the guys were loading equipment.

'Marlon, this is Pen. She's the Night Angel.' The bass player stopped what he was doing and stared at me. He was older than the rest of the band. His hair was shaved at the sides with a crown of short dreads.

Hi,' he said and then went back to work. What did Melody mean – I was the Night Angel? She was treating me like I was a good friend as if she had no memory of what happened in London. Maybe she didn't. She'd been drunk.

'I can't believe it, Mel,' I said. 'The band, you're so good. That was amazing.'

'Yeah,' she gave me her Cheshire cat grin. 'We're starting to make some money even. Thanks to Marlon. I told you I'd be famous didn't I,' she laughed.

'Yeah, you did,' and I laughed too. Somehow it was impossible to stay mad at Melody.

'You still dancing on the night streets?' she asked.

'Not so much. I'm doing dance at college now.' I could see Frieda walking towards us and I beckoned her over, 'with Frieda.' I said as Frieda approached looking, for the first time since I'd known her, a bit unsure of herself.

'Frieda, this is Melody. She lives up the road from me.' Frieda's eyes were huge with wonder. I couldn't help feeling a bit pleased.

'Not anymore Angel,' Melody said.' I moved to Digbeth.'

'Ready Mel?' the bass player called her. They'd packed the kit into the van.

'Give me your new number - your old one doesn't work.' Melody got out her phone. I paused for a moment. Did I want Melody back in my life? Frieda elbowed me and glared with an 'are you insane?' expression. I gave Melody my number.

'Mel. Come on, we need to go.'

'In a minute Marlon,' Melody shouted back. Then to me, 'I'll call. We're playing at The Midnight Bell on Friday. I'll put you on the guest list.' The van was reversing onto the road. Melody ran after them, hopped into the front seat and they drove off.

Frieda was looking at me like I'd grown a second head or turned green and scaly.

'So how do you know her again?' she asked.

'Where's your Mum,' I couldn't see Anna.

'She's gone home, she says bye. Let's get something to eat, I'm starving.' Frieda started moving away from the stage.

'The speeches haven't finished,' I realised.

'I'm done. Speeches are meh, and I need the lowdown on you and Melody.'

We headed back towards Temple Row where there were pop-up food stalls lined along the pavement. Frieda was vegan, so we queued up for bean burgers.

'So, she used to live near you?' Frieda wasn't going to let this one go, but I was reluctant to tell her the whole story. I felt vulnerable and churned up. Disturbing memories were haunting my head. If I was truthful, I'd look like a naive victim whereas right now Frieda was impressed.

Maybe Melody had changed. I was trying to be more understanding and less critical. Maybe I should give Melody a second chance?

To keep Frieda at bay I said, 'Yeah. You know Mick, the guy I told you about, the one who's gone off travelling? He was best mates with Melody's boyfriend. They were in a band together.' I wasn't lying just offering a partial truth.

'Okay, Wow. Pen Flowers, you're a box of surprises.'

'She wasn't any good then. Their band was pretty shit.'

'You know she writes her own songs?' Frieda said. I shook my head. A day of surprises for everyone.

'Pen, Pen.' Vivienne had found us. She and Louis wove their way through the people now leaving the park in their hundreds and joined us in the burger queue.

'I saw you by the stage. Can you believe that was Melody? She's like really got her act together.'

'Yeah,' I agreed and made the introductions. We got burgers and found a bench to sit on. Vivienne and Frieda were both so friendly that they immediately started finding out about each other. I sat and ate my burger and let them get on with it. I liked the feeling of my old school friend and my new college friend getting on. The different parts of my life coming together made my world more whole. Louis wasn't saying much, so I asked him what he thought of The Night Angels.

'Yeah,' he said, 'they're not bad. I've seen 'em before.' I wondered why, if he'd seen them, he hadn't said anything to me and Vivienne. Maybe he didn't recognize Melody. He was quiet, not like his regular jokey self. Usually, he'd be teasing me or Vivienne about something. Maybe he was feeling angry and churned up. I knew he'd been stopped a few times by the police for no reason. I wanted to say something but was worried I'd get it wrong, so we sat in silence while Frieda and Viv chatted away.

Frieda told Vivienne that Melody was playing in Digbeth on Friday night.

'We could meet up earlier in town and go together.' Vivienne suggested. Louis didn't look enthusiastic though he didn't say anything. Two minutes later he stood up saying they needed to go, and Vivienne rushed after him. She was right, he did seem a bit off.

On the bus home, I checked out The Night Angels on my phone. There was a clip of Melody singing a song called 'Night Angel'. It was a ballad, soulful, but with a wild energetic riff on the chorus line, and an underlying sense of despair.

She was there by my side
When I needed her most
Night Angel, Night Angel
Holding me tight
Guiding me home
Night Angel, Night Angel
When I was so alone
When I was so alone
She heard my prayer
Was somehow there
Night Angel, Night Angel.

Melody's voice made the hairs on the back of my hands prickle. Tears were running down my face by the end of the song. I got off the bus outside The King's Head pub where I'd first found Melody collapsed on the steps. She'd been so drunk I thought she'd barely remembered. I couldn't work her out. I'd assumed that she'd been using me but maybe I did matter to her.

I walked slowly down Lordswood Road and turned into Knightlow. My body remembered the nights I'd spent dancing out my troubles on these streets. I lifted my arms and made a few skip steps. I hadn't been night dancing for ages. A longing to feel the night air on my skin stirred in my heart.

I stayed up late listening to Melody's Night Angel song over and over. It was raw and painful and beautiful – like Melody herself. When I was sure that Mum and Thomas were asleep, and I couldn't hear any cars, I crept out of the front door.

There was a full moon. A giant white orb dangling above the treetops, making the night as bright as day with her strange, magical, silvery light. I must be at least part wolf because the full moon always called to me. The full moons had different names. This was a Hunter's Moon, signifying change.

The street was empty, so I danced up the centre of the road following the path of the moonlight. I was Diana, the virgin huntress, arching my back to shoot arrows into the sky, a swift and silent predator. But what was I hunting?

I turned into the back alleyway that ran behind the houses. A fox was strolling across the path ahead of me. She stopped and stared. Her eyes were amber green and her paws black to the knee as if she'd been dipped in paint. How still she was. Unafraid. She looked offended at having her nightly ramble interrupted. We shared a moment then she stepped carefully into the shadows and disappeared. Did she have a mate? My fellow night dancer? Or did she hunt alone?

Melody's voice sang inside my head. Why was I destined to dance the night streets alone? I didn't want to be a lonely huntress. I wanted to be loved. I arched my back again and then flung myself into the air, leaping towards the moon, calling to her to bring me a lover so that together we could explore the mysteries of the night.

6

Back in the mundane world of daylight, I had the first rehearsal of my dance sequence for the play. I'd worked myself up into a nervous state. Having bold, dangerous ideas was one thing, but putting them into practice was alarming. Frieda was helping me. I'd choreographed these low-down wide stance stomping movements using hip circles and body ripples. They were blatantly sexual and with Frieda doing them they looked mega cool, but I dreaded persuading the girls at Kings to try them. I wished Frieda could play Tituba, the slave accused of voodoo, because she could do things with her buttocks that were frankly amazing. She was teaching me how, but I had a long way to go to achieve her muscle control.

'Why don't I come to your rehearsal,' Frieda offered, 'then we can perform the routine together so everyone will see how it should look.'

'Are you sure?'

'And I'll get to nose around your school,' she grinned. Frieda wanted to know everything about everyone. She'd asked me endless questions about Melody, and Vivienne and Louis too. She was the most genuinely friendly person I'd ever met. She really liked people.

Mrs Mulligan said it was fine for Frieda to come to the rehearsal. At four o'clock when lessons finished, I met Frieda at the end of the school drive and walked her up to the main hall. She was wearing her usual jeans, trainers, and hoody and laughed at me in my smart navy-blue skirt and blazer. In the sixth form we had more freedom over what we wore but jeans, trainers, and hoodies were all on the forbidden list.

Coco, Tamasin, and the other 'bewitched' girls were already in the hall. Vivienne had stayed back because she wanted to watch. She rushed over to say hi to Frieda while I plugged my phone into the music system. I'd found a piece that was mainly drumbeats, whistles, and bird calls that I thought would work as a soundtrack.

'Right, everyone,' Mrs Mulligan called for attention. 'I've asked Pen to choreograph a short dance sequence which will be a prologue to the first act. Over to you Pen.'

I breathed in; nervous explosions of energy were detonating in my tummy. This was the first time I'd choreographed a dance for other people. They were looking at me with varying degrees of anxiety and suspicion. They weren't even dancers. I wished Tamasin wasn't in the group. She hated dancing and was glowering at me from behind her glasses.

'Ok,' I began. 'I've been looking at African dance. The concept is that Tituba is teaching us some of the dance rituals she'd learned as a slave in Barbados.' I was speaking too fast, and my voice had a stupid wobble that I couldn't control. I took another deep breath and tried to smile. 'So, I've researched the New Orleans Mardi Gras dance clubs for African-inspired moves. They should, sort of, be deliberately provocative and shocking for a Puritan community. This is Frieda who's at dance college with me.'

Frieda smiled and waved. She didn't look in the least bit nervous. Her confidence made me bolder. My voice got steadier.

'We're going to show you the routine – Frieda will be Tituba who'll be on a raised platform here.' I blocked out the space where the raised area would be. 'Then the rest of us are down here copying her. We'll demonstrate the whole thing and then break it down into individual moves. Don't worry there's only three steps to learn.'

I picked up my phone to start the music but was distracted by the side door opening. Grant Barker had arrived early for his rehearsal. He walked down to the front and sat next to Vivienne. I could really have done without him being there. I looked over at Mrs Mulligan hoping she'd ask him to leave but she just smiled at me encouragingly. I hesitated.

'Ready, Pen.' Frieda prompted me, and I pressed play. What the hell – we just had to go for it. Luckily Frieda's undulating buttocks were so mesmerizing that no one watched me as we demonstrated the routine.

'Fabulous,' Mrs Mulligan called out the moment we'd finished. 'That should wake up the governors. What a way to start the show.' She clapped her hands and laughed. 'I want to learn the moves too.'

Grateful as I was for her jumping in with an enthusiastic response, teaching Mrs Mulligan to do hip grinds felt wrong.

Rosa, a plump girl with hair braided into waist-length dreads, who was in the year above me, was playing Tituba. I'd been concerned that she might be offended but she was straight in there with Frieda, getting stuck into the gyrations. She didn't have Frieda's skills, but she was giving it a go.

While Frieda went through the routine with Rosa, I was left with the other five girls. I got them to drop into a wide-legged squat and then showed them how to turn and stamp and circle their hips as they moved. Mrs Mulligan joined in, and I had to turn away as she thrust her crotch in my direction.

I looked over to Vivienne seeking support. Grant was

whispering in her ear and she laughed. His eyes were fixed on me. I felt myself blushing but then realised he wasn't looking at me but at Coco dancing behind me. She had caught hold of the routine quickly. She'd obviously done ballet. She could even do body ripples, managing to look sexy and elegant at the same time. Unlike most of the others, she was in time with the beat.

Everyone was having a go. It didn't matter if they weren't great because it made sense of the story if they looked awkward. They were doing something alien and scary. Only Tamasin was struggling. She was so self-conscious that it was painful to watch. Her movements were stiff, she couldn't let go and relax. Seeing me watching her she began to muck about doing Gangnam-style galloping horse movements and then stopped entirely. I went over to help her.

'I suppose this is your idea of revenge.' She glared at me. 'Is that why Vivienne's here so you can both laugh at me?'

'Of course not.' She was upset and I wanted to be encouraging. 'You've nearly got it. You just need a wider stance and then stamp forwards one foot at a time.' I demonstrated the first move. 'You don't have to be perfect.'

'I'm not making a twat of myself.' Tamasin stood arms folded across her chest, refusing to join in. I didn't know what to do.

Frieda appeared by my side. 'How's it going? I'm Frieda.' She beamed her megawatt football stadium smile.

'Tamasin.' Surprisingly Tamasin smiled back.

'You gotta drop your ass to the ground and get real low and then thrust with your hips,' Frieda put her hands on Tamasin's waist and encouraged her to squat down. 'Now see push your pelvis forward, like you were fucking.'

Tamasin laughed a slightly nervous and high-pitched giggle, not at all like her usual cool bark. But she didn't resist, and she didn't give up. With Frieda's hands still on her waist, she did the steps. I moved off to help the others. Frieda was such a flirt. I'd known Tamasin forever, so I forgot how pretty she was with her blonde curls and on-trend glasses. She was getting hands-on personal tuition.

Once everyone had mastered the basic moves we ran through the whole routine to music. Grant and Vivienne applauded when we finished, and Mrs Mulligan said she was pleased.

'Looks cool.' Frieda declared. 'Another couple of rehearsals and it'll be a riot.' She was clearly angling for more invites.

Vivienne, Frieda, Tamasin, and I walked down the school drive together leaving Coco and Grant to rehearse their love scene.

Frieda and Tamasin walked ahead of me and Viv.

'What did Grant say to you?' I asked, 'He was whispering and then you laughed.'

'At Mrs Mulligan grinding. He says she's always thrusting herself at him in rehearsals.'

'Oh.' I hoped he'd said something about the dance.

'You're very interested in Grant Barker these days,' Vivienne challenged me.

'No, I'm not!'

She shrugged, 'keep your hair on. Those two have hit it off.'

Ahead of us Tamasin and Frieda were screaming with laughter. Thank goodness for Frieda. If Tamasin had made a scene and walked off, I wouldn't have known what to do.

*

The next day at college Frieda wanted to know everything about everyone.

'That Coco is a stunner. Holy moly, what a beaut! So, are she and that pretty boy an item?'

'In the Play they're lovers. In real life, I don't know.'

But she was mainly interested in Tamasin. I ended up telling her the whole story of how we'd been best friends and then fallen out. How Tamasin had posted the Giant Arse video and how I'd been so angry that I'd hit her. Frieda was a good listener. When I finished talking she was quiet, turning the information over in her head.

'I liked her,' she said eventually. 'I think she wants to make up with you. She told me how talented she thought you were.'

'She did?' I was surprised.

'Yep, let's invite her to come with us to see The Night Angels.' She pulled a mock innocent face that was so cheeky I laughed.

I'd only known Frieda for a couple of months, but I felt as if we'd been friends our whole lives. It was like the first time I had avocado on toast. I'd never tasted avocado before, but it immediately became one of my all-time favourite foods. Frieda was avocado on toast with a squeeze of lemon and a grind of pepper, so right that I couldn't imagine life without her.

I still felt wary of Tamasin, but I couldn't resist Frieda's smile.

'Okay, but don't get too excited, I'm pretty certain she's straight.'

7

Mum was locked in the bathroom.

'I need to wash my hair,' I shouted through the door. She'd been in there forever. I hoped she wasn't having a breakdown.

'I'll be out soon.'

'I'm going out tonight you know,' I reminded her.

'I know, calm down,' she opened the door and steam billowed out over the landing. 'You've got plenty of time.'

'Have you been having a sauna in there?'

A headache-inducing mixture of toxic scents blasted my nostrils. Mum must have been oiling, spraying, and creaming with enthusiasm. Her head was wrapped in a towel. I pushed past her into the bathroom.

'Everywhere's steamed up and dripping wet. How am I going to get ready?' Mum came back with an armful of clean towels and handed them to me as she picked up the wet ones from the floor and put them in the laundry bin.

'You're not the only one going out,' she said and went downstairs.

What did she mean by that? Mum never went out. Not going out was her thing.

I was out of the shower and taking inventory of the Martian landscape on my left cheek - two new eruptions and one crater - when Mum called up the stairs.

'Pizza's ready.'

I put on my dressing gown and ran down to get mine

before Thomas helped himself to the largest slices. Mum was in the kitchen dressed in a tight black dress with a plunging v- neckline. She'd blow-dried her hair into a shiny bob.

'What's going on,' I demanded.

'Pollo – the one you like. And I've made a salad.'

'No, I meant with the outfit?'

'Mike's taking me out for dinner.' Mum's cheeks were strangely pink, either guilt or too much blusher. She busied herself cutting up pizza avoiding my stare.

'Thomas,' she yelled. 'Come and get your pizza.'

'Who's Mike?' I asked though I knew exactly who he was. His leery gaze was seared into my psyche. Mum shot me a suspicious look.

'My driving instructor.'

'Should he be mixing business with pleasure? Isn't there a law against dating clients?'

'Not if they're over eighteen,' Mum snapped back.

I took my pizza upstairs to brood over this latest development. I hadn't considered Mum seeing other men. Dad, yes. I'd prepared myself for him getting a girlfriend. But not Mum. She didn't go out of the house; how could she have a boyfriend?

She'd nicked the hair dryer so I had to rescue it from her bedroom, the one she and Dad used to share. I had a vision of Mike lying naked in the bed. What if he stayed the night? My stomach went into spasm, and I nearly chucked up a mouthful of pizza. Disgusting images were flying through my head. I realised the worst aspects of this divorce had only just begun.

I was nearly ready when Mum called up the stairs.

'Pen, I'm off now. Mrs Bell's in with Thomas.' Mrs Bell was our next-door neighbour.

From the landing I looked down into the hall. Mum had her fake fur coat on and red lipstick. You'd think she was starting a new career as a sex worker. Mike was standing next to her by the open front door.

'You've got money? You've got your phone charged up?' She shouted.

'Yes, yes, okay.'

'Now call me or text me if you have any problems and you're to be back by midnight.' Mum said.

'Okay.'

'Well have a lovely evening.'

'You too,' I managed to say while secretly hoping that she'd have a full-on panic attack and that would be the end of Mike.

I heard him say, 'you look lovely,' before Mum closed the door behind them.

It wasn't even December, but the Christmas lights were already up in the city. Bands of yellow and white starbursts zigzagged across the street. Usually, the decorations cheered up the dark wet nights but for some reason known only to the City Council, they'd chosen to have lights that flashed downwards in vertical stripes like electric rain was falling and falling, forever falling. The descending movement worked against any uplifting effect of the neon and made me think of hopes being dashed into oblivion on the pavement. I couldn't blame Mum for wanting to meet someone now that Dad had left. But I found the idea of a man who wasn't Dad coming into our house disturbing. It made me feel lonelier than ever.

I was the last one to arrive at the Bullring. Vivienne, Louis, Frieda, and Tamasin were standing in a group chatting and laughing. I felt a weird stab of jealousy. They wouldn't know each other if it weren't for me but they were getting on fine without me. Even my friends had paired off leaving me on my own.

I didn't want to appear miserable, so I put on a fake cheery face and bounced up.

'Sorry, I'm late,'

'No problem, we've been having a laugh,' Vivienne said. Louis led the way towards St Martin's church and down into Digbeth. Frieda, with her long legs, kept pace beside him and Tamasin, Vivienne, and I followed. I was in the middle with Tamasin on one side and Vivienne on the other. As far as I knew these two had never been out together before.

'Melody was so professional at Black Lives Matter.' Vivienne said. 'I mean, I knew she was into music, but she was such a mess, I thought her talk was BS. She seemed like one of those vulnerable types - on a mission to self-destruct. Louis was saying the bass player is a really good musician.'

'She was always pretty serious about music,' I said, asserting my greater Melody knowledge. 'And mega ambitious.' But I'd never imagined her being successful. Maybe I should have. I'd been on the painful end of her ruthless streak. She'd do anything to get what she wanted.

We turned off the main road and walked along an empty side street with brick arches on one side and industrial units on the other. Spooky. I was glad Louis was with us. The damp cold air was making my hair go frizzy and cling to my face. Hanging out with Tamasin again, going to Melody's gig while Mum went out on a date. Everything felt strange and off balance.

As we reached the bottom of the street, I heard music. The thump of a distant bass vibrated in my chest. Turning the corner, the high brick walls of old railway arches were painted with colourful graffiti. Giant faces loomed out of the night. Strings of bare electric light bulbs were slung across the road and bright spots reflected off the shiny paintwork on the parked cars. The street was dancing with light. Groups of people moved along the pavements weaving between the parked cars. Neon signs over industrial metal doors named the clubs inside the industrial units. Birdies, Roxy's, Mamas, Luna Nights. The energy in the street was so high I felt as if the pavement was bouncing. My mood lifted.

The Midnight Bell was a small square building painted dark blue with a round neon logo of a bell over the entrance. There was a queue of people waiting to get in, but Louis led us to the front, and I spoke to one of the bouncers.

'We're on the guest list,' I said.

'What's your name?'

'Pen, Pen Flowers plus four.'

Those standing at the front of the queue were staring at us. I felt guilty as if we were pushing in, which in a way we were.

'Can't see anything,' he said.

Typical of Melody, now I'd be letting my friends down, and we'd look like idiots.

'Are you sure? Melody said she'd put me on with four guests. You can see her text.' I showed him my phone.

'Look for yourself.' The bouncer showed me his list and I saw Angel + 4.

'Oh, that's me. Melody calls me Angel.'

Louis nodded to confirm what I'd said. The bouncer seemed to believe us. He opened the door. Frieda appeared at my side and squeezed my arm.

'I'm so made up by this,' she beamed her lighthouse smile.

The bouncer let us in through the roadside door to a

small outdoor courtyard with a canvas roof. People were standing here drinking and smoking. We pushed through them to the second set of doors and into the club. No wonder they were keeping people queueing outside. The place was packed. There was a bar at the back of the room and a small stage opposite. Unless we got to the front, I wouldn't see anything, and I couldn't see any way through the congealed mess of bodies. But Frieda wasn't daunted. She did her thing; big smiles to everyone as she moved them aside and ploughed on. The atmosphere in the room was hyper, with a buzz of anticipation. I thought about Melody's filthy flat in Bearwood and tried to match it to this exciting, steamy room. Louis fought his way to the bar and came back with a young woman with short, cropped hair who was helping him carry the drinks.

'This is Harriet,' he said introducing her.

'Hi,' she smiled, a short brief twitch of the lips, and then started looking around the room while Louis told her our names. When he introduced Vivienne, her eyes darted back. There was some weird tension going on. Usually, Viv would be all over a new friend of Louis, making them feel welcome. But instead, she retreated moving closer to me. Luckily Frieda was as friendly as ever so there were no awkward silences, but Viv was obviously unnerved by Harriet's arrival. There was no opportunity to talk as the house lights dimmed and a spotlight focused on the DJ.

'Get ready for the next big thing from Birmingham. Home-grown and incandescent, let's give a real Brummy welcome to our very own Night Angels.'

The guitarist Yogi, the drummer, and bass player appeared on stage and started to play a compelling disco beat. We were standing close to the speakers and the noise was deafening.

When Melody ran onto the stage and began to sing it

was as if she was already a star – there were wolf whistles, men shouting her name, hooting, and howling, a farmyard of animal noises. She looked incredible in thigh-high leather boots and a black sequined leotard with her natural auburn hair blazing copper under the lights. I'd been traumatized by the thought of being on stage in a leotard, but Melody had no problem with it. She looked as comfortable and relaxed as I'd ever seen her.

Frieda was totally smitten. She was dancing but her eyes were locked on Melody's face. Tamasin kept glancing at me and then up to the stage, frowning as if she were trying to work out how I could possibly be friends with Melody. I had trouble believing it myself. I'd been impressed by the band at the demonstration but here, playing with their full set up, they were astonishing. They did a cover version of 'Build me up buttercup' that was poignant and sad. Melody had a way of looking as if she was singing just to you. She sang 'don't break my heart' with such depth of emotion that my heart broke open and the sadness and anger I felt at Dad leaving home bubbled into my eyes.

No one would ever spot me in a crowd but Frieda with her height and quiff and cool dance moves would always get noticed. I was next to her to the left of the stage near the front. Melody spotted us there as she stopped to drink water between songs and gave me a grin and a thumbs up. I say water but knowing Mel it could as easily be vodka.

It seemed incredible that in just over six months Mel had gone from singing with a dodgy schoolboy band to this. You didn't get to be this good without hours of practice. I couldn't imagine Mel having the discipline.

They'd been playing for about forty minutes and were nearing the end of their set when Melody walked over to

Yogi and whispered something to him, and he signed to the others. I recognized the intro to 'Night Angel'. I wasn't alone because there was a scattering of applause and some cheering. Their signature song was obviously popular.

Melody walked to the front of the stage and started to speak while the band kept the intro going quietly in the background. The room hushed to listen.

'So, tonight is a BIG night for me,' she said.' One Hundred Days Sober!'

A huge roar went up from the crowd.

'Thank you but hey, one day at a time.' Another roar of recognition as if this was some form of catchphrase. 'But tonight's also special because I've someone I'd like to introduce to you.' She came over to the corner of the stage where we were standing. 'Pen,' she said and put out her hand. I froze but Frieda pushed me forward. I found myself walking up the steps and onto the stage. Melody slung her arm around my shoulders and walked me into the spotlights.

'This is Pen. When I was still drinking, she found me one night, collapsed on the street. Off my head, totally out of it. And this young woman, a stranger, didn't ignore me, didn't rob me, didn't even call the police. She got me up and walked me home and made sure I was safe. Please meet the Night Angel.'

There was an explosive roar of applause and cheering that filled the small room. I wanted to put my hands over my ears. How could Melody possibly hear to sing? I was also blinded by the lights. I couldn't see anything. I felt embarrassed and emotional and didn't know what to do. My arms hung uselessly by my sides – I gave a shrug and a quick smile in the direction of the dark space in front of me and as soon as Melody took her arm from my shoulders, I rushed down the steps and out of the light. Melody turned her back to the crowd and raised her arms to show her angel wings and then started to sing Night Angel.

Down on the club floor Frieda and Vivienne were straight in there.

'You never told me that,' Frieda whispered.

'She hasn't even told me,' Vivienne sounded offended looking at Frieda like why the hell should Pen tell you? I wanted to laugh I was in such a whirl. A few people nearby stared at me.

'It was no big deal,' I whispered back. It really hadn't been. Mel had been drunk plenty of other times after. It wasn't a life-changing moment or anything like that. But the song showed that it meant more to Melody than I'd realised. When she finished to huge applause, she spoke into the microphone.

'We all need to be Night Angels for each other.' And then she sang the anthem song she'd sung at the protest. 'Together we, fly free.' Everyone in the audience was holding hands or linking arms over each other's shoulders. We joined in. I was in the middle with Frieda on one side of me, her arms over mine and Tamasin's shoulders. On my other side, Vivienne and I held hands while Louis put his arms around her on one side and Harriet on the other. Vivienne was squeezing my hand very tightly and I thought something was upsetting her even though she was smiling and singing as Melody encouraged the crowd to join in the chorus.

It was their last song, and they left the stage, but people were stamping and clapping for an encore. I had to leave to get the last bus.

'You guys stay,' I said.

'Aren't you going to wait and see Melody?' Frieda asked. I shook my head.

The others decided to leave with me, and we made our

way to the exit. The audience cheered as the band came back on stage.

There was a log jam in front of the doors as other people were already leaving. Bodies were crammed together to funnel through the narrow gap. Being small I hated these crushes: at armpit height, I was hemmed in on all sides unable to see and shuffling along as if my ankles were chained. I had to fight the urge to go crazy and push my way out. I was one stampede away from death by trample. It was alright for the tall ones like Frieda and Louis who could see what was happening. I heard Vivienne say hi to someone and peering around Louis's broad back I saw Grant Barker in front of us with his arm around the waist of a raven-haired girl.

'Oh, hi Viv,' Grant said but he looked straight past Vivienne and was staring at me as if he'd noticed me for the first time. His eyes crinkled as he smiled and winked at me. Then the crowd swept him away in front of us.

'Who's Grant with? I recognize her.' I asked Vivienne

'Priya, year 11. His girlfriend, though I don't know for how long.'

'What do you mean?

'Well, he and Coco are extremely friendly these days.'

What a player. Flirting with me in front of his girlfriend and getting off with Coco behind her back. Did he think he was irresistible?

Out in the night air the fear of being flattened faded. A layer of sweat cooled on my skin. We walked away from the club doors until there was enough space to gather and say our goodbyes.

Tamasin called an Uber to take her home and as Frieda lived in Balsall Heath which was on the way, Tamasin said she'd drop her back. We waved them off and Viv and Louis walked with me to my bus stop. Louis's friend

Harriet tagged along. She was older than us and talked a lot, going on about how difficult it was to be back in Birmingham after being away at Uni for three years. She was keen to emphasize her superiority. I didn't much like her. Vivienne was unusually quiet.

8

'I know something's going on between them.' Vivienne was in her bedroom, pacing around in her tiger print PJs. I kept missing parts of what she was saying.

'Sit down Viv. I can't hear you properly when you're charging around.' I could understand why Vivienne wouldn't want to stare at my unwashed, half-asleep face but she'd chosen to FaceTime me at nine on a Saturday morning.

'With Harriet?' I backtracked.

'I just told you,' Vivienne almost screamed at me. She had got herself wound up so tight you could have used her to drill for oil.

'Calm down, I'm trying to catch up here. Please sit down and speak slowly.'

Vivienne held her phone so I could see her. She looked terrible with red swollen eyes and her skin so pale that it had a greeny-grey hue against the vibrant purple of her bedroom walls.

'I've been awake all night,' she said. 'Trying to decide what I should do.'

'He seemed fine last night. On good form.'

Vivienne leaned into the screen so close I could see the hairs in her nostrils.

'What you've gotta grasp Pen is that Louis was heartbroken when Harriet dumped him. She was his first love. They go to the same church; his Mum loves her.'

'And Louis is crazy about you now. You're the most well-matched couple I've ever seen.'

'She wants him back and that's why he's gone weird on me, I know it.' Vivienne was gnawing her fingernails as if they were chicken wings.

'Don't chew your nails,' I reminded her because she'd asked me to. 'Sit on your hands.'

She did and I found myself looking at a clump of frizzy bed hair and the bedroom ceiling. I addressed the hair. 'I think you're making this into a big issue. When it isn't.'

'You think so?' Vivienne quietened down.

'He's just being friendly. Besides you're loads prettier than she is.'

'Am I?' Vivienne's face came back into view looking happier but still like an extra in a vampire film, droopy and bloodless.

'Defo. Are you seeing him later?'

She nodded.

'I wouldn't make a big deal about it if I were you.'

'Thanks Pen,'.

Mum and Thomas were in the kitchen making American-style pancakes. Thomas had recently got into cooking which was excellent news because this pushed Mum into making more effort.

I sat at the table checking my phone.

'You have a nice evening?' Mum asked. I had messages from Frieda and Tamasin.

'I said – did you have a nice evening?' Mum repeated at an increased volume.

'Yeah,' I answered.

'Well, I had a nice time too,' she said sarcastically. I looked up at her but didn't say anything. There was no way I wanted to know any details. Thomas brought the pancakes across and there were even blueberries and maple syrup out on the table. Mum was singing along to the radio.

'When's Dad coming to pick us up?' Thomas asked. We exchanged a knowing look. I knew I was being childish. Mum had every right to date other men, but I had a bad feeling about Mike. Also, I didn't think it was fair that Mum, who couldn't even go out of the house on her own, had somehow managed to get a boyfriend while I remained forever single. I let out a heavy sigh. At least there were pancakes.

'These are really good Thomas.' I was being hugely encouraging about his cooking for entirely selfish reasons.

We met up with Dad on Saturdays. If Birmingham City was playing at home Dad took Thomas. This week they were away in Norwich, so we went out for lunch instead to a new Turkish cafe in Harborne where you sat on low benches stacked with velvet cushions. The place wasn't really Dad's style, but I was keen to try it out.

Only seeing Dad once a week was weird, like meeting up with a distant cousin. Someone related by blood but without much to say to each other. Dad now lived in a two-bedroom flat in the old part of Harborne. The idea was that Thomas and I could stay over. So far, we hadn't done that. I was sure Dad liked being on his own. He could listen to jazz and do his local history research without being disturbed. Meanwhile, Thomas and I were left dealing with Mum. It wasn't fair that he'd escaped.

'Mum went out last night,' Thomas said between bites of burger. I glared at him, but he took no notice and carried on. 'With Mike.'

'Did she?' Dad didn't seem upset. He didn't ask any follow-up questions, just went quiet and then began interrogating Thomas on how he was doing at his new school. Now that Thomas was at senior school, he got his share of the pressure to achieve. Dad never asked me about dancing. Not ever.

I looked forward to seeing Dad but often came away disappointed. He didn't seem at all sad about not living with us. At least he saw us every week which was more than Frieda's Dad had ever done. I should try and be more positive.

At school on Monday, I passed Vivienne in the corridor on my way to History.

'How did it go with Louis?' I asked.

She spread her fingers and rocked her hand in a so-so gesture. I noticed that the no-biting of her nails wasn't working.

'I'll tell you later. I'm late for Psychology.'

In History class Tamasin was waiting for me.

'You're famous,' she said handing me her phone.

There was a photo of me with Melody on stage at The Midnight Bell with a headline – Local Band Reveals Secret Behind Name. There was a paragraph about Melody and the band and then one about me.

Good Samaritan, sixteen-year-old Pen Flowers, found singer Melody Jones collapsed outside the King's Head pub in Harborne at 2 am in the morning and walked her home safely. Melody says, 'She just appeared out of the night and helped me. I thought she was an angel. I wrote a song about her called Night Angel and Marlon thought that would be a cool name for the band.

I felt embarrassed. She was making out I was some kind of heroine when I wasn't. I sat down next to Tamasin for the first time this term, as if we were back to being friends.

'The Night Angels are amazing,' she said. 'Friday night was ace – thanks for getting us in. Everyone is well impressed.' Knowing Melody was improving my street cred. 'Frieda's cool.' Tamasin was fishing for gossip, but I wasn't going to tell her anything.

'She is,' I agreed as Miss McBride, the history teacher, arrived.

We stopped talking and concentrated on the aftermath of the English Civil War. We were looking at these cool revolutionary groups called The Levellers and Diggers. I couldn't believe how radical their ideas were. In the seventeenth century, they fought against the 'slavery of property' and believed in the common ownership of land. If only they'd been successful then maybe people wouldn't have spent the next three hundred years destroying our planet.

After class, we had a free period before English and Tamasin suggested we walk up to the High Street to get a drink. I was surprised but agreed.

The morning was cold but bright, with that honey-coloured autumn sunlight that gave everywhere a nostalgic glow. We were a little awkward around each other as we walked down the school drive and up to the shops. The conversation kept lapsing into silence as we stepped around sensitive areas like cracks in the pavement.

'What did you make of Miss McBride's new eco shoes?' Tamasin asked.

'Truly hideous,' I laughed. 'With that added weird flower detail to draw attention to them.'

'She must get them from a hideous shoe specialist.'

I laughed again and we lapsed back into silence. We passed the park and were halfway up the hill when she started speaking.

'We've never talked since, you know,'

I nodded, waiting. Tamasin went on. 'I've missed

being friends with you, Pen. I know I messed up. I've got other friends but they're not close like we were. I can't talk to them like I could with you.'

I wanted to say that it had been her choice to drop me, but I kept my mouth shut and concentrated on being kind. Tamasin hated showing weakness. This was the first time I'd ever heard her admit to any vulnerable feelings. Maybe if she was more open we could be friends again. If it wasn't another booby trap.

'My Mum said I should talk to you and "build bridges",' she made inverted commas in the air. I smiled because I could just see Mrs Fox, saying it. 'Mum's all about talking stuff through, and Vivienne said she thought I should too.'

She'd been getting advice from Vivienne! Not just the Diggers and Levellers going for radical change. Tamasin used to be so rude about Vivienne. We were entering a new world order. I walked on for a bit not saying anything. We turned into the High Street. Part of me wanted to brush over what had happened so that this awkwardness would end, and we could go back to talking about shoes. But if we were ever to be friends again, I needed to be honest.

I took a deep breath.

'The thing is Tamasin, I get that you're sorry but if we're going to be friends, proper friends, like someone I know I can trust, then you need to realise how important dancing is to me. It's the thing that makes me happy.'

Tamasin didn't look at me, keeping her eyes on the ground. I went on.

'You don't have to feel the same way. Why should you? But you need to respect my feelings.'

We were outside the coffee shop now.

'I'll get these,' Tamasin said and opened the door so that a gust of hot air lifted my fringe. 'You want to try their special Christmas hot chocolate?'

'Sure.' I followed her inside and waited near the door while she queued and paid. She'd recently had her hair cut into a short curly bob and had new retro-shaped tortoise-shell glasses. Her look had shifted from girly into a geekier style. She handed me the hot chocolate and we walked back towards Kings. She was taking her time over her reply.

'Your dancing obsession,' she said, and I bristled but she went on not even noticing. 'Came out of nowhere and then took over. You know I can't dance, I'm crap at it. So, it was difficult for me. I could tell you were good. Seriously good. Frieda says even at college you're the best in the class. I was jealous. I was afraid you were leaving me behind and...' Tamasin's voice choked up and she coughed. 'And I just felt so angry inside, I can't explain. I've been unhappy for ages.' Her eyes were tearing up. Tamasin crying!

I put my arms around her and pulled her to me, manoeuvring my hug around our cups. There weren't many people I was taller than, but Tamasin was one of them. She was genuinely upset.

'Tell me about angry and unhappy? That's my special-ty.' I said making her give a watery snort of laughter. 'We've still got loads in common.'

'You've spilled chocolate all down your coat.'

'No use crying over spilt chocolate,' I said feeling profound and scrubbing at my puffer with a napkin.

At lunchtime Tamasin, Vivienne, and I hung out as if we'd been best buddies forever. Vivienne was happy to talk about Louis in front of Tamasin. They seemed to have become friends without me noticing. Must have happened on Wednesdays when I was at college. They were both doing Drama A Level.

Vivienne launched into her woes. 'I tried not to make a

big deal about Harriet. But I couldn't stop myself. Louis said they were just friends, that he couldn't ignore her, and I was being paranoid. Then he said if I wouldn't believe him it was pointless to talk anymore. He left early and hasn't phoned or texted since. I'm sure something's going on.'

Vivienne was more agitated than I'd ever seen her. I felt sorry for Louis. She was wound up about the play and this business with Harriet was a total projection. Her character, Elizabeth Procter, had been betrayed not her. She was attacking the skin around her nails with her teeth, speaking in between bites.

'The thing is I've got rehearsals every night this week and then the dress rehearsal this weekend and then tech rehearsal and then the performances, so I won't get to see him for two weeks.' She was close to tears. For once I felt like the most stable dry-eyed person present.

Tamasin and I looked at each other to see who was going to answer. She left it to me.

'That's a good thing. You'll be free to concentrate on the play, and Louis'll miss you and get over whatever is bothering him. He's coming to the play?'

'Yeah, I've got him tickets for the final night.'

'You know Mrs Mulligan's having a cast party at her house afterward.' Tamasin shifted the focus.

Vivienne's love of Mrs Mulligan had grown ever more intense during the rehearsals. She was an ideal way to distract Vivienne from Louis's imaginary infidelity.

'God yeah, I can't wait to see what her house is like – I bet it's gorgeous.'

I had the second rehearsal for the opening dance sequence. This time without Frieda's help. It went okay. Rosa as Tituba was giving the moves her best and the other girls, particularly Coco, were enjoying getting down and dirty.

Even Tamasin was having a go.

Once we'd finished Grant and Coco had a rehearsal. As Tamasin and I were leaving the hall there was a commotion in the corridor outside. A girl with long dark silky hair was being pulled away from the hall door by two year elevens.

'What's all that about?' I wondered out loud.

'Priya's messed up because Grant dumped her. She thinks he's having a thing with Coco.'

Why was I always the last person to know what was going on?

'And is he?'

'Probably. Who knows, who cares?'

Tamasin was unmoved by Priya's despair and walked past her sobbing figure without a moment's pause. I felt sorry for her. She must be really cut up to make such a humiliating public demonstration of her feelings. But Tamasin was right, none of this was my business. What did it matter who Grant Barker was dating?

9

Frieda was ridiculously excited about my photo in the paper. She was showing the other students The Night Angels story on her phone as we got changed for dance practice.

'Pen's a real-life superhero. She needs an outfit with a cloak,' Frieda teased. I wished she'd stop making a fuss. I didn't know the other students very well and didn't want them to think I was full of myself. As I yanked up my leggings the skin on the back of my hands prickled like it did when I was scared.

Helping Melody hadn't happened the way the newspaper story said. I wasn't a Good Samaritan. I'd seen Melody around in Harborne and I wanted to get to know her because she looked exciting. Her being drunk gave me an excuse to speak to her - that was the truth. There was one story out in public but a different one in my heart. I felt ashamed like I was a fraud. I'd texted Melody to say how good the gig was but she hadn't replied. She wasn't a reliable friend.

But I liked her music and suggested to Frieda that we use the Night Angel song for our end-of-term dance project. Whatever ambivalence I felt about Melody, the song was beautiful with a disturbing discordant undercurrent that worked against the lyrics. Predictably, Frieda loved the idea.

After an hour of excruciating ballet with our technique teacher we were left to work on our own pieces. I wanted our duet to be spectacular. But because of the school play,

I hadn't had much time to work on it. The play took up way too much space in my life. Dancing wasn't getting enough attention.

Mr Thorne, or Joe as he liked us to call him, was a small compact man only two or three inches taller than me but without one millimetre of fat over his sculpted muscles. He was going bald so kept his head shaved but he had a black arrow of a goatee and intense dark blue eyes. The way he focused on a detail of a foot or hand out of line was alarming. He was obsessed with timing and body alignment. I thought of him as a scalpel, a dance surgeon, cutting and exposing, sharp and deadly. He was a friend of Frieda's mother and Frieda said Joe was a laugh. I'd seen no evidence of this.

Frieda and I started improvising. I had a vision of how the dance could look but the moves were ambitious. There was a back-to-back lift I'd done with Tartan Fling that I wanted to try. I explained how it worked to Frieda and she immediately hoisted me onto her back and spun me round with both of our arms outstretched. In the mirror, we could see how well the move worked. Frieda, who did martial arts, was stronger and fitter than me. When I tried to lift her onto my back and do the same thing I staggered as I turned. Stretching my arms out was agony and I could only keep them extended for a few seconds.

Joe came over to watch us. I could've done without his sharp little eyes watching me flounder. He pointed out the muscles in my core that I should use.

'You need to strengthen your abdominals and your back muscles.' He told me. 'At the moment your legs are strong, but the rest of your body is in serious need of attention.' He moved on to lacerate someone else. I felt like the weak link in our team. But I gritted my teeth. Hating him gave me the energy to keep trying.

At the end of the session, I was a right sweaty Betty and was on my way to the shower when Joe called me over.

'A word with you, Pen. When you've changed.'

Frieda and I exchanged glances.

'What do you think he wants?' I asked her.

'No idea.'

He was waiting for me in the dance studio. I hoped whatever he wanted wouldn't take too long as I'd still got an hour's bus journey home and a load of homework to do before tomorrow. If he was going to have a go at me that wasn't fair. I was trying my hardest.

'Frieda told me you've done some work with Jock Briggs. I can see that in your approach,' he started.

'Oh, do you know Jock?' I asked trying to be friendly in a Frieda style.

'Our paths crossed briefly,' Joe swiped my question away. He was in full-on teacher mode. 'I want to discuss your intentions after A Levels.'

I breathed in and answered honestly. 'I want to go to the London School of Contemporary Dance where Jock went, and then either join Tartan Fling or start my own company.' This sounded audacious in the face of Joe's scrutiny. But I'd spent hours dreaming up my future.

'You want to be a professional dancer?' His eyebrows went up like pointed tents.

'And a choreographer.' I tried not to waver even though he was looking at me like I was a body on an operating table.

'What's your training schedule?' he asked.

'I'm sorry?'

'Dance classes, practice sessions, gym training – talk me through your current programme.'

'Well, I do adult ballet on Monday and then I have Wednesdays here at college, plus I'm choreographing a dance for the school play. I work on my own ideas when I have time.'

He nodded.

'How many hours in all?'

'Maybe nine or ten,' I said exaggerating massively.

'You've got a natural flair for dance, plus an intelligent and creative mind.' Even though Joe was saying complimentary things I could see the blade of the 'but' coming before he raised the knife. 'But your technique is virtually non-existent and your body,' he turned down his mouth in sorrow. 'A dancer must be an athlete. Your body is your instrument. You need to practice, practice, practice. You lack strength, flexibility, and stamina. If you're serious about being a professional dancer, you should be training a minimum of twenty hours a week. I can see from your body that you're not.'

I didn't know what to say. I wasn't lazy or unwilling, but I couldn't see where to fit it in. I spent two hours on the bus every day to and from school, we had a ton of homework, plus Saturdays were the only time I saw Dad, and then there was the stupid play. I was filling up with despair as if the fire brigade had turned industrial-scale hoses on my inner flame. I'd never make it as a dancer.

'I don't know how to do that,' I said in a tiny panicky voice that I didn't recognise. Joe, the scalpel, smiled.

'Of course you don't. That's why I'm offering to train you. If you're prepared to put the time and effort in, then I think I can turn you into a dancer.'

I was overwhelmed. Mr Thorne was offering to give me special coaching. I didn't know what was stronger, my gratitude or my fear. I hesitated for a second but then leaped in.

'Thanks, I am. I truly, truly, am, whatever, thanks so much.' I stammered out.

Joe laughed and the next minute I was committing myself to getting up an hour earlier every morning, doing two nights a week plus four hours at the weekend. Becoming a dancer was going to hurt in so many ways.

On the bus home I put my earbuds in and listened to the 'Night Angel' track, staring out of the window not focusing on the outside, just letting the neon Christmas lights blur into stripes of colour against the dark sky.

My body was humming. I loved the way I felt after a day in the dance studio. Feel-good endorphins whizzed around inside me and even though Joe had criticized my body I could feel a sheath of muscles like a corset holding me tight inside. I felt strong and sexy with the life force surging through me. Imagine how I'd feel once I was training twenty hours a week? I'd need an outfit and a cloak I'd be so super-powered. But then how was I going to keep up with the new schedule without dying?

I was deep in my own complex inner world when someone tapped me on the shoulder. I looked up to see Grant Barker standing there smiling at me. I hadn't even realised that he was on the bus. I popped out one earbud.

'Come and see the Bournville Christmas tree,' he said and held out his hand.

I put my hand in his and he led me down the stairs and off the bus.

10

I've no idea why I followed. I was still dreamy, preoccupied, my head full of music and he was so certain and confident. He summoned and I obeyed. 'Night Angel' was still playing in one ear as hand in hand, laughing, we ran across Bournville Green towards the Christmas tree.

The tree was a giant Cedar – dark and lush, planted outside the Quaker Meeting House and decorated every Christmas with thousands of lights. This year they'd gone for blue and gold. We raced towards the deep bluey green twinkling shadow as if we were entering a magic cave, a portal into a new dimension.

Often crowds were gathered around the tree but tonight there was just Grant and me. I breathed in the piney scent.

'It's like being in a Hans Christian Andersen fairy tale,' I said. In reply Grant leaned forward and kissed me. We'd barely ever spoken. I didn't know if he even knew my name, but his lips were slowly and gently touching mine.

What kind of kiss was this? Friendly, ironic, a dare? Coming out of nowhere, cold, and warm at the same time, sweet and somehow innocent but also amazingly sexy and totally unexpected. A kiss that got firmer and fuller as I closed my eyes and surprised myself by kissing back. I returned the pressure. Our lips lingered, nothing urgent, not going anywhere, just hanging out until we had to part to breathe. A good kiss. A very good kiss. Wow! Nothing like this had ever happened to me before.

We peeled apart. I opened my eyes and looked up at Grant who was staring back at me, his green eyes scrunched with laughter lines.

'Do you even know my name?' I asked.

'Everyone knows your name Pen Flowers,' he said. 'You're famous.' He was teasing me. I didn't know if he meant because of The Night Angels newspaper photo or the Giant Arse video so I blushed and pulled away. But he reached out and touched my arm.

'Your bus,' he said nodding over my head at the road behind us. We ran back to the bus stop just as another number eleven drew up. Its doors opened with the farting sound of air escaping from a tyre. I got on and Grant stood there smiling at me as the glass panels slid closed between us.

'See you.' He mouthed as the bus pulled away.

I climbed up to my usual seat at the front of the top deck and through the window saw him looking up from the pavement. He winked at me.

What had just happened?

I put in my other earbud and went back to counting the bars of 'Night Angel'. I needed to steady myself. Why had I let Grant Barker play me like that? What was I thinking?

The kiss was like a shiny bauble on the Christmas tree. I left the experience hanging in the dark. I could feel the impact on my body. Every molecule was now on full alert. My face, reflected in the bus window, grinned at me like an idiot, with a smile so wide it hurt. There was a fizzy sensation in my belly that hadn't been there before.

Part 2

Dance of the Night Angel

11

I wasn't going to think about The Kiss. Too dangerous. The kiss existed in another dimension. I told no one about it, not even myself. But in that elsewhere space the memory floated, emitting a warm glow as if I were smiling inside.

The alarm catapulted me from a cocoon of deep, delicious, darkness. Sadly, there was no longer space for dreaming - my life was too busy. Getting up at six in the week was bad enough but getting up at seven on a Saturday was much worse. My pillow had never been more loving; parting from its soft embrace was brutal. Did I want to be a dancer this much?

The house was silent as I dressed. Downstairs in the kitchen, the empty cereal box was scrunched up in the recycling. Thomas was in the living room on his PlayStation

'You've eaten all the cereal. You could've left me some.'

'There wasn't much.'

So, breakfast was off the menu. I opened the fridge and was confronted by a vast emptiness. Only a going-orange bit of cheese and the crusts of a loaf of bread. All the fruit had gone. Typical. How was I going to get a dancer's body on a diet of mouldy cheese and stale bread? I got out a glass and banged the cupboard doors.

Mum appeared in her dressing gown while I was drinking milk and putting together a pathetic, unappetising sandwich.

'There's no food in the house. You know I've got my

first training session this morning and then the dress rehearsal for the play.'

'The Tesco order's coming this morning.'

'That's no good for me I'm getting the 7.30 bus. I'm supposed to eat nutritionally balanced meals to build muscle.'

'Stop shouting Pen. I'm sorry, okay, I'm not perfect. I'll give you some money and you can get what you want.'

She handed me a £20 note which I pocketed.

'And get yourself fish and chips or pizza for tea. Thomas is staying over at Dad's. I'm out with Mike.'

It wasn't enough that she saw him every day for her driving lessons. She had to go out with him at weekends. Mike-the-Menace had been around our house far too much recently. There was something sleazy about him. The way his eyes combed over my body made me put on my baggiest sweatshirt.

'If you spent more time ordering food before we ran out and less time dating, I'd stand a chance of making it as a dancer.'

Mum started to shout back.

'You want me to be trapped at home, imprisoned, a 24/7 servant!'

'No, I don't.'

'I'm trying to get better. Don't you want me to be happy?'

Not if her happiness involved Mike.

I slammed the front door shut as I left. Resentment and self-pity fuelled my sprint to the bus stop. Why did I have to have such a useless hopeless mother? A proper mother would drive me to my first training class. She'd be encouraging. Tell me there was no need to be scared. She'd make me a lentil salad with nuts and healthy green veg. In my dreams.

*

Joe was waiting for me in the dance studio. By then I'd woken up. I wasn't afraid of working hard. I was ready to give my heart and soul to being a dancer. I liked physical exercise, that feeling of pushing your body to its limits. With Tartan Fling we'd danced for hours every day and I'd never been happier. But I was anxious at the thought of being alone with Joe-the-scalpel.

'Let's warm up,' he said the moment I entered. He led me through a gentle ballet-inspired routine. Then we did thirty minutes of stretching exercises which he said I needed to do every day to improve my flexibility. How did he expect me to squeeze these into my timetable? I'd have to get up in the middle of the night to do forward bends.

'We'll have a five-minute break before we start on your core training.' Joe fetched two balls, one large, one small, from the corner of the room and placed them near us.

I glugged back half my water bottle feeling certain that the worst was yet to come.

'What do your parents think about you being a dancer?' Joe asked.

'Mum thinks it's great. She was a ballroom dancer when she was young. Dad's not keen. He wants me to do history at university. They're separated.' I added unnecessarily.

'Recently?' Joe asked and I nodded. 'That's tough.'

I hadn't expected sympathy from Mr Thorne. If I thought about Dad never coming home a dark hole opened inside. What if Mike moved in?

'What music are you and Frieda using for your duet?' Joe asked and I was grateful for the change of subject.

'Have you heard of The Night Angels? They're a local band – we're using one of their songs.'

'I like the idea of using a local band. I'll look forward to hearing the track.' I could see why Frieda said he was easy to talk to. I was starting to like him.

'Okay, let's get to work on your core.' He jumped up.

The things he made me do. Hundreds of abdominal exercises, crunches, sit-ups, leg lifts, press-ups, planks, everything I was worst at. He wouldn't let me give up. He held my feet down and barked counts. Any idea of liking Joe vanished. We were in a sado-masochistic relationship in which he had the power, and I had the pain. He treated my body like a lump of clay that he was sculpting. My agony was of no interest to him.

When we'd finished the floor exercises, he asked me to stand on a weird wobbly ball with a flat top. Keeping balance and not falling off was difficult but I wasn't doing too badly.

'Now we're going to go through your leg exercises.'

I jumped off the ball pleased to be moving onto something I felt confident about.

'No, get back on the ball, do them while balancing on the ball.'

'That's impossible!' He was joking surely. But he didn't even reply just waited unsmiling. I fell off again and again.

'I can't do it,' I said, the fury rising inside me.

'You need to find the muscles, once you engage your core, you'll be able to lift your legs.' Joe was oblivious.

I'd never felt so useless. If he was training me in falling over he was doing a great job. By the time I'd fallen off a trillion times, I could just about manage to stand on one foot and lift one leg six inches for three seconds. It took massive concentration and I had to squeeze every single muscle I possessed.

'Okay good, now balance on two feet again.' By now simply standing on the ball felt easy. Joe threw a small leather football-sized ball at me. It was super heavy and slammed into my belly. I caught it but wobbled like crazy and seconds later tumbled to the ground.

'Up,' he said, 'then throw the medicine ball back.' The brute kept chucking the monster ball right into my middle and knocking the breath and balance out of me. Rage surged through me. I channelled my whole being into hating Joe and managed to catch the ball without falling and chucked it back at him with all the force I could. I wanted to knock him over.

'Now we're getting somewhere,' he said, smiling as if he understood how angry he'd made me. By the end of an hour of this torture which had nothing to do with dancing, sweat was pouring off me.

'Okay,' Joe said, 'you can take a ten-minute break and then we'll finish with some technique and that's probably enough for today.'

My muscles were shaky before I even began this last session. At least finally I was dancing. Joe played a phrase of music and demonstrated a sequence I had to copy. He was an excellent dancer. His technique, as far as I could tell, was perfect but he didn't have that magical quality that Jock brought to his dancing. Joe was textbook precise but there was no inner flame and inner flame was what, for me, dancing was about. For Joe it was counting bars and drilling moves like a machine. This was dancing as if you were in the army, left, right, left, right, stop, turn, fire. A storm was rising inside me.

'No, no, no, you keep missing the beat. You're not counting. The jump starts on beat 4,' Joe corrected me.

I hated counting. I needed to feel the music so that my moves came out of the expressive moment – that was how Jock had taught me. Counting like this killed everything dead.

'Jock says you need to feel the music and let the timing emerge naturally.' I fought back.

'You still need to count, or you'll get lost on complex sequences and if you want to choreograph for other dancers, you'll need to give them counts. No counting no dancing. Your mate Jock counts like everyone else. It's only after counting has been drilled into you that you can afford to be casual about it. I want you to count every piece of music you listen to. Go to sleep counting, wake up counting.'

I wanted to tell him to count me out. But I didn't of course. Even though my whole body was hurting and only rage gave me the energy to continue, some part of my brain knew that Joe was giving up his Saturday morning to teach me. I couldn't even pay him any money. I should be grateful, but it was hard to be grateful to someone who was making you feel like you wished you were dead.

We ended the session by dancing a difficult sequence together. I almost got the timings right and while Joe didn't go as far as actual praise, he did say I'd worked hard, and he'd see me again on Monday at 7.00 am. He went off to get changed leaving me alone in the studio.

My muscles started to wobble by themselves. I couldn't stop them. I seemed not to have bones anymore. I was total jelly, melting down onto the floor like a giant amoeba. The door to get out of the studio was so far away I'd never get there. Maybe someone could scrape me off the floor and scoop me into a plastic bag and carry me.

I didn't know how I was going to stand up, let alone get showered and walk back to school and do the dress rehearsal for the play.

A long hot shower followed by hot chocolate and a muffin on Kings Heath High Street gave me just enough life force to make it up the school drive. I was glad that

Joe's training had left me too exhausted to be nervous. Even so a cloud of butterflies erupted in my belly as I walked into the hall.

The Christmas tree kiss that I wasn't thinking about had made a sudden and spectacular entrance. One idea had taken over my entire brain - any minute now, I'd be face to face with Grant Barker.

12

The school hall was packed with people. Movement in every direction, so that I didn't know where to focus and for a few seconds couldn't make sense of the space. Most of the chairs had been pushed to one side, just a few rows left at the front, and the main body of the hall had been divided into separate areas each filled with frenetic activity. Two boys walked past carrying a painted backdrop, a landscape of tidy green fields. Mr Andrews, who was down by the stage, called them over and directed them up the steps. A group of girls were painting two more large canvases spread out on sheets on the floor. One was the interior of a wood-beamed house. The sound of loud hammering was coming from somewhere. I scanned the clusters of people for Vivienne but couldn't see her. I didn't know what I'd do if I saw Grant. There was a bubbly sensation in my belly as if I'd drunk a can of coke too quickly.

He wasn't in the hall.

Mrs Mulligan's voice dominated the low hum of chatter. She was at the back of the room behind a rail of costumes.

'You're meant to look like a Puritan not a prostitute, lace that up to the neck. Your hair needs to be out of sight.' Her voice was high-pitched and tense.

There was no sign of Coco or Tamasin, none of the people in my scene. Where were they? I felt lost, and anxious.

'Hi Pen,' said a quiet voice at my side. I turned and

Vivienne's friend Ed was smiling at me. 'I've been waiting for you to get here. Can you come and look at the set for the dance sequence? I need to check that it's safe. We're starting in twenty minutes.'

'Sure.' I followed him, glad to have something to do. Ed moved purposefully towards the stage threading his way through the clumps of people. He didn't part the crowds like Frieda with a smile and a nudge and a cheeky elbow, he just approached, waited and people moved out of his way. Following behind him, I wasn't sure how he did it, a path simply opened in front of him.

Once we were on the stage he called up to the balcony at the back of the hall.

'Can we have lighting cue one for the opening scene, please.'

The overhead lights went out and the stage was striped with green light streaming through slotted panels on either side of the stage.

'Wow, this looks amazing,' I said. 'It's like being in a forest.'

Ed nodded and the tips of his ears went pink. Viv was right, he was a sweetie.

'Can you try the platform for Tituba?' he asked me.

I jumped up and ran through a few of Tituba's dance moves. Getting into a low squat made me wince. Joe's training session had probably left me permanently damaged. As I moved the platform shifted slightly.

'We'll need to wedge that,' Ed said. 'Okay thanks.' As he turned to leave, I caught his arm.

'Do you know where everyone is? I can't find Vivienne.'

'She might be having her photo taken. They're doing cast portraits for the programme in the foyer. She was already in costume when I saw her last. You need to be ready to go in ten minutes. Girls' costumes are at the back of the hall.'

'Great thanks. You know everything,' I said, and he laughed.

'I think that's the stage manager's job.'

'Ed, can you come here?' Mr Andrews called.

'Got to go.'

I made my way to the costume rail in the far corner of the hall and found Tamasin looking appalled as she stared at her reflection in a full-length mirror. She was wearing a shapeless white cotton sack with a drawstring neck.

'This is what we're expected to wear for the opening dance,' she said. 'You've got one too.'

Along the rail were hangers marked with characters' names. I had a white sack the same as Tamasin's and a brown laced jacket and matching skirt plus a white Puritan collar and cap. I changed into my cotton shift. I had no idea how I was going to dance because just lifting my arms to pull on the sack sent arrows of pain through my shoulders and down my back.

Once inside the shift I looked in the mirror and had the same reaction as Tamasin.

'See what I mean?' she said tying up the tunic top that fitted over the white shift. Hers was a dark grey colour. The dresses weren't as bad as the shift. You could at least pull in the lacing to give them some shape and I quite liked the big white collars and cute little caps. Mrs Mulligan came whirling up,

'Let's see.'

Tamasin and I turned towards her, and she shouted with laughter.

'I've never seen you two look so demure. Excellent. Go through and get your photos taken then be ready to start in five minutes.' And off she raced. In honour of the dress rehearsal, she was wearing a flappy kimono-type robe over her usual black roll neck and leggings. Pink and red cranes took flight across her back. Tamasin and I looked at each other and shrugged.

We found Vivienne out in the corridor. She had a similar outfit to ours only hers was a pretty cornflower blue.

'You look good,' I said, trying to work out why she seemed different.

'Thanks,' she said, 'you too, both of you.'

I realised what it was.

'Vivienne you're so skinny.' With her hair tucked up into the white cap her face was a long pale oval. She looked taller and older, worn down with sorrow. She had completely transformed herself into the character of Elizabeth Proctor.

'Yeah, see,' she turned round and showed us that her skirt had been pleated and fixed with safety pins. 'They've had to take my dress in by two inches.' She waited with us while Tamasin and I had our photos taken.

'You nervous?' I asked as we walked back to the hall. She was unusually quiet.

'I'm worried I'm going to throw up I'm so scared. I've been having nightmares that I've forgotten my words.'

'You'll be brilliant Viv; I know you will.' I squeezed her hand. I didn't feel nervous about the play. I had such a small part it didn't matter how bad I was. I was about to ask Vivienne if she'd seen Grant when a loud buzzer went off.

'That's the call,' Viv said, and we ran back to the hall.

'Starting positions,' Mrs Mulligan shouted, and Tamasin and I sprinted to the far side of the stage. Coco and Rosa and the other girls were already waiting in their shifts, running on the spot to keep warm. Tamasin and I stripped off our dresses and hung them on a rail put there for this purpose. Ed had thought of everything.

Mrs Mulligan stood in the middle of the stage and called for silence. She spread her arms wide so that her robe swirled around her like she was conjuring a rabbit from her sleeve.

'Okay, I want absolute focus. This is the dress rehearsal which means no matter what happens the show goes on as if this were a real performance.' She paused checking that every eye was fixed on her. 'I'll be in the audience watching with Mr Andrews and we'll give detailed notes at the end. Ed will cue you in. Please listen for his instructions. I want you to give this everything you've got. Break a leg.'

She ended with a dramatic flourish of her flapping sleeves, then clapped her hands and vaulted off the stage. I'd have laughed if she'd broken her leg. She was such a show-off.

The lights went out in the hall and the green woodland lighting faded up on the stage.

'Starting positions,' Ed said quietly behind us and then to me, 'watch my hand and I'll cue in the music.'

We ran onto the stage. Even though there was no real audience some of the backstage people were sitting in the hall or had gathered in the wings to watch. I was focused on Ed when Grant walked up and stood behind him, wearing a leather jerkin with his hair combed back off his face. He looked rugged and sexy, and he winked at me. Ed was waving his arm to get my attention and signalling three, two, one, with his fingers. The music started and our dance began.

I was pleased with how well everyone danced. Even Tamasin remembered the moves and Rosa, as Tituba, was raw, and earthy. Coco managed to look arrogantly sexy.

When the music finished, and the lights went down we ran off the stage. There was sniggering from the hall. Some people were just so stupid. Did they not realise that the dance was deliberately provocative, that was the whole point? Why the need to giggle like twelve-year-olds?

I didn't have time to stay annoyed because we had to get our Puritan dresses on for the first scene. Coco was straight on for the opening lines, and I followed a few minutes later. Just before my entrance Grant came up behind me and put his hands on my waist.

'Great dancing,' he whispered in my ear. 'Couldn't take my eyes off you.'

There was some teasing hidden in his words. I felt flustered and rushed onto the stage in a right state. Luckily Mrs Mulligan thought I was acting and later praised me for being 'real' when she was giving out her notes.

When I had to do my flirtatious exit, I swayed my hips and looked directly into Grant's eyes as I walked towards him, dropping him a curtsy, and then brushing my hand along his arm as I left.

'Good morning, Mr Proctor,' I said with a confident cheeky smile.

Grant's eyebrows shot up. This acting business allowed you to behave in ways you couldn't as yourself.

The scene between Grant and Coco was hot and steamy. They behaved as if they wanted to rip each other's clothes off and it didn't look like acting to me. I wasn't on again until near to the end of the final Act. As I made my way towards the backstage steps, I saw Ed.

'Was that okay?' I asked him. 'The dance?'

Ed's face flushed.

'Yeah, very good,' he mumbled not looking at me directly. 'May need some costume adjustments.' He rushed onto the stage to reset for the next scene.

*

I sat on my own at the back of the hall watching the show and eating my stale cheese sandwiches. Vivienne's big scene with Grant was at the start of Act Two. As Grant's betrayed wife she needed to win the audience's sympathy away from the beautiful, sexy Coco. Competing with Coco was a tough challenge.

The moment Vivienne walked on stage the atmosphere in the hall changed. I don't know how she gathered the attention, but everyone stopped what they were doing and watched her. Up until this point Coco and Grant's scene had been the most watchable, but Vivienne was mesmerising. You couldn't take your eyes off her. And it wasn't just because she was my friend. The room had gone totally silent.

On stage Viv had disappeared. Instead, a thin, angular woman moved awkwardly towards her husband. I felt her heartbreak. Her struggle to trust again. Elizabeth Proctor could have come across as cold and judgemental, but Vivienne's portrayal trembled with restrained passion. Grant did all right, but he was like a schoolboy playing a man's role. He couldn't come near the truth of Viv's performance. When the scene finished, I couldn't stop myself I jumped up and clapped, and I wasn't the only one, several people joined me.

At the very end of the play, as Grant was taken away to be hanged, Vivienne had the last line. She turned to the audience her eyes full of tears that she didn't let fall, pausing for ages before she spoke. She held the room in breathless anticipation.

'He have his goodness now. God forbid I take it from him.'

My cheeks were wet, and I had to scramble in my bag for a tissue to blow my nose.

Mrs Mulligan called us into the hall for notes. Vivienne was surrounded by a crowd of girls telling her she was amazing. How fickle were the winds of popularity? I remembered when Vivienne spent every lunch time in the library on her own because no one would talk to her.

Outside the sky was already dark. The play had gone on for hours. Mrs Mulligan was bound to make a performance out of giving us notes. I wanted to get into a hot bath as soon as possible to soothe my brutalised muscles.

'Let's start with the dance scene,' Mrs Mulligan began. Around me people started to laugh. I was sitting between Vivienne and Tamasin. Grant was opposite me and he looked straight at me, his face split into a grin. I turned to Tamasin, but she looked as confused as me.

'Yes, well,' Mrs Mulligan coughed and laughed herself. 'The dance was perfect, wonderful start to the show, but we are going to have to reconsider the costumes. Unfortunately, they proved to be transparent under the stage lights.'

My body went rigid. It was like being shot. Why did things like this happen to me? I turned to Vivienne who whispered.

'You may as well have been naked. At least you had a sports bra on. You could see Coco's nipples.'

Now all I needed was for a film of it to end up on the internet. Mrs Mulligan clearly had the same thought.

'If anyone has by any chance filmed the dance,' she glared around the room, 'delete it immediately. If I discover so much as a single photo posted on social media, I promise immediate expulsion. And I mean this – immediate expulsion. Does everyone understand?'

No wonder Grant was laughing his head off. I considered refusing to perform the dance. But Mrs Mulligan spent so long on her notes that by the time she'd finished I lacked the energy to make a fuss. All I wanted to do was go home. I got a 'good' for my flustered entrance but loads of people got terrible comments and I felt sorry for them. Grant had a list of stuff he had to do better. The only person who came out bathed in butter was Vivienne, of course.

I took my time getting my stuff together. Vivienne was talking to Mrs Mulligan, but Tamasin insisted on walking down the drive with me. I was hoping to be alone in case Grant appeared. But there was no sign of him, and he wasn't on the bus.

13

The play was a huge success with sold-out audiences every night. Within the world of Kings, Vivienne, Grant, and Coco became superstars.

Vivienne's parents were there for every performance. Mum came with Mike to the Thursday night show. She even drove us home, crunching the gears a few times, but with Mike telling her what to do, she managed. She had her test the week after Christmas and according to Mike, she was bound to pass.

I didn't want Mike at the show. We were wearing leotards under our shifts now but I still found it hard to dance sexily with him watching. I should be glad that Mum had someone to be with because I hardly saw her anymore. With the extra dance training and the play, I was getting up at six in the morning and not getting home until after ten at night. But why did she have to choose a sleazebag like Mike?

On Saturday Dad and Thomas came to see the show. Thomas was staying at Dad's afterwards while I went onto the cast party at Mrs Mulligan's house. Frieda was also coming to the show and the party. I was far more excited about the party than the final performance.

When we did the opening dance for the last time, we got a round of applause. For the final curtain call the whole cast lined up on stage and the main characters stepped forward for individual bows. As Vivienne took her bow the room exploded. People stood up and cheered. Probably Mr

Cooper started it, but the entire audience got to their feet. Shouts of 'bravo' had nothing to do with a proud Dad and everything to do with Viv being such a talented actor.

I felt a bit sorry for Grant because he had the final bow and had to follow Vivienne's reception. He handled the moment with dignity by stepping forward to take over Viv's cheers and almost immediately bringing the whole cast forward while the audience remained standing. He came over as generous and modest.

Once we were changed Vivienne, Tamasin and I met up with Louis and Frieda and headed over to Mrs Mulligan's house. It was a large Edwardian detached house surrounded by a thick hedge, and what looked like a huge garden. Her husband was a director at BBC Pebble Mill Studios. They were doing all right. The fancy entrance hall had stained glass panels and a snazzy tiled floor. The elegance of the space was lessened by a giant heap of coats and bags that had been dumped there. We added ours.

Viv led the way deeper into the house towards the noise of people talking. She stopped to nose into every room we passed. The living room had a relaxed arty feel with large abstract oil paintings on the walls, bookshelves on either side of a fireplace and old battered leather sofas covered in throws and cushions.

'Oh my God, I love this house. Look at this Louis, look at those books, that painting. This is how I want our house to look.' She gave a running commentary on everything she saw.

The kitchen at the back of the house was gigantic, opening onto a conservatory that opened onto a patio. Even though it was freezing there were people standing outside drinking and vaping.

I scanned the room. Most of the cast and crew were

there but there was no sign of Grant. Maybe he was outside. Mrs Mulligan spotted Vivienne and called her over. Louis went with her, while Tamasin, Frieda, and I wandered through the conservatory into the garden.

There were a couple of free-standing patio heaters and people had gathered around the pools of warmth. Frieda turned herself in a 360 degree circle taking in the setup.

'So, I've never been in a house as big as this, and what about the garden? I can't even see where it ends. What's happening down the bottom there?'

'Looks like a pond.' Tamasin had her new contact lenses in and was squinting into the distance. Without her glasses, she looked conventionally pretty but because I was used to her with specs, her face looked naked. Her newly exposed greeny-grey eyes kept blinking which gave her an alarmed expression.

'Let's go check it out,' said Frieda heading off and Tamasin followed.

'I don't want to get my trainers muddy,' I shouted after them. 'And it's freezing. I'm going back inside.' I was wearing a strappy, floaty top and besides I had plans of my own.

More people had pressed into the kitchen. A crowd of boys I didn't recognize were clustered around Mr Andrews. I spotted Ed talking to Rosa and when I smiled at him he came over.

'Show wus good tunight,' he spoke with a Brummy accent which I hadn't noticed before.

'Yeah, the audience seemed to like it.' A group had just come through from the hall and I stood on tiptoe to look over their heads and check if anyone more interesting had arrived.

'Your dance scene went down well.' Ed was twisting his can round and round. The conversation felt like a painful effort. He wasn't his usual calm self.

'Yeah,' I replied wondering how I could get away.

'Viv,' he gestured towards her across the room. She was standing with Louis next to Mrs Mulligan, with a balding man whom I assumed was Mr Mulligan, and a tall slender woman with long brown hair dressed entirely in black. 'Has been spotted.'

I looked back at Ed; my attention caught.

'That woman's an agent who Mrs Mulligan invited to see Vivienne and she wants to sign her up. Mr Andrews just told me.'

'That's amazing.' I stared over at the group. Vivienne was talking animatedly to the tall lady in black with Mrs Mulligan interjecting and Louis standing listening. Wow. Maybe she'd be famous soon?

'Have you seen Grant anywhere?' I asked. Ed paused for a moment and took a swig.

'He was here earlier, in the front room.' He turned abruptly and walked back towards the crowd around Mr Andrews. I thought that was a bit rude to leave me standing alone. I tried to catch Viv's eye, but she was absorbed in her conversation. I pushed through the mess of people blocking the kitchen doorway and headed towards the front room.

I didn't really expect to find Grant there. The room was empty, but the wood-burner was blazing away. I stood by the fire warming up and checked out the titles of the books. I curled up on one of the sofas with a book of Sylvia Plath poems.

Out of the ash I rise
With my red hair
I eat men like air.

I didn't know why but I felt depressed. Maybe I was just tired. I'd been looking forward to this party, but here I was alone in a room feeling miserable with no one to talk to. Get a grip Flowers! I should go find Frieda and get the dancing started.

I went back to the kitchen. Still no sign of Grant. Vivienne was sewn to Mrs Mulligan's side. Frieda and Tamasin must have stayed out in the garden. I decided to risk my trainers. There was a path running down the side of the lawn towards the pond and a cute little wooden summer house.

I triple-stepped down the path to keep warm. Being out in the dark reminded me of night dancing. The sky was clear and I could see the stars of the plough constellation above us.

There were no lights on in the summer house, but I heard voices. As I got close I saw Frieda and Tamasin were glued, face to face, in a full-on clinch. I stopped abruptly. Frieda clearly fancied Tamasin, but was Tamasin bi? Should I have expected this?

I turned around and walked quickly back to the house not wanting to disturb them. This could get messy. What if Tamasin broke Frieda's heart? I'd feel responsible. Frieda was so open and loving. Maybe it was just a moment, like Grant and I under the Christmas tree. I wished I hadn't seen them.

Back in the kitchen Mrs Mulligan and the agent were still in the corner but there was no sign of Viv. I was in a room packed with people but felt the loneliest I'd ever been.

I drifted out into the hall. I'd lost the ability to talk to people. Superficial bullshit, making sounds just for the sake of opening your mouth.

I needed the loo but there was a queue for the downstairs toilet, so I thought I'd explore upstairs. At the top of the staircase was a wide landing with a polished wooden floor. I heard laughter coming from a room marked PRIVATE. On another door was a notice with TOILET written in big black letters.

The bathroom was as big as my bedroom with a raised porcelain bath and black and white tiles on the floor. A giant old-fashioned key locked the door. If I had this house, I'd live in the bathroom. It was sumptuous, with dark blue walls and a jungle of lush green house plants along the windowsill. I was tempted to pour myself a bath and spend the rest of the party in here. I heard voices outside. I recognised Coco.

'I need to pee,' she was saying, and the door handle rattled.

'In a minute,' I called.

I heard Grant say, 'there's another one downstairs.'

I waited until they'd gone then opened the door. From the landing, I watched them at the bottom of the stairs. Grant had his hand resting on Coco's back, his fingers tucked inside her skirt waistband.

My stomach somersaulted. I decided to get my coat and go. I was so stupid. The coats and bags were in a giant jumble sale pile. I couldn't find mine and was ploughing through puffers and fake furs when Ed came up.

'Vivienne's looking for you,' he said.

'Tell her I'll call her tomorrow.' I found my coat.

'She's in a bad way.' Ed's face was full of concern.

'What's happened?'

'She's through here.' Ed led me down a turning off the hall to a small dark room at the side of the kitchen where there was a washing machine and a sink. The overhead light was off but, in the light spilling from the hall, I saw Vivienne crouched in the corner between the washing machine and a freezer.

'She asked me to get you.' Ed said.

'Thanks,' I touched his arm.

'If you need me, I'll be in the kitchen.' He left us alone and I squatted down beside Viv.

'Babe, what's the matter? Where's Louis?'

Vivienne clutched at the front of her dress bunching it up in her fist.

'He's finished with me Pen.'

'No that can't be. I don't believe it. He loves you.'

'He says I'm obsessed with Mrs Mulligan.' This was true but not a reason to dump her. 'He doesn't like her, thinks she's a pretentious snob. He says I've changed.'

'That's bullshit. What's the matter with him? How dare he do this to you tonight? Ed told me you've got a London agent interested in signing you.'

Vivienne nodded but kept sobbing. For a moment I listened to the sound of the fridge whirring and Viv breathing heavily through her mouth.

'I wonder if Louis feels threatened. He might be worried about losing you?'

'I'm sure it's Harriet,' Vivienne was rubbing the centre of her chest as if she was in physical pain. 'He wants to get back with her. Oh, Pen, I love him so much my heart is literally breaking. I wish I'd never done the play.'

I sank down onto the floor and put my arm around her so she could sob into my shoulder. The tiled floor sent arctic waves up my body so that I had a vision of myself turning blue from the bottom up. Some party this had turned out to be.

'Don't say that Viv, don't let Louis spoil that. You were wonderful. I was so proud of you.'

'He's always been weird about Harriet, won't talk about her. But Pen, I can't bear it. That he loves her more than me, that kills me.'

'If he does, he's an idiot.' I was furious with him.

'He feels guilty,' Vivienne sobbed, 'that he doesn't love me anymore after all his promises. Or maybe he never did. Not how he loved Harriet.'

I didn't know what to say. Ever since I'd known Viv she'd been with Louis. I thought that they were the perfect couple.

I'd shared one stupid meaningless kiss with Grant, but I felt rejected and miserable. I couldn't imagine how dreadful this was for Vivienne. But offering wisdom and compassion was challenging when you were ninety-five percent ice. There were limits to the amount I was prepared to suffer for the sake of friendship.

'Viv, I'm freezing to death down here. Let's get out of this crap party.'

14

How wise I'd been to not read anything into the Christmas tree kiss. Even wiser to not mention it to anyone. On Monday morning the news of Grant and Coco getting together at the party was all around the school. By Tuesday the story sweeping the corridors was that Priya had swallowed a bottle of paracetamol and been rushed to the hospital. Luckily no lasting harm to Priya. No way was I ever going to let some man mess up my life like that.

Grant and his girls, whom he was or wasn't dating, were of no interest to me. I had far more important concerns. Frieda and I were performing our duet at college and the marks counted toward our A Level grade.

I'd been listening to Melody singing 'Night Angel' over and over. Despite her public display of friendship, she hadn't bothered to call or text. Immersed in the music and dwelling on the night I'd met her, I realised that we needed to increase the darkness in our choreography. I could hear in the music that weird mix of vulnerability, ruthlessness, and danger that I associated with Melody. In our duet, Frieda was playing the Night Angel and I was playing the Melody role.

'We need to increase the sense of underlying menace.' I played Frieda the part of the track I wanted to use. 'What do you think?'

Frieda listened to the section a couple of times. 'Yeah,' she said slowly, 'that could work. The music's got a bite to it.'

I loved the way Frieda picked up on stuff. She was such a 'let's do it' sort of person. We set to work improvising a new sequence. By the time we finished, I reckoned we'd made a powerful piece of work.

The duet would be marked by Joe Thorne plus an external examiner. My luck was in because Mrs Hadley, my old dance teacher from school, was the examiner. Mrs Hadley was famous for her over-the-top blinging outfits but today she was in a sombre grey dress with only her rainbow-coloured hair to dazzle.

Everyone in the class had to present a piece of original choreographed work. Craig, the college technician, was there to film us. Joe liked to use the videos when he was giving feedback. Our slot was halfway through the afternoon. We'd decided to wear street clothes for our dance so there was nothing exposing. Frieda was in white tracksuit bottoms with a white crop top, and I wore black leggings and a black roll neck. We were using black and white to emphasize the theme of simple dualities – good/bad, night/day, angel/devil. Our dance didn't dramatize the words of Night Angel, instead it created a disturbing narrative suggested by my uncomfortable relationship with Melody.

Frieda's Night Angel was a powerful physical creature – her moves were based on a swan we'd watched in Cannon Hill Park whose huge wings were protective of her young, curving and holding, but also terrifying when raised in anger at a passing dog. Frieda danced her Night Angel like that swan, mighty, maternal but menacing. She was stunning. I couldn't have dreamed up a better dance partner.

I'd based my moves on the fox I'd seen when I was out night dancing. She'd been such a delicate scavenger, looking both vulnerable and bold. Reading up on them, foxes would often catch their prey by playing dead, that's why they had a reputation for being cunning. If Melody had a spirit animal, it would be a fox.

We wanted our dance to be full of ambivalence and to play out like a thriller. The audience should keep wondering if the Night Angel was a force for good or evil and then right at the end when they realised the angel was loving and protective there was a twist and the fox/Melody victim turned into the aggressor.

Our dance was athletic, dramatic, and daring as we flung our body weights against each other in tumbling, circling movements. We wanted to express the complex emotional nature of women's relationships with each other, the support and the conflict, the tenderness and anger, as they work out who they are in comparison to each other.

We finished with a final image of me, thanks to my strength training with Joe, holding Frieda upside down like a hunter showing off his catch, with her magnificent arms or wings trailing, lifeless on the floor. We'd got this idea from an old oil painting of dead birds hung on a door. Frieda's Mum, Anna, was always recommending artwork we should look at. She'd even found a painting of a fox playing dead. I ended with an aggressive look of triumph on my face which was partly acting but mainly the effort of not dropping Frieda on her head.

When we finished there was total silence. The other performances had been applauded. Frieda and I looked at each other. What had we done wrong? We'd nearly killed ourselves creating this piece.

Eventually, Joe started the applause and then the other students joined in. Maybe we'd shocked them into silence.

After everyone had performed their pieces, Joe gave feedback. He said ours was an original, and powerful piece of work, but we needed to work on our balance and that some of our transitions were clumsy. I was disappointed but Frieda laughed at me.

'He has to say something bad. You could tell he was knocked out. We aced that my little powerhouse - A* coming our way.'

I loved Frieda's confidence. How had she developed such certainty? Did she drink it with her mother's milk? It seemed as natural to her as breathing. I wished I could glug it down, like Alice in Wonderland with her 'drink me' bottles, so that I could grow that big, kind, self-belief in me.

On my way out of the building, I saw Mrs Hadley leaving and ran to catch up with her. We walked back towards Kings Heath High Street together. When we were out of sight of college, she squeezed my arm.

'I shouldn't say this, but your piece was fabulous. Joe told me you were doing extra training with him. I can already see the difference in your dancing. I'm so proud of you. Don't give up, promise me you won't?'

Why was she worried about me giving up? After this afternoon's dance, I had a bonfire inside me. I could have been naked at the North Pole I was so charged with energy.

'Of course, I won't!'

'Good, I've seen so many talented young women give up. They get a boyfriend, or they have a knockback, and they let go of their dreams.'

'Not me.'

Once I parted from Mrs Hadley, I tangoed down the road to Vivienne's house.

Vivienne was supposedly off school with a cold. Heartbreak was not considered a legitimate reason for absence. Mrs Cooper was home from work and opened the door. She gave me one of her bosomy hugs.

'She's upstairs. She'll be glad to see you. Go up. Do you want a cup of tea?'

'Oh yes, please. How is she?'

Mrs Cooper shook her head and her stiff bob swung in a slow-motion wave.

'Not good. Not good at all.'

The Coopers lived in a small, terraced house with just two rooms upstairs reached by a steep staircase that bisected their living room and back room. Vivienne's bedroom was a lurid purple grotto. Her bed, on which she sat hunched up in her dressing gown, was generously endowed with bright, fluffy cushions. She was clutching a shaggy violet cushion to her chest.

I sat down on her dressing table stool.

'Everyone's talking about how you were the star of the show.' I told her. 'Truth, no lies.'

She shrugged in a so what gesture.

'Have you heard from Louis?' I asked, knowing this was what she wanted to talk about. Vivienne shook her head.

'He won't answer my calls. He's sent a text saying he needs space to sort himself out. I don't know how to go on.'

'What about that agent? Have you heard from her?'

'I've got to get some professional acting photos done.' Viv sounded as if she'd been given a prison sentence.

'Well, that's exciting,' I reminded her.

'Look at me.' Vivienne pushed me aside and pulled a face at her reflection in the dressing table mirror.

'What roles would I get? Zombie? Crazy woman?' She collapsed back into bed.

'Terminal illness,' I suggested, 'specializes in deathbed scenes – Shakespeare's packed with them. In fact, I think you're onto something.'

Vivienne managed a watery chuckle.

'Oh Pen, you won't believe me but honestly, if I could have Louis back, I wouldn't care if I never acted again.'

She was right I didn't believe her.

'I just don't get it,' I said. 'I'm sure he loves you.'
Viv whispered in her brink-of-death voice.
'It's Harriet for sure. She wants him back.'
'She seemed a bit,' I thought for a moment. 'Bossy, in that way teachers can be, talking down at you, like you're in their class.'
Vivienne brightened up.
'Yeh, that's what I thought. Boring on about herself.'
'Louis will soon realise she's dull, dull, dull.'
'You think so?' Vivienne asked.
'Certain. Meanwhile, you need to transform yourself into a creature of astonishing beauty, so Louis gets an eyeful of what he's missing.'
Vivienne leapt out of bed, cushions flying dangerously.
'You're so right Pen. I need to fight for him. Who does she think she is – waltzing back to Birmingham and expecting she can have him back at the snap of her fingers? He's not a dog. He's MY boyfriend.' Viv's indignation filled the room. I was relieved to see the return of her usual boisterous self.
'Harriet doesn't realise what she's up against. Vivienne Cooper, star of stage and screen.'
'Thanks Pen, you've fired me up.' I got a damp hug and managed to snaffle a piece of Mrs Cooper's delicious chocolate cake before I got the bus home. I was pleased to see Vivienne have some too. I'd been worried that she was developing an eating disorder, but it turned out to be method acting. Now the play was over she was back on the carbs.

On the bus home, my phone rang. Melody had finally condescended to get in touch.
'Yo Pen, lovin' the dance film,' she said.
'What dance film?' I asked, confused.

'You and your tall mate dancing to 'Night Angel'.'

I didn't speak because I didn't know what she was talking about.

'It's on YouTube.'

Maybe the college had posted something.

'We've put it on our website,' Melody continued, 'and the fans are loving it. So, here's what I wondered. Can we project your film on Friday when I do 'Night Angel'? We're at The Midnight Bell again.'

I was whirling inside, my mind dashing from one thought to the next so that none of them registered.

'I'll put you on the guest list. It'll be good publicity for you. Is it okay? Marlon wants it sorted.'

'Who's Marlon?'

'Our manager, the bass player.'

'I'll ask Frieda and let you know.'

'Love you Angel. See you Friday, my little dancing superstar.' And she was gone.

Frieda knew about the film, of course. The college had posted a clip of our dance on their YouTube Channel and there'd been some reposts. She was totally up for Melody screening the film and for going to the gig on Friday Night.

'What have we got to lose? I get that Melody's tricky but if she's using us, we can use her right back. I'll invite Tamasin, see if Viv wants to come.'

She didn't.

'If I bumped into Louis with Harriet I'd die. If they're there together don't tell me. I don't want to know.' Viv said on the phone, sounding more like herself. 'Mum and I are going to do a home spa evening, face mask, hair mask, pedicure, nails, eyebrows, the works.'

A quiet cosy night at home after this manic term was

what I needed. I wanted to get into bed and pull the duvet over my head and sleep until Christmas morning. I considered telling Frieda I wasn't going but then Mum told me that Mike was coming over so I made myself get ready.

I looked monstrous. I had dark rings beneath my eyes and probably the worst outbreak of spots I'd ever had across my left cheek. Even plastering my face in thick foundation, they blazed red. The foundation made me look like a ghoul, so I wiped it off. I'd have to leave my real true spotty self on show.

On the bus into the city, I rested my inflamed cheek against the cool glass of the window and closed my eyes. Everyone else was busy falling in love. They all had someone special to care about. Even heartbreak was preferable to being totally ignored. Why was I so meh that none of the boys at school were remotely attracted? By the time the bus arrived in the city, I had imagined myself into a pit of despair that would take some climbing out of.

I walked down into Digbeth and turned into Heath Mill Lane. The food smells hit me first: curry spices, fried chicken, and burgers. Music boomed from behind the brick fronts. I imagined the walls of the units pulsing and started to feel the kick of excitement in my belly. I did a little skip step and started to swing my hips, eyeing up the passing boys.

Frieda and Tamasin were waiting for me outside The Midnight Bell. Standing with them was Grant Barker.

'Hi Pen,' he said and by way of greeting, he kissed me on the mouth, not a lingering snog, but not a peck either. A definite 'I have intentions' mouth clamped on mouth. Behind Grant's head, Frieda's eyebrows shot up and she grinned at me.

Tamasin said. 'As Viv's not coming, I told Grant we could probably get him in for free.'

We walked straight to the front of the queue. Grant had his hand on my back as I walked by his side. The bouncer remembered us and waved us through. It was like being famous. Grant and Tamasin went to get drinks while Frieda and I made our way through to the front by the stage.

'What's with you and pretty boy?' she asked squeezing me at the waist.

'What's with you and Tamasin?' I fired back.

She just laughed.

The evening I'd been dreading turned into one of the best. Tamasin and Grant did impressions of Mrs Mulligan. I almost wet myself.

'No darling,' Grant adopted a high posh voice, 'you need to be more thrusting; you've got to enter into the words, penetrate the character.'

'Oh, Mrs Mulligan,' Tamasin pretended to be Grant, bashful and impressed, 'you're so strong!'

They made a great double act. I whispered to Tamasin.

'What happened with Coco?'

She shrugged, 'ask Grant?' I didn't.

Grant stayed with us for the whole evening. He kept brushing against me as we danced. When The Night Angels came on, he stood behind me, his body pressed against mine with his hands on my shoulders. The video of Frieda and I dancing was projected on a giant screen that hung above the stage while Melody sang 'Night Angel'. Watching myself, huge and blurry, felt strange, I couldn't connect my physical presence in the room with the digital version above me. Grant whispered in my ear.

'You're one sexy dancer.'

His breath was warm on my skin and maybe I imagined it but maybe he touched the lightest, feathery flutter of lips against my neck. Tingling sensations ran right through my body from my toes to my scalp. I realised I was holding my breath. I wanted to turn and kiss him, but I didn't dare. I could be reading the signals wrong. What if this was just like the Christmas tree kiss?

As we were leaving Grant asked for my number.

I was on the bus home when my phone pinged. It was Grant asking me out on an actual proper date.

15

At two o'clock on Tuesday, it started to snow. Just tiny fluttering dots of white to start with, like blossom falling, but then harder. Normally I'd love a white Christmas but what if Grant cancelled?

'Where is he taking you?' Mum asked. I was sitting by the living room window watching the flakes settle on the garden.

'I don't know.'

'Well, I hope he's not driving far. The roads will be treacherous.'

I was amazed when Grant said he'd pick me up. I didn't even realise he could drive. He couldn't have had a licence for long.

The snow continued throughout the afternoon and by four was lying two inches deep on the drive and the traffic on our road was crawling. I kept checking my phone. Nothing. I hadn't told anyone about this date, not Vivienne, not Frieda, certainly not Tamasin. Some part of me didn't believe it was going to happen.

By ten past four, the snow was falling in thick white swirls against the now inky sky. The road had a coating of slush, and the car tyres made a wet slurpy scrunch. There was no sign of Grant. I didn't even know what colour car he had. I gave up watching from the front room and went upstairs and lay on my bed staring through the window at the snowflakes downward dance over the lilac tree. I was destined to be a lonely spinster.

My phone bleeped - a voice message. I couldn't bear to listen.

'On my way, with you in ten.'

My stomach took off, a swoosh of snowflakes spiralling upwards. I checked my face in the bedroom mirror. Spots were better, and hair was good. I practiced my smile. I looked better when I smiled. I jumped down the stairs two at a time and pulled on my puffer jacket, shoved a beanie and gloves in my bag. Money, phone, lip gloss, I was ready. I had no idea where I was going but I felt as if I was stepping over a threshold and entering a new world.

A small white car pulled onto the drive behind Mum's red Fiesta. Grant got out looking tall, lithe, and gorgeous with the snowflakes settling on his curly brown hair.

'Bye Mum,' I shouted pulling the front door closed behind me. Grant was on the doorstep underneath the porch, and he put his arms around me and pulled me in tight and kissed me as I'd never been kissed before. As if I was the most beautiful woman in the world. Like he wanted to drink me up.

'I've been wanting to do that for weeks,' he said.

I thought about Priya and Coco. He read my mind.

'But it was complicated. Come on.' He took my hand, and we ran down the drive. The snow was wet on our faces. Running, snowflakes, holding hands, I could hear the music. I didn't need to pretend to smile. The corners of my mouth were practically touching my ears.

'I didn't know you could drive,' I said as Grant started the engine and pulled out onto the road. I knew almost nothing about him.

'I passed my test this morning,' he grinned.

I gasped, 'but what if you'd failed?'

'You were the incentive to pass,' he said, 'first time.' The sat nav interrupted telling Grant in a posh woman's voice to turn left.

'Where are we going?'

'Stratford-upon-Avon, the Royal Shakespeare Company. They've got a South African Theatre Company doing *The Tempest*, with puppets and dancing. Supposed to be incredible. I thought you'd like it.'

'Wow,' I said, 'how wonderful. Thanks.'

Grant was concentrating on the road, driving carefully. The windscreen wipers juddered across the window, heavy with snow. He'd done this for me, getting the tickets, passing his test, and driving us there. I'd never had anyone do anything like that for me before. And this was Grant Barker, the funniest, sexiest boy in the whole school. How had I suddenly become the luckiest girl in the world?

'How far is it?' I wondered out loud.

'Sat nav says forty-five minutes but might be slower tonight. I checked the roads before I left and they're okay. We've got loads of time. The show doesn't start until seven.'

We were on the dual carriageway into the city. Grant was weaving in and out of the traffic, overtaking when necessary and following the satnav's instructions without any signs of panic even though the snow made it hard to see and he was leaning forward to peer out onto the road. Compared to Mum he was Lewis Hamilton, so confident and sure of himself. As if he'd been driving for years.

'My Mum's learning to drive. She's got her test after Christmas and she's in a total panic about the snow. You're way better than she is. How long did it take you to learn?'

'I've been driving go-karts since I was a kid. My Dad's a mechanic, so we've always had cars around. I wanted to be a racing driver when I was younger.' I was ready for his whole biography. I wanted to know everything.

'What made you stop?'

'Just lost interest.'

'What about now? What do you think you'll do now?'

'Thought I might give acting a go,' he said.

'I didn't realise you were serious about acting?'

'I wasn't but that agent who came to see the play wants to sign me up.'

'As well as Vivienne?' My voice revealed how surprised I was, and I saw Grant's mouth tighten. The car was silent for a while, and I wished I could eat back my words. I tried to make up for my gaff.

'Congratulations on the agent, that's brilliant. Viv has to get professional photos done. What about you?'

'Yeah.'

We were picking up speed zooming through spaghetti junction, the car banking made me lean over towards Grant and touch his arm. I remembered the trip to London with Melody. Me, Yogi and Mick in the back of the beetle. I'd been such an innocent back then. Mick wasn't in the same league as Grant.

'Is this your car?' I asked.

'Nah, Mum's. But she's cool about lending it to me.'

'I want to learn as soon as I can.'

'I'll teach you.' He put his hand on my thigh. We were on the M6 now and there weren't many other cars because of the weather. I worried about him driving one-handed. But I wasn't complaining. Just the weight of his hand on my thigh, the warmth through the material of my jeans, was sending the most amazing sensations through my body.

The snow kept falling, thick and fast, blown by a fierce wind it splattered across the windscreen. Grant was concentrating hard, and we travelled in silence. Outside was this wild weather and inside we were suspended in a tiny tin cocoon for two, like a space capsule rocketing alone through the universe. I'd remember this moment forever.

'Are you okay?' I asked putting my hand over his on the steering wheel for a moment.

'What do you mean?'

'These have got to be the worst driving conditions any new driver has ever faced.'

He laughed.

'I love it,' he said, and I believed him. His face was lit up with the energy of the storm.

'Me too, such a crazy thing to do – drive through a blizzard to watch Shakespeare. This is the kind of wild adventure I've yearned for.'

Grant looked at me briefly, then back to the road.

'No shit Pen. Loads of girls'd be freaking out – in fact, I can't think of any girl apart from you that wouldn't be.' I thought for a moment. Yeah, Vivienne and Tamasin would probably be anxious. I didn't know about Frieda.

'Not me. Bring it on.'

The vibes in the car were way high; there was electricity, there was chemistry, there was meteorology, there was even bloody geography, every scientific scale known to mankind was peaking. I had never felt so alive.

We had the blizzard world to ourselves but every so often a car would pass and briefly light up our intimate bubble. I examined Grant's profile, his high forehead with silky black eyebrows, a long straight nose, full pouty almost girly lips, and a sharp straight jawline. A long face with sharp bone structure, fabulous long-lashed eyes, and creamy skin. He turned and caught me watching him, smiled, eyes crinkling into laughter lines, mouth growing wide, a mobile face full of humour. I wanted to touch him, so I reached out and put my hand on the back of his head and stroked the short hair at the nape of his neck. He relaxed into my hand.

'That feels good,' he said, 'keep doing that.'

*

We arrived safely in Stratford and parked in the theatre car park. The snow had stopped but after the warmth of the car, the wind was arctic and slashed at my face. I was pulling on my beanie when Grant threw a snowball splat into my face.

'What the…' I screamed, spitting out ice, and another came flying my way. I dodged and scooped up a fist of crunchy fresh snow then flung it at Grant. We chased each other around the parked cars. I did a lot of screaming.

Grant had a handful of snow he was threatening to put down the back of my jumper. I ran from him as fast as I could, squealing like I was six again and Dad was tickling me. He cornered me against the theatre wall but let the wet snow fall from his hands as he pushed the length of my body back against the red bricks.

He kissed me, pressing his body against mine. I had my arms around his neck pulling him into me. Even though it was freezing and the middle of winter I opened like a rose to the sun, wider and wider. I wanted him inside me, not just in a sexual way, but like I wanted every door inside me to open to him, so that he had access to all of me, knew every beat and pulse of me, so that my sense of aloneness would melt like the snow on our hands.

I had never felt anything remotely like this for Mick. My whole body was on fire. This man had done something to my insides that was as intense as one of Joe's training sessions - but way more pleasurable. This was like dancing only better. If Grant had wanted to screw me, there and then, I would have been up for it.

Other people were walking past staring at us, so we did the adult thing and joined the queue to get in. Everything made us laugh, but mainly the others in the queue. Grey heads and glasses lined up in pairs. We were about fifty years younger than everyone else. Would we be like that in fifty years, looking at our phones, reading the programme, not talking, not kissing, not touching even, standing together but oblivious of each other? I never wanted my relationship to be like that. I pulled Grant close, so we were standing chest to chest, his arms around me, and my face snuggled into his shoulder.

Everything about that night was charged with magic. The all-black South African cast used these huge, paper puppets as moving scenery. They were waves of the sea, and clouds of the storm, creatures of the forest, and spirits of the air. The puppeteers moved like dancers. I loved it, so beautiful and clever.

Grant and I held hands throughout the show, and I squeezed his hand every time there was something I really liked which was pretty much always.

'That was the most astonishing, amazing theatre I've ever seen. Thank you.' I hugged him.

Travelling back home in the car, I felt as if we'd known each other for years and at the same time as if I was cupping in my hands a tiny shoot, newer than new, but vigorous, bursting with energy.

When Grant dropped me home, he asked if I'd like to come over on Boxing Day. I wanted to leap in the air and scream. This was really happening. I mean obviously, I was a feminist and all that, self-determined and not needing a man to define me or give me worth, blah, blah, blah, but hey I could still celebrate the pursuit of love. Could it be that I, Pen Flowers, finally had a proper boyfriend? Was it possible that I had Grant Barker as a boyfriend. I was the luckiest, happiest, most sexually excited woman in the world.

16

All day Christmas Eve while Grant was at his grandparents', we sent each other funny memes and had flirty text banter. When he got home, he called me at midnight to be the first person to wish me a happy Christmas. I was in a relationship. I was no longer alone in the world. Grant was the best Christmas present I'd ever had. I drifted off to sleep as if carried downstream in a gently rocking boat filled with rose petals.

On Christmas morning Dad always made bacon sandwiches for breakfast, and we ate them while opening our presents. I have a thing about bacon sandwiches and Dad's were the best. Grilled streaky bacon, which was crunchy but not burnt, layered up with crisp, shredded lettuce and thinly sliced tomato with mayo to sandwich everything together between lightly toasted sourdough bread. Dad's bacon sandwiches were an art form.

This year Mum made the sandwiches. Thomas and I were in our pyjamas in the living room and when she handed me the plate, I thought I might burst into tears. She'd used the same limp, sliced bread we had for our packed lunches. There was just bacon inside, nothing else, big pink slabs with the fat still white because she hadn't cooked it for long enough. Not a hint of crunch anywhere. When I lifted mine up to take a bite it wilted over my hand, drooping like a dying tulip. My disappointment was so acute I couldn't hide it. I put the sandwich down.

'You love bacon sandwiches.' Mum was immediately suspicious.

'I'm trying to go veggie,' I said.

'You weren't vegetarian when Dad made the sandwiches. Mine not good enough?' She glared at me, her eyes spitting hot fat.

I wanted to scream back that her sandwich was disgusting. But this was Christmas Day, and we hadn't even got to nine o'clock yet, so I kept quiet and even managed to get a few bites down.

We were waiting until Dad came round to open our presents. There are some things in life that shouldn't change and how you do Christmas is one of them. Every Christmas of my life so far had followed the same pattern but now everything was messed up. Mum wanted us to get dressed in our best clothes instead of staying in our jimjams like we usually did. Thomas was as unhappy as me about this, but we could see that Mum was teetering on the edge of a total meltdown, so we complied.

As I changed into my jeans and new top which was as fancy as I was getting, I could feel the anger sparking inside me. Mum was treating Dad as if he were a guest rather than the parent who had lived with us for the past sixteen years. I wondered how Grant and his family spent Christmas. Maybe next year I could be with him.

When I got downstairs, I realised why Thomas and I had been forced to dress up – so that Mum could. She was dolled up as if she were going out with Mike, in her plunging V-necked dress, wearing makeup and pointy shoes with heels. She looked ridiculous for first thing on Christmas morning. She obviously still wanted Dad to find her attractive. I was sure he'd have preferred us to be relaxed and not wound into a state of high tension. Mum was behaving like Mrs Mulligan, directing a show that she'd imagined in her head. I foresaw disaster travelling our way faster than Santa's magic sleigh.

The presents under the Christmas tree were from Mum. Dad arrived carrying his gifts. That was weird – separate presents. We sat around in the living room with cups of hot chocolate. Mum had put the radio on so that there was a background hum of jingling Christmas music that I knew would wind Dad up as much as it did me. Thomas handed round the presents so that we each had a pile in front of us. I decided to open Mum's first in case she took offence at going second. I was relieved to find she'd given me a new dance kit that I genuinely liked.

'Oh, Mum these are gorgeous, I love them.' I ran over and hugged her.

'I checked with Vivienne to see if they were the right ones, and she said you'd like them in black.'

'Brilliant Mum, they'll be perfect for college.' But Mum wasn't listening to me she was watching Thomas who had opened his present from Dad first, revealing the recently released PlayStation upgrade that he'd been drooling over.

'Mega, Dad, thanks.' Thomas was pink with pleasure. Mum was looking at Dad as if she was going to kill him. I was too scared to open my present from Dad, but Mum switched her raptor gaze onto me.

'Aren't you going to open yours then?', she said.

I undid the wrapping paper slowly - a new laptop. No more having to share our crappy old computer with Mum and Thomas. A shiny silver lightweight high-spec laptop of my own. I opened the box and hugged the streamlined shape to my chest.

'Oh Dad,' I whispered, 'this is wonderful.'

Mum exploded. She was up on her feet shouting.

'We agreed on a budget. How dare you? You've done this to humiliate me. You've got to outdo me, haven't you? Never miss an opportunity to put me down.'

'Mum don't,' Thomas and I spoke at the same time.

Dad stayed calm.

'Sit down Jenny, there's no need for you to get upset.'

'Don't you dare patronise me. You've broken our agreement.'

'Look they're my children and I don't live with them anymore so if I want to treat them, you can't stop me.'

I thought Dad was making a fair point. Getting us decent presents was the least he could do after abandoning us.

'I love your present just as much as Dad's.' I said, trying to help.

Thomas had ripped open his present from Mum, a new dressing gown.

'Me too,' he said, clearly lying, but doing his bit to restore peace.

'You're buying their love.' Mum was still at top volume. 'To compensate for not being here. If you really loved them, you'd spend more time with them.' Mum was right but I didn't object to bribery in the form of laptops.

'You're spoiling Christmas for everyone.' Dad said.

'I am! You already have!' Mum screamed and then Dad stood up.

'Enough. I don't need this.' He walked out. Then Mum ran upstairs to her bedroom. We hadn't even opened the rest of the presents.

I didn't know who I was angrier with, Dad for leaving or Mum for making him. You'd think they could manage to hold it together for one day for Thomas's sake. He was only eleven. His big blue eyes had filled with tears. I put my arms around him.

'Come on let's open our presents and not worry about them.'

I did what I could to protect Christmas dinner. I basted the turkey that was already in the oven and when

Mum didn't appear I put the roast potatoes on and got the vegetables ready. Mum came down in time to make gravy. It wasn't much of a meal. Mum had turned Dad's old music room into a dining room. The shelves where Dad had stored his vinyl and CD collections were empty. The three of us sat around the big table wearing paper crowns, reading out the unfunny cracker jokes. I'd never missed Dad more.

My stupid selfish parents had managed to turn the best Christmas ever into the worst.

There were no buses on Boxing Day, so Grant came to pick me up. He lived between Kings Norton and Selly Oak which explained why he sometimes got off the number eleven in Bournville and walked or sometimes got on another bus in Cotteridge. His house was bigger than ours, detached with a double garage, large windows on either side of the front door, and a neat square lawn surrounded by tidy flower beds. It was in the middle of a new estate full of identical houses. Mini mansions sitting in their own small plots. Grant parked on the drive next to a large navy BMW.

The only other boyfriend I'd had was Mick and I'd never gone to his house. I'd only had one date with Grant but here I was walking along the carpeted hall to meet his family. He must be serious about me. My tummy fluttered.

Grant got his looks from his Mum who was tall, slender, with dark silky black hair. She had the same eyebrows and good bones. I felt short and stubby beside her. She was standing by the door to the living room ironing a big pile of washing – on Boxing Day. That seemed a bit sad to me. She looked up and smiled, and said hello, but carried on ironing.

Grant's Dad was in the living room watching the

biggest TV screen I'd ever seen. It took up most of one wall. A fist the size of a pumpkin smashed into a man's head that was bigger than my whole body. I jumped back in alarm. Then a mouth like a car tyre was opening and closing.

'Who's this then?' Grant's Dad waved us in.

'Pen,' Grant answered but didn't move from the door.

'Pen? That's an odd name!'

'Short for Penelope,' I said.

He was plump, broad-shouldered, and fair-haired going bald. The only thing Grant appeared to have inherited from him was his curls.

'Come in, come in, do you want a drink? Coke, tea, a beer?'

'We're going upstairs.' Grant moved away.

'Righty oh, see you later then.' His Dad went back to watching the film. His Mum didn't say anything, just smiled at us and kept on ironing while staring at the big screen. If Grant had come to our house my Mum would have been all over him, asking him questions, and chatting away. Maybe Grant's parents were used to him bringing girls home. Maybe he'd brought lots of different girls back. I pushed the thought away.

Grant's bedroom was huge, the size of mine and Thomas's put together. It was directly above the living room with a big rectangular window looking over the drive. I could hear the telly from below and Grant's Dad talking. The room was dominated by a double bed and on the wall above the headboard was a poster of a sports car curving around a dramatic cliff-edged road. Grant saw me looking at the car.

'That's the Aston Martin I'm going to buy with my first movie pay cheque.'

Grant flung himself onto the centre of the bed and lay

there, hands behind his head watching me. Cars were clearly a big thing with Grant. I'd never much thought about cars. I moved slowly around the room. His was way tidier than mine. But then maybe he'd cleaned up knowing I was coming. I would have if it was the other way around. Along one wall was a fitted wardrobe and a desk unit, with cupboards and bookshelves. There were a few books about acting and lots about films; *The Greatest 100 Movies of All Time*, *The Story of Marvel Studios*, *Making Movies*.

'You're a film buff?' I asked.

Grant nodded. 'So, Sherlock Flowers, what else can you deduce?'

There were two framed black and white photos, one of Grant in costume as John Proctor and the other of a group of young women in some sort of musical. The girls were dressed in 50s style costumes. The photo looked dated. I picked it up and looked carefully.

'Is this your Mum?' I pointed at a slim young woman at the back of the group.

'Well done. She was a professional dancer. That's the touring show of *Grease*.'

'She was a dancer? Like me? Wow, she's beautiful. You look like her.' I wondered if that was why Grant liked me. Because I was a dancer.

Grant came over and took the photo off me and put it back on the shelf. He kissed me and pulled me towards the bed, but I held him off. I was nervous about the giant bed and what might happen there.

'I'm still investigating,' I said. 'My Mum wanted to be a dancer, ballroom, but she gave up. Maybe I could talk to your Mum about how she made it.'

'She didn't do it for long. There's no money in it.' Money was obviously important to Grant.

On a table in front of the window was a professional-looking video camera like the one the college technician used.

'Is this yours?'

'Christmas present.'

'Wow.' His parents must be loaded. Their house was large and full of expensive things but it wasn't posh like Tamasin's nor arty like Mrs Mulligan's.

'I've got a present for you.' Grant pulled open a drawer in the fitted unit and handed me a parcel.

'But I haven't got you anything.' This was only our second date. I wouldn't have had a clue what to get him.

'Doesn't matter. Open it.'

The present was a woollen scarf and matching bobble hat in a dark rich red. I held them to my cheek.

'They're lovely. Super soft, thank you so much.' I felt my breath catch. This almost made up for the horrors of Christmas Day. Grant took the hat from me and put it on my head then wrapped the scarf gently around my neck and pulled me towards him. We kissed. I opened my eyes to drink in his smile.

'To remind you of our first date in a blizzard.'

How did he know that I loved soft cosy things? I had to stop myself getting gushy.

'Yeh and the ice down my back.'

Grant laughed and picked up the camera.

'And now I'm going to film you doing a strip tease.'

'Get lost.'

'Naked apart from the hat and scarf.'

'With your Mum and Dad downstairs.'

'Makes it more fun.' He was making his eyebrows dance up and down.

'Yeah right.' He was circling around me pretending to film.

Standing in the middle of the room my hands felt too

big for my body. I didn't know where they should go. The way Grant was staring at me made me flustered. My palms were hot and sticky. I walked over to the window away from him and the video and stared out at the houses opposite. There were still a few lumps of greying snow on the roadsides. I wished Grant would put down the camera. The two cars on the drive beneath were parked side by side, one black one white, one little one large, his and hers. Why did men always get the big cars?

Grant was virtually a stranger; I didn't really know him and yet I was in his bedroom. Did he expect me to have sex with him now? What if we had sex and then he dumped me? I wanted to stop thinking too much, to just be happy like I'd been in the car to Stratford. But I couldn't stop myself. The intimacy here was too intense, threatening.

Grant put down the camera and led me to the bed. We both lay down and he put his arms around me. We kissed again but I couldn't let go.

'Relax,' he said, 'don't look so worried.'

'I'm a virgin,' I blurted out. 'I've never had sex.'

Grant stroked the side of my cheek and then ran his finger down my arm and onto my hip.

'I know,' he said.

How did he know? Did I have a neon sign on my forehead flashing out 'sexually inexperienced'. Grant was stroking my leg and smiling at me.

'There's no rush, we're not going to do anything you don't want to. It's just cool being close.'

I was pretty sure he'd had sex with Coco at the afterplay party. Why didn't he want to have sex with me?

'I don't understand why you want to be with me.'

What was it with me? I dug my nails into my palms. Why did I end up saying whatever was in my head?

'I mean there's loads of girls prettier than me.'

'But you're sexier,' Grant was pushing up my jumper, putting his hand underneath my t-shirt, stroking my breast. He pulled up the t-shirt. 'Pretty breasts.'

As his mouth touched my nipple my body went crazy. Whoosh, bang, wowser, a goddam Olympic opening ceremony of fireworks exploded.

'Ay Corona,' I shouted for no reason apart from the energy had to go somewhere. Grant laughed and we were wrestling, faces pressed together, mouths everywhere. I stopped worrying and let my body enjoy these new sensations.

Grant drove me home. I was still a virgin but very ready not to be. Grant was the one saying we shouldn't rush. I was all in for the complete experience.

We were nearly at my house when out of nowhere Grant asked me how long I'd been friends with Melody Jones.

'I'm not sure we are friends. Not really, not like with Viv or Frieda. But I knew her before she was in The Night Angels.'

'Everyone thinks The Night Angels are going to be huge.'

'She always wanted to be rich and famous.'

'What's she like?' Grant asked as he pulled into our street and parked outside the house. I sat for a while with the sound of the engine idling filling the silence.

'She's got this vulnerability that's compelling, breaks your heart. She's had a tough childhood. But that's made her ruthless. I don't know that she's got any sense of loyalty or morality. She reminds me of a fox; you want to stroke her like you would a dog, but if you did, she'd rip your hand to pieces.'

Grant whistled, 'sounds dangerous.'
'Yeh, I'd say she was dangerous.'
'Exciting though.'
'I can do without the excitement, thanks. I've learnt my lesson with Mel.'

We must have talked her up because late that night I got a message from her wanting to meet up.

17

I was desperate to see Vivienne and tell her my news. New Year, New World Order. Vivienne was single, and I had a boyfriend.

I headed into the city centre. By Moor Street Station I got tangled in a gang of shoppers heading for the sales. They were boisterous and energised by their mission to spend. The sun was low in the sky, lemon-bright, giving long dramatic shadows to Birmingham's puffer-clad, padded-out bargain hunters. The last of the snow had melted. I bounced up the hill blowing my breath into the cold air.

Vivienne was waiting for me on the steps facing the town hall.

'You know sometimes I don't recognise you these days – you're so thin.' I said hugging her now slender body.

Viv laughed. 'Just two pounds off a size 10.'

'Let's get lunch, I'm starving.' She needed feeding.

We went to a pizza place where Viv had a salad in the middle of winter.

'You're crazy,' I told her. 'I thought the dieting was for the play. Why are you carrying on?'

'My agent says if you're slim you get put up for the lead roles. Plump and you're 'character'.'

'That's gross. But get you – 'my agent says' - I thought Louis was your priority?'

'Yeah.'

'Well, he loves your curves.'

'I still got curves. I get loads more eye work now I'm thinner.' Vivienne appeared to be glowing. There was no sign of the pre-Christmas tragic victim. I had to admit she looked good; smug, sleek, and shiny.

'Just don't get too thin.'

'It's all right for you, you can eat what you want because you burn up a million calories a day with your dancing.'

I was stuffing my face with pizza.

'I just like eating. Loads of dancers get anorexia. What's the story? You've seen Louis?'

'Yep, and he'd missed me as much as I'd missed him,' Viv smiled.

'So, you're back together?'

'Well,' she gave a great sigh.

'Viv, get on with it! I don't need the Shakespearian embellishments.'

'Okay, I was totally right. Harriet's still in love with him but he's in love with me. But he doesn't want to hurt her.'

'So, it's a fight for the heart of Louis Evan Brown?'

'Exactly,'

'Which you're obviously going to win.'

Vivienne grinned at me and even ate a dough ball.

'Obviously,' she agreed.

'Because Harriet's boring.'

'I going to give him the space to realise this. I'm not going to make a fuss about him seeing her. Meanwhile, I'm going to look gorgeous and let him know that other men are interested.'

'You're turning into a diva.'

'Good.'

'I too have news!'

'Do tell,' Vivienne settled into her active listening

posture. She tilted her face down and looked up at me, eyes open wide, lips parted, ready to express heartfelt empathy. I laughed.

'You're looking at a woman with a boyfriend.' I told her.

'Grant made a move then?'

'How did you know?' I was cheated of my big reveal.

Vivienne shrugged. 'One of the things I love about you Pen is you're utterly transparent.'

This didn't seem like such a positive attribute to me.

'He drove me to Stratford to see a South African version of *The Tempest* – it was incredible.'

'Very cultured for a first date.'

'Oh, Viv it was just the most amazing night.'

'Be careful Pen.' Viv's pretend empathy had shifted into something real.

'What do you mean? I thought you liked Grant?'

'I do but he's..'

'What?' I interrupted, unable to stop myself.

'Keep your hair on. Grant's a laugh, but don't you think he's a bit lightweight for you?'

'No.' I'd expected her to be impressed. 'He chose the theatre because of the dancing in it. He got me a present I really like. He's kind and thoughtful.'

'Alright, Okay,' Vivienne backed off. 'Don't get wound up, maybe he's got hidden depths I've not seen. Good for you. Enjoy! But don't take it too seriously.'

'What do you mean?' This conversation was not going the way I'd imagined.

'Well, Grant likes attention. He's not exactly the steady type, is he?'

'Like Louis?' I fought back.

'Well, Louis is steady. It's because he feels loyal to his ex that we've had these problems. He's only ever had two serious girlfriends, Harriet, and me. Whereas Grant's had flings with half the school.'

'He has not.'

'Tamasin, Priya, Coco, and now you, all in the last six months.'

'He and Tamasin were just friends.'

Viv pulled an 'Oh Yeah' face.

'Tamasin's gay,' I blurted out then felt terrible. This wasn't my news to share.

'So you know?'

'Yeah, and you?'

She nodded. 'Told me ages ago. Funny I never liked Tamasin. I hated the way she treated you, but since we've been doing Drama together, I've got to know her better. She's not as spoilt as I thought. I feel sorry for her. She hasn't even told her parents because she's worried about how they'll react.'

I felt weirdly jealous that Tamasin had opened up to Viv.

'You know Frieda and Tamasin are an item now.'

Vivienne blinked a few times and her nose twitched. She scratched her ear. Finally, I'd managed to surprise her.

'I didn't but I guess it was pretty obvious.'

'I'm worried Tamasin's going to break Frieda's heart. That she's just experimenting to be cool.'

Vivienne went quiet, a sign of deep thought.

'I don't know, she seems genuine to me. And heartbreak's always a risk. Love hurts. I'm still in pain.'

I chewed over the conversation with Vivienne as I walked down to Digbeth to meet Melody. Why had she been so negative about Grant? I'd expected her to be happy for me. She knew how much I wanted a proper relationship. I acknowledged that I'd thought Grant was a player before I realised how sensitive and caring he was. Vivienne would come round when she saw how happy he made me.

The café was easy to find. Giant orange and yellow graffiti declared that Soul Food was for sale inside. The walls were bare brick and a wooden bar was clad in corrugated iron. Vintage bikes and car parts hung from the ceiling. Melody was waiting for me. The table where she sat was made from reclaimed wood marked with old paint and the trails left by woodworm.

I had barely sat down before she told me she was getting married and wanted me to be her bridesmaid!

'At the Registry Office. Just with the band, no big deal. I don't have any girlfriends. Marlon said I should ask you. The press will be there.'

Her request was so unexpected I couldn't speak. I thought about the night I'd spent on the streets in London, abandoned by her. Melody was rattling her bangles as she ripped a foil teacake wrapper into shiny red and gold squares. She looked up at me and her pale grey-blue eyes were huge. She was quivering like a reed in the wind. Maybe she was also remembering.

'Will you?' she asked.

How awful to have no one to invite to your wedding. I was powerless.

'Of course,' I said. Then thinking about my new coupled-up status, I added, 'can I bring my boyfriend?'

'Sure you can.' Melody switched in an instant into happy mode. 'See these colours?' She laid out the foil squares in a pattern on the bare planks of the table. 'What about I wear gold and you wear red? You'll look good in red with your dark hair. I'll sort your dress. Marlon and I will pay for everything.'

'How did you two meet? Tell me about him?'

'Yogi got me an audition with the band. Marlon's the

manager. He's a brilliant musician. Got us the gig at The Hare and Hounds and then at The Midnight Bell. He's a genius at promotion. He suggested I get you up on stage and tell the Night Angel story.'

'Is he kind? Does he look after you?'

'He makes sure I go to AA meetings,' Mel grimaced. 'And he won't let us have any booze in the house.'

'You've not known him for long then?' I wondered why the rush to get married.

'No,' Melody went quiet and looked over my shoulder her eyes fixed on the street outside. 'Now I'm not drinking,' her voice was so low I leaned forwards to hear her, 'it's like I'm on a ledge and in front of me there's a sheer drop with no bottom. Marlon's the only thing holding me back from the edge.'

The sadness in Melody's voice was like a punch in my chest. I didn't know how to respond and reached for my super jolly voice.

'I'm glad things are working out for you. Everyone says you're going to be massive.'

'Yeah,' Melody sounded distant. 'Guess so.' Then she grinned, shaking her head, and switching back to the Melody of my old night dancing days. 'Getting hitched will be a laugh. I've never been married.'

As I walked away from the café, I wondered why I didn't feel happier for her. My body was seething with emotions I couldn't connect with. I felt as if my lungs were full of water like there was something heavy on my chest. Maybe I was picking up on the darkness inside Melody. I often felt Mum's emotions. Though ever since Dad left, I had my own inner black hole.

18

The next day Mum had her driving test. She was in a total state. Her left hand constantly pawed at the table while I tried to eat breakfast. I wanted to stab it with a fork just to keep it still. Nervous energy flew from her like stinging rain. The well-being people should provide me and Thomas with psychic protective clothing.

I was sure she'd flake. But when Mike arrived to pick her up, she went with him out of the door. I had to admit that Mike was reassuring. I guess he was used to people being nervous before their tests.

'Do you think she'll pass?' I asked Thomas.

'No chance.'

I agreed with his assessment.

But we were both wrong. Two hours later she burst through the door jangling her car keys.

'I passed.'

We did a family victory dance in the kitchen.

Mike must have bribed the examiner.

Grant's parents were out that evening, so we were going to watch a movie on their giant TV screen. I wondered if tonight might be 'the night'. My body demonstrated a mixed response to this idea. Below the waist I was all – bring it on – above the waist my heart was in a flutter.

Mum said she'd drive me over. Driving with Mum on her first solo trip was enough to cause palpitations even without thinking about losing my virginity. To say she was a nervous driver was like saying water is wet. Passing her test was a massive deal and I was proud of her. But I fully expected every junction to be my last.

Conversation was impossible. We were both fully concentrated on survival. By the time we got to Grant's house, I had post-traumatic stress having lived through at least three near-death experiences. There was a muscle jumping in my face. I wasn't starting the evening at my calmest.

'Will you be okay getting home?' I asked her.

'Should be.'

'What about your agoraphobia, being out on your own?'

'Somehow, it's easier in the car. I feel safe.'

I almost laughed out loud. Just showed how mentally unstable she was.

'Mike's coming round tonight to celebrate. We can pick you up.' Mum offered as I got out of the car.

'That's okay,' I said. 'Grant said he'd drive me home.'

Mum waited while I walked up the drive and pressed the doorbell. Grant came to the door, and I waved for her to go. She pulled off to the sound of gnashing metal and made erratic progress down the street.

'Your Mum's a terrible driver.'

'Tell me about it!' I hoped she'd make it home.

We kissed in his hall.

'Your parents here?' I asked.

'They left already.'

Grant was an only child like Vivienne, though his parents weren't as doting as hers. The family had a successful garage business that sold second-hand cars. Both of his parents worked there even at the weekends. Grant seemed to spend lots of time on his own.

'So, we have the house to ourselves?'

'We do,' Grant did his suggestive eyebrow wriggle. I thought maybe we'd go straight upstairs, and a nest of snakes began writhing in my belly. Grant had other plans.

'You like pizza?'

'Sure – who doesn't.'

I followed Grant into the kitchen and was blinded by reflected light from bright shiny surfaces. An extravaganza of white goods lay before me. The room smelt of bleach. A line of machines: blender, mixer, juicer, coffee maker, were spotlessly clean as if they'd just come out of their boxes. They must have raided John Lewis in the sales.

Grant slid a pizza out of its packet and into an eye-level electric oven.

'You've heard about the *Great British Talent Show*?' His voice was excited. He leaned against the kitchen counter with his arms folded. I could see the jut of his hip bones above the waistband of his jeans. Even in this non-contamination zone of a kitchen, he was effortlessly sexy. Why were we wasting time on pizza?

'No,' I said stepping forward and putting my arms around his neck, so we stood hip to hip.

'I'd have thought Viv would have told you.' He moved away from me and got two cokes from the fridge. I shook my head.

'The BBC is making a new talent show and they're having auditions here in Birmingham. Lydia, our agent, thinks Viv and I should enter. They're filming in four cities and three acts from each place get to compete in the national finals.' Grant handed me a coke.

'I saw Viv yesterday; she didn't mention it.'

'Lydia thinks we stand a good chance. You have to send in a video and Mrs Mulligan's husband is going to help with ours. He's a director. The best videos are selected for a live audition and then ten acts are chosen for filming. This could be my first big break.'

'And Viv's up for it?'

'Course she is.' Grant's face asked if I was an idiot.

'You didn't want to do it with Coco?'

I appeared to have confirmed my stupidity.

'Come on Pen, get real; Viv is a way better actress than Coco. You know that.'

Of course I knew that. I gulped back a mouthful of coke and the liquid seemed to coat my teeth and make my mouth feel scratchy. This evening wasn't heading in the direction I'd hoped.

'Also,' Grant went on. 'And don't take this the wrong way, I know you and Viv are tight, but Viv's not much competition in the looks department. Whereas Coco…' he shrugged. 'I want all eyes on me.'

I didn't like it when Grant was arrogant. I stepped away. He came after me putting one hand on my waist and pulling me towards him. He tucked my hair behind my ear and then leaned down to kiss my neck. His lips were like butterfly wings just brushing the surface of the skin beneath my ear.

The effect was immediate like he'd pressed a secret button that switched my body on to quiver mode. A rush of energy so fierce and intense that I couldn't control it surged through me. I pressed my mouth hard against his and bit his lip. I wanted to tear him to pieces and howl like a wolf. What was happening to me?

The oven alarm pinged, and Grant wriggled away laughing.

'Easy Tiger.'

I could feel my heart beating fast. I was wet. As if I'd weed myself. I turned away frightened by the intensity of my body's response. Who knew that the skin beneath my ear would prove the gateway to such powerful desire?

*

We sat in front of the giant television screen eating pizza. Grant wanted to watch an old nineties film of *Romeo and Juliet* starring a very young Leonardo DiCaprio.

'This is great,' I said impressed. 'Really sexy.' My body was on fire. I put my hand on Grant's thigh. 'He's gorgeous – like you.'

'I was thinking Viv and I could do a scene from *Romeo and Juliet* for the talent show.'

'Aren't you going to do your scene from *The Crucible*?'

'Nah, Lydia thinks we need to do something well-known and romantic.'

I imagined the scene we were watching with Grant and Vivienne. 'You'd make a great Romeo but I'm not sure Viv's an obvious Juliet.'

'She could do it.' Grant said.

'Sure, Viv could play any part,' I agreed. 'But I think she needs a character with a bit more, I don't know, power to it. So that she can show her full range.'

'Whereas it's fine for me to be a vacuous pretty boy?' Grant moved his leg away from mine.

'I didn't say that!'

'You make it so obvious you think Viv's a better actor than me.'

'I think you're both brilliant.' I said quickly. How had I managed to upset him? The atmosphere in the room had transformed in an instant.

'You want another coke?' Grant asked getting up.

'No, I'm okay thanks.'

When he came back from the kitchen, he sat in the armchair away from me and kept his eyes on the screen. The film flowed on, but I was no longer immersed in the story.

What had I done? I kept darting glances at him. His

fringe hung down over his face so I couldn't read his expression. Even his hair was conspiring against me.

The oozy sensuality had drained from my body. Now I was tense and jumpy instead. All I'd done was express my opinion. What was so terrible about that? But I did think Viv was a better actor than Grant and I'd hurt his feelings.

I wished I could turn back time and swallow everything I'd said. How could I make things right? Maybe this was it – our relationship over before it had even started.

The double death scene at the end of the film was apt for the tragic atmosphere in Grant's living room. Anyone looking in would think that the carpet was strewn with the corpses of our closest friends. A funeral parlour was livelier.

'You okay?' I asked as the film finished and Grant got up.

'Sure,' he said switching off the TV and the room went dark. He didn't sound okay, he sounded sulky.

'Amazing film, thanks.' There was a weird pleading in my voice. Where had this pathetic girl come from?

'I'll take you home,' Grant said.

'I can get the bus.'

'I said I would.'

I could have been his Auntie. Should I call him on his sulky weirdness? But what if he said that this was it – we were over? I'd only just told Vivienne we were going out. And there was Melody's wedding. I needed to rescue our relationship.

We were on the dual carriageway into the city driving in total silence when I had an idea.

'Why don't you do a scene from *Wuthering Heights*?'

'What are you talking about?' Grant was dismissive but at least he spoke to me.

'You and Viv as Cathy and Heathcliff. One of the all-time great romances.'

'Never heard of them.'

'You must know the old Kate Bush song 'Wuthering Heights'.' I sang a few bars very badly and waved my arms about hoping to make him laugh. He kept his eyes on the road. 'We're doing the novel for A Level. She's wild and passionate and he's intense and ruthless. They have this incredible soul connection that's stronger even than death. It's got all sorts of levels because he's an immigrant and orphan and she's rich and spoilt.'

'Sounds interesting.'

'You'd make a brilliant Heathcliff. He needs to be super sexy. There've been loads of film versions with the best actors playing him.'

Grant didn't say anything, but the quality of his attention changed. One of the invisible glass panels between us slid down. I waited, holding my breath.

'Okay, I'll mention it to Mrs Mulligan and Lydia. See what they think.'

He was thawing. I kept reaching out.

'I saw Melody yesterday,' I said.

'Melody Jones?'

'Yeah, she's getting married, and she's asked me to be her bridesmaid.'

Grant laughed then and I did too, sounding slightly hysterical.

'I know. Ridiculous. She's only having a small do. The band, and a few friends. You're invited.'

'Cool.'

'She's marrying her manager, Marlon. He's the bass player in The Night Angels.' To try and re-establish intimacy with Grant I shared my reservations. 'It was weird, but I didn't get the sense that she loved him. The marriage sounded more like a business arrangement.'

'I guess she's pretty ambitious.' Grant was chatting with me again. My jaw unclenched and the frightened rabbit tension melted away from my face.

'Yeah,' I agreed. 'She is. But even so, marrying someone to help your career's a bit extreme.'

'I'd say Melody was extreme.' Grant said and I laughed.

'You're so right,' I risked putting my hand on his thigh and he didn't move his leg.

When we arrived at my house he leaned over and kissed me, a full-on serious kiss and the last of the fear fell away. My body flared.

'Let me know the date of the wedding,' he said before driving off. We were still going out.

The house was in darkness as I let myself in. Mum and Thomas must have gone to bed. I got a glass of water from the kitchen and made my way upstairs. I didn't feel sleepy. The strangeness of the evening was running figure of eight loops around my heart and brain. I couldn't think my way out of the charged-up agitation inside me. Why had Grant reacted like that? And why had I been so desperate to placate him?

As I reached the landing a man came out of the bathroom, and I screamed.

'Sorry I didn't know you were back.' Mike was dressed in jeans with his chest bare, and his belly hanging over the waistband. I wanted to look away, but my eyes seemed glued to his nipples and the grey sprouting hairs around them. I managed to wrench my gaze up to his face. He was smiling at me.

'Grant's parents were out, I heard?' What business of his was that? 'You had a good night then!' Mike spoke in a leery way, standing too close to me. I stepped back and felt my face heat up as if I were feeling guilty. He laughed, looking over my body as if he were imagining me and

Grant having sex. I pushed past him and slammed my door shut. For the first time ever I wished I had a lock on my bedroom door.

What was he doing wandering around our house dressed like that? Then I realised that he might be staying the night, that maybe he and Mum had had sex. I shook my head like a wet dog trying to fling away the terrible pictures.

If I'd been agitated before I'd bumped into Mike, now I was roaring. I rampaged around the room. For the first time in months, I opened my bedroom window and climbed out onto the flat roof and down the lilac tree into the alley.

The night air welcomed me like an old friend, and I danced my anti-Mike rage up the road.

19

By the time I got up the next morning, there was no sign of Mike. Mum was singing show tunes, and dancing around the kitchen cooking pancakes. Thomas and I exchanged looks. I decided not to say anything. Mike didn't make an appearance for the rest of the school holidays so there was no need to get into a fight about him.

On my first day back at college Frieda was pumped up, her energy as full on as Mum's.

'So did you and Grant 'get it on' baby?' She made suggestive movements with her hips. I punched her in the arm.

'We've had a few dates,' I admitted, not wanting to big things up. My relationship was too precarious to boast about. 'What about you and Tamasin?' I turned on her.

Frieda pretended to swoon in my arms.

'I'm in luuurve,' she drawled. 'That girl is so smart and funny. And have you seen the size of her house?'

'Gold digger!'

Frieda punched me then, much harder than I had her.

'Ouch,' I said. 'Careful she-hulk.'

She grinned. 'I've never been out with anyone rich before. Tam's got no idea how privileged she is. She hasn't a clue what it's like to be poor. She'd never heard of Universal Credit. And when I challenge her, she gets like so defensive. But the arguing's fun.'

Was I also privileged? Dad worried about money but as far as I knew we had enough to pay the bills. What if Dad stopped paying maintenance for us?

We were warming up in the dance studio waiting for Joe to turn up for our technique class. Frieda had her foot on my shoulder stretching her hamstrings. She was so much taller than me that I made a convenient resting post. She switched legs and I lifted my right leg for her to hold so that I could stretch out too.

'Have you heard about this new *Great British Talent Show* that's looking for acts?'

Of course, Frieda - she who knew everything - was bound to know. I nodded. I knew exactly what was coming next.

'We should enter'. She took her leg off my shoulder and lowered mine to the floor. I lifted my other leg and Frieda raised it until I was practically doing the splits from standing. 'Don't you think? We can win and become rich.'

I shook my head.

'Grant and Viv are going for it,' I said.

'And about a million other people. But that doesn't mean we shouldn't. I've looked on the website. They want you to send in a video and get someone to propose you. We can use our Night Angel video and ask Joe to be our sponsor.' Frieda had her stubborn look on, jaw jutting slightly forward.

'Talent shows are so tacky and it's not even a dance show.'

'If you're selected for filming you get five hundred quid. And if you get through to the finals it's two grand! I could take Mum to Portugal to see Avo – my granny.'

How could I resist Frieda's pleading eyes?

Joe, Mr Thorne as I still called him, rushed in.

'What are you waiting for, starting positions at the bar.' He was the late one, not us. A loud aggressive rock track blasted from the speakers and Joe began a fast warm-up routine.

I could see trouble ahead. But how could I stop Frieda having a shot at the money. Maybe Jock Briggs would be our sponsor? I didn't know how Grant would react if Frieda and I entered. I had a feeling that he wouldn't like me competing with him. Probably neither of us would be selected and then it wouldn't matter.

'Pen are you with us this morning or orbiting space?' Joe snapped at me.

'Sorry, Mr Thorne.'

I brought my attention to my feet.

When I got home that night Thomas was on his PlayStation in the living room and there was no sign of Mum or tea.

'Where's Mum?' I asked.

'Upstairs,' he said not looking at me and keeping his head down. There was something wrong with him. I moved closer.

'Have you been crying?' I asked.

'No,' he said, obviously lying, as his eyes were red-rimmed. I put my hand on his shoulder.

'Is it Mum? Has she hit you? Is she in a bad way?'

He shook his head and muttered.

'Kids at school – calling me fat.'

My stomach jumped as if I'd been kicked. I couldn't bear the idea of Thomas being hurt. 'How dare they! You're not fat. I'll come and beat them up. I've got moves you know.'

I demonstrated some fast martial arts techniques that Frieda had taught me, and Thomas laughed. I squeezed his arm.

'Seriously Thomas, that's messed up – I hate bullies. Try and ignore them but if it gets worse promise you'll tell me, and I'll get onto Mum, or maybe Dad, to sort it. You can't let bullies get away with it.'

I moved away thinking I'd get changed into comfy clothes.

'Any sign of tea?' I asked.

Thomas shook his head sadly. 'I'm starving. I ate some bread and butter.'

'Is Mum in bed?'

'Yep.'

'I'll see what I can find in the freezer.'

I should go and see Mum, find out what was wrong. But I couldn't face her on an empty stomach. I'd done so much dancing I had a serious calorie deficit.

There were oven chips and some eggs I could fry. I opened a tin of baked beans. I didn't know whether to make any for Mum, so I told Thomas to ask her. He didn't want to go up either. He shouted from the bottom of the stairs.

'Pen's making tea if you want some.'

I was putting the food onto plates when she came down. She looked awful. Her hair stuck out in a great frizzy lump at the back of her head. She was still in her dressing gown and nightie. One of her eyes was red, red-rimmed from crying like Thomas, but also bloodshot, an actual bright red eye. There was a crazy mad woman standing in our kitchen who sadly happened to be our mother.

'Let's sit at the table, shall we?' I put on my bright chirpy voice. Given the state of Mum and Thomas, I thought I'd better try and lift the mood. 'You know I have college today – dancing,' Mum didn't give any sign of remembering but I carried on anyway. 'You'd have enjoyed today because we did Latin rhythms like Mambo and Rhumba and Cha-cha-cha – '

'Look at this.' Mum interrupted pushing her mobile phone across the table.

There was a load of texts from Mum to Mike, versions

on the theme of - where are you, call me, but getting increasingly more desperate. There was just one from Mike.

Please leave me alone. I'm blocking your number.

'He ghosted you?' I asked.

Mum started crying.

'Well, I always knew he was a sleaze bag! You're better off without him.' I was furious on Mum's behalf but pleased if this meant Mike was now out of our lives. Only, I could do without Mum having a full-on breakdown. She wasn't eating her food, just pushing the beans around the plate with her fork. Her head was drooping, doing her broken doll performance.

'Why aren't you dressed? Didn't you have Wellbeing today?' She'd been getting better, passing her test, managing to go out of the house on her own.

'I cancelled,' Mum said. 'Wasn't up to it.'

My heart was pounding, and I could feel a weird muscle twitching in my cheek. My face heated up from trying to hold down a molten mass of seething energy.

'But you were doing so well - you mustn't give up.' I managed to keep my voice calm.

'Don't start on me Pen, I can't handle you having a go at me.'

'I'm trying to help,' I said.

'Well, you're not,' she glared at me. I'd had enough. What was in my head came out of my mouth before I could stop it.

'You can't let some ridiculous, stupid, disgusting man stop you getting better. It isn't fair on me and Thomas.'

'You don't know what you're talking about.' Mum was shouting now.

'Yes, I do. I hated Mike, he was a pervert and you're being pathetic. Why keep texting him – it's humiliating.' I was shouting back.

'Don't shout,' Thomas said. 'Both of you stop shouting.'

'Look at Thomas. He's upset because he's having a hard time, but you don't even notice because you're too self-obsessed. Why don't you try looking after him for a change, instead of expecting us to look after you!'

I left the room slamming the kitchen door as hard as I could. At least Mum shouting was better than her being weepy and limp. I didn't regret what I'd said. She'd be furious but maybe that would fire her up and she'd sort herself out.

I banged around my room. Maybe I should go and live with Dad. His flat would be lovely and calm. He'd be listening to jazz and working on his research. I could sit at the table next to him and get on with my homework. He'd even cook a proper tea.

Once Mum and Thomas had gone to bed, I went out into the streets again. There was a fierce bitter wind that stung my skin when I faced up Knightlow Road, so I turned and danced in the opposite direction moving west towards the mansions on Westfield Grove.

I didn't much like this road. You couldn't see the houses because they were blocked from view by high hedges and tall stone walls with electronic gates. They made me feel like I was a criminal creeping along with malicious intent. The pavements were dark from the long shadows of the walls. Probably there were hundreds of CCTV cameras recording my dancing and any minute police cars would come screaming down the road to arrest me. Was dancing in the streets illegal?

Probably the resident bankers would have me charged with suspicious activity. These high walls were built to keep people out and made me think about all the refugees huddled at borders in the freezing cold. Kept out of safer, warmer places by walls and guards with guns. We lived in such a monstrously unfair world. What could I do to change it? I didn't just want things to be better for Mum and Thomas and me, I wanted them to be better for Frieda and Anna, for everyone. I wanted the world to be a kinder, fairer place. But what could I do? I hated feeling so useless.

I kicked out at the monstrous grey stone wall surrounding a large, detached house on the corner.

About two hundred metres along Westfield Grove the road divided and there was a grassy island in the middle. On the island grew an ancient oak, at least three hundred years old. They must have split the road to preserve it. The tree was spectacular, throwing amazing shapes with its giant twisted branches against the night sky. Solar up-lighters bathed the bare limbs in a ghostly green glow as if the tree itself was emitting light. This tree was the only reason I ever came down here. Harborne would once have been full of trees like this but somehow only the super-rich got to keep them. In most places, they'd been torn down. All over the world beautiful trees were being hacked down to make way for the relentless spread of the human plague.

I danced around the tree and then I moved in, pressing myself against the bark and stretching my arms around the trunk I wanted it to know it was loved.

Closing my eyes, I relaxed into the tree feeling its strength, imagining deep roots travelling down into the earth, spreading out beneath me. I travelled with them and drank in stability, endurance, calm. This oak was the antidote to Mum.

A car engine revving hard burst through the stillness and braked to a halt beside the island. A man's voice shouted 'tree hugger' through the rolled-down window. Out of the car tumbled three young men, students at the university probably. Complete strangers.

'I love a tree hugger,' shouted the leading man. They ran across the grass and flung themselves at the tree. Joining me they stretched their arms around the trunk.

'Love this tree, man,' said another. On either side of me, unknown men took hold of my hand. We stood for a second linked around the tree.

'Yeah to the Mighty Oak,' shouted the first boy. They didn't smell of alcohol, but I thought they were probably stoned. I felt perfectly safe. A minute later they left.

'Power to the trees, Sister,' the one who did the talking handed me a leaflet. 'Come to the protest,' he shouted as they drove off.

Stillness returned.

I laughed out loud and patted the tree.

'You've got a host of admirers.' I told her.

The leaflet was for an Extinction Rebellion protest day in the city centre. An idea started to form, just a spark, a tiny acorn of an idea. Maybe there was something, some small way I could help the world. My mood was totally transformed. Yeah to the Mighty Oak.

20

Grant had gone horribly silent, no more flirty texts and nightly calls but we had exams, so I guessed he'd be busy revising. I was determined not to behave like Mum with Mike, sending millions of texts because I felt insecure. I was insecure, but I hoped that if I acted as if I wasn't, the feeling would go away. I didn't even know if Grant wanted our relationship to be public or not. Viv, Frieda and Tamasin knew but no one else. I should stop worrying about Grant and get on with my own life.

Keeping up with dance training and schoolwork was stretching me wider than 180-degree splits. Undone essays were breeding in the depths of my bag. Every day I slipped further behind with my revision. Luckily on Thursday mornings I had a double free period when Vivienne and Tamasin went off to drama class. I watched them head towards the drama studio. Mrs Mulligan's A Level group was a tight little posse of golden girls. Tamasin and Viv had loads of in-jokes that I didn't get. Doing dance meant I was divided. Wherever I was, whether at school or college, I felt like I was missing out on something.

I found an empty table in the sixth form common room and spread out my books. I was hoping I might see Grant, but although there were lots of boys sitting around working, there was no sign of him.

I had a history essay about the English Civil War that was due in tomorrow. I was focusing on one of the revolutionary groups, Gerald Winstanley and The Diggers. I loved that they'd taken back the common land to grow vegetables for everyone. They showed respect for the earth and believed in fairness. Even though they'd been defeated, and their houses and crops burnt down by wealthy landowners I wanted to argue that their ideas had survived and were still relevant today. Given the total inability of our government to care for nature and the vast inequalities in wealth I should start a 'Bring back The Diggers' campaign. I was struggling with my opening paragraph when someone tapped me on the shoulder.

'Pen,' Ed was standing next to me holding a pile of books, 'sorry to disturb you but is it okay if I share your table? I've got a free period now.'

'Sure,' I smiled and moved some of my books to make space for him. His books couldn't have been more different from mine, a stack of hardback text books with strange algebraic formulas stretching down the pages.

'What A Levels are you doing?' I asked.

'Maths, Physics and Environmental Science.'

'Wow, intense. Environmental Science sounds good. Do you learn how to save the planet?' I was joking and Ed laughed.

'Well, yeah that's the plan. What about you?'

'History and English here, and Dance at City College.'

'Is that why you're not here on Wednesdays?'

'Yeah,' I was surprised he'd noticed.

'Are you going to be a dancer then?' He seemed genuinely interested.

'I want to. And choreographer. My problem is I started late. Most dancers have done ballet since they were like two, so I've got a lot of catching up to do. My Dad wants me to do a history degree.' How come I was giving Ed my life story? He didn't seem to mind.

'You'll be fine, that dance you choreographed for the

school play was the best thing in it.'

'You think so, really?'

'Sure,' Ed sounded like he was sure and for some reason, I instantly felt less insecure. Maybe everything would work out okay.

'Thanks Ed,' I smiled at him, and he smiled back. He had a sweet face with his too-short hair and sticking out ears the colour of raw sausages.

'What about you? What do you want to do?' I asked, really wanting to know.

'You laugh about it, but I do want to improve the environment. I'm going to be a Structural Engineer, at Imperial College London if I can get the grades. It's the best place in the UK. I want to build bridges. I love bridges. Since the beginning of civilization, humankind has built bridges. We should be reducing our reliance on cars. There are so many great things we could do if only the Government invested wisely. There's a way of making floating bridges that can be used in flood zones to evacuate people. The challenge is to adapt to the climate emergency but do everything possible to prevent further damage.' I liked the way Ed's eyes had narrowed and were glinting as he spoke. 'Do you know the Queensferry Crossing outside Edinburgh is 1.7 miles long? That's the longest balanced cantilever in the world.

I didn't and shook my head.

'And it's beautiful, have you seen it?'

'No, I've never been to Scotland.' I'd never heard Ed speak for so long nor with such passion. His whole face was neon pink. There was a lot going on inside that funny square head of his. I hadn't expected Ed to be the passionate type.

He laughed at himself, 'Sorry, I get a bit carried away about bridges. The world's in such a mess but bridges are hopeful, joining two places together, overcoming obstacles, connecting people.'

'I've never thought about bridges but you're right, they're special. Bringing the separate together – I like that. I might nick that idea for my next dance project.' My inner squirrel popped up and stashed another acorn in the secret store.

'I won't charge you,' Ed said, his face returning to a more normal shade.

'Thanks,' I was busy juggling images in my head. I looked at Ed and he grinned at me.

'If I'm going to get into Imperial, I'd better get down to work,' he opened his book.

I went back to The Diggers. I wanted to tell Ed about them. But he had his head down writing. Vivienne was right, he was a good guy. The more I got to know Ed the more I liked him.

There was something very calming about working near Ed. I crossed over a bridge and left my negative thinking on the other bank. I was able to concentrate, and the essay flowed onto the page without any problems.

I was just writing the conclusion to my essay when two hands came over my eyes and the world went black. I felt a flutter of lips on my neck just above the collar of my shirt and desire in one swift pull unzipped me. I gasped.

'Guess who?' Grant whispered taking his hands from my eyes. I turned up my face and he kissed me on the lips, a deliberate possessive kiss. So, I gathered, kissing him back, our relationship was going public.

Ed shut his large textbook with a bang.

'All right Ed,' Grant nodded at him, 'how are the sums?' Ed was gathering up his papers. He ignored Grant.

'See you here next week?' I asked Ed.

'Yeah, maybe,' Ed replied, sounding uncommitted.

'Got Physics,' he said and moved away at his usual steady pace. Grant sat down in his place.

'Ed cracks me up,' he said. 'He's so inert you just can't get a rise out of him.'

'I like him,' I said.

'Yeah, everyone likes Ed, there's nothing there to not like. You may as well like a lump of rock.'

I didn't want to get into another fight, so I just kept my opinion to myself. Already I was developing relationship skills.

'Do you know where Vivienne is?' Grant asked. 'I've spoken to Mrs Mulligan and Lydia and they like your *Wuthering Heights* idea. I need to talk to Viv about it. Will you help us write the script?'

'Course I will. I'd love to.' If I helped with their audition, maybe he wouldn't mind that me and Frieda were entering as well. 'She's in the drama studio, we could go and find her?'

Grant put his arm around my waist and kissed me again. Other people in the common room were looking over. By this afternoon everyone in the Boys' and Girls' School would know that Grant and I were an item. Together we headed across the playground toward the drama studio. I felt as if I'd grown a few inches taller and there was a sassy sway to my hips as I walked.

21

Vivienne loved the idea of doing *Wuthering Heights*. The three of us spent our lunchtime working on the script. Grant was obsessed. The *Great British Talent Show* was all he talked about. I kept meaning to tell him that Frieda and I were also entering but somehow the right moment never materialised.

I sent Jock Briggs our Night Angel dance video and asked him if he'd be our sponsor. I was on the bus home when he called.

'This is good, Pen. Great connection between you two.'

'Thanks.' Praise from Jock meant more than anything else in the world.

'I like the underlying aggression. You need to work with that. You have levels of intensity that you've only just begun to explore. Don't be afraid of your power. Give that fierceness space.'

I didn't know how to respond.

'I'll try. But will you be our sponsor?'

'Sure, though I'm surprised. I wouldn't have thought this was your thing.'

'Frieda wants to enter. To win the money.'

Jock laughed.

'Fair enough. Of course, put me down if it helps.'

'Thanks that's brill. How's the new show?' I asked.

'Getting there. You'll have to come to the launch.'

'I'd love that.'

'Okay. Remember what I said. Use that aggression - not many female dancers have it.'

'Yes.' I said and he rang off. Why was aggression my thing? I wanted to be graceful and loving. Fierce and angry wasn't exactly adorable.

On Friday evening Mum announced she had a surprise for us. We were going somewhere in the car.

Ever since our fight, I'd been avoiding conversations with her. She appeared to have recovered from the Mike episode. Her bloodshot eye had faded, and she was back to getting dressed and cooking tea. Now that she could drive, I hoped Mike was out of our lives forever.

I let Thomas sit at the front, so I wouldn't have to speak to her. Ideally, her surprise would involve a takeaway, my preference would be for a Chinese. I contemplated spring rolls and duck pancakes. But instead of driving into Harborne High Street, Mum took the turning onto the M5 link road.

'Where are we going?' I leaned forward to ask.

'Wait and see,' Mum said.

I didn't know much about driving but I was sure that the fierce whine of the engine and the juddering suspension indicated the need for a gear change. There was a nasty scrape of metal against metal as Mum pushed the gear stick forward but after that, the engine settled into a comfortable background hum. She managed the transition onto the motorway without any problems.

'Thomas, my phone has the directions.'

Thomas switched on the navigator and the posh bossy lady whom we'd nicknamed Helga told us to leave the motorway at the next junction.

'This is the way to the Lickey Hills,' I realised.

Mum didn't reply. Driving and talking at the same time

was still beyond her. I stared out of the back window as the directions led us away from the motorway, away from streetlights, away from any evidence of civilization, and into the empty blackness of a country lane. Mum was doing well to find her way in the total dark. Our car headlights threw forward circles of light, revealing high banks with hedges and a few scrubby trees.

'Take the next turning on the left,' instructed Helga. There was a farm gate left open and a gravel track with trees planted on either side. We turned in and the headlamps created a spooky tunnel out of the tree branches.

Mum had slowed to a walking pace.

'You have reached your destination.' Helga informed us.

There was a low white farm building on our left. I could hear dogs barking. I guessed we weren't here for spring rolls. This would be the perfect setting for a murder. Mum parked by a barbed wire fence, and we got out. She led the way through the gate and up to the front door without her hands doing any jerking.

When Mum rang the doorbell, the dogs inside went crazy. Thomas was as confused as me. The door opened and a middle-aged woman wearing jeans and a grubby sweatshirt opened the door.

'Jenny?' she asked.

'Yes, and this is Penny and Thomas.' Mum pushed us forward.

'Come in, come in.' The lady turned, 'they're in the back.'

We followed her along a dimly lit corridor. The house stank of bleach and underneath that there was a fusty, sweet, animal smell. She opened a door into a white tiled room and in the corner on a blanket was a chocolate Labrador lying on her side. She raised her head to look at us but didn't get up. On the blanket next to her were a tangle of little fury blobs.

'Puppies,' I whispered. 'Oh, Mum.'

'You get first choice,' said the lady smiling at us. 'None have gone yet. There's four boys and two girls.'

'I want a boy,' said Thomas.

'Can we pick them up?' I asked.

'Of course you can. They're a little bit sleepy as they've just been fed. Sit down and they'll probably come and investigate.'

I looked over at Mum and I didn't think I'd ever seen her so happy. She and Thomas were already kneeling. One of the little balls unrolled and grew paws and a nose and floppy ears and snuffled toward me. I squatted down and picked up the little black bundle.

'That's a boy,' the dog lady said. 'The only black boy. The other three boys are chocolate, two black girls.'

He was warm and soft, wriggling in my hands. I held him first against my chest and stroked his head and then held him out in front of me so I could look at his face. A little pink tongue popped out and licked my nose.

'Hello to you too. Oh my God Mum, they're adorable. Do we get one each?'

'Just one.' She used her no-point arguing voice.

'This one then,' I said, knowing for certain. Love at first lick.

I passed him on to Thomas. 'He's the boldest, the leader of the pack.'

Thomas held him and he barked - a playful excited yap. He grabbed hold of Thomas's finger and growled.

'He wants to play.' The lady said.

Thomas put him down on the floor and faced him on his hands and knees and growled back. The puppy charged at him clamping his mouth around Thomas's hand.

'He bit me. Wow, he's got mega sharp teeth.' But Thomas wasn't upset. 'I like him.'

'Looks like he's chosen you,' the dog woman was nodding.

Mum had a go, picking him up and holding him snuggled into her neck. She put her face to his fur.

'I love the way puppies smell. So new, like babies.'

'Can we have him, Mum?' Thomas was pleading.

More of the other puppies were getting up and running toward us. I picked up a little fat chocolate furball. He was fluffy, not as silky as the black one.

'Their Dad was a black poodle so they'll probably be curly and shouldn't shed.' The lady told Mum. 'But you can never tell how they'll turn out. Everyone's different.'

'Like children,' Mum said. She was still holding the black one who seemed after his energetic five minutes to have fallen asleep again. 'So, this is the one we want?'

'Yes,' Thomas and I said together.

We couldn't take him home with us as we had to wait another four weeks until he was weaned. Driving home I was in the front seat next to Mum.

'What shall we call him?' She asked.

'Heathcliff.' I got in first.

'Get lost,' Thomas was outraged.

'How about Shadow?' said Mum.

'What about Bouncer?' Thomas suggested.

I thought about the way the puppy had bounded over towards us wagging his whole body.

'He does look like a Bouncer.' Mum said. 'Pen?'

'Yeah okay.' I agreed.

'Bouncer he is,' Mum said.

We drove for a while in silence thinking about little Bouncer, soon to be the newest member of our family.

'Thanks Mum,' I said. 'Getting Bouncer is a brilliant surprise.'

'I finally got something right then?' She gave me a quick sharp look and then turned back to the road. 'Does anyone fancy a Chinese?'

Maybe Mum wasn't a total disaster.

22

I hardly saw Grant for the next week. He and Vivienne filmed their video over the weekend and then on Monday exams started. Even so, Grant spent several evenings at Mrs Mulligan's house working with her husband to edit the video. I was impressed by how much effort he put into their submission. Frieda and I had just sent our video in as it was. I didn't think we stood a chance. But I hoped that Grant and Vivienne would get through after all the work they'd done.

I was glad when the deadline passed and we could forget about it. The BBC said they'd let people know within two weeks which acts had been selected for the live auditions.

Dance A Level only had one written exam. We had to evaluate the work of two choreographers. I chose Jock Briggs as one of mine. Words poured out of me. My wrist ached from writing so fast. I described his improvisational methods and how I agreed with him that dance should be actively engaged in political issues. Doing an exam about dance was no hardship because it helped me to work out what I believed. When we'd finished, Joe said that instead of our usual studio session we could have free time to start work on our next project.

Frieda and I decided to walk into Cannon Hill Park. It was one of those beautiful winter days when the world was washed in shades of white and grey. In the playground, a toddler's bright red coat and her mother's deep blue sari popped against the faded sky. The afternoon sun was low making our shadows long and pinheaded. Both Frieda and I preferred to do our thinking in motion.

'Mum and I came here every day when I was little. Whenever I see kids playing on the swings, I get a warm feeling inside.' Frieda bounced along beside me, her shadow stretching way out in front. I had no memories of being outside in a park with my Mum. 'And I did my first dance classes there at the MAC.' Frieda nodded at the square brick building. I hadn't done any dance classes as a child. We'd danced in the kitchen. Mum was always dancing with us but always inside the house. Maybe that was why I loved dancing outside so much.

'I've had an idea,' I said, 'for our next project.'

'Oh, here we go!'

'Well,' I wasn't sure where to start. 'You know when we first danced together, and you said we should do a protest dance?'

'Ah huh,' Frieda had slowed down her pace, so I knew she was listening.

'And you know that Tartan Fling's new dance is about how we need to respect the planet.'

She nodded.

'For my History A Level, I've been studying this revolutionary group called The Diggers who believed in the common ownership of land. And that got me thinking about how humans have changed throughout history in their relationship to the earth. So, I thought we could create a dance that was like a speeded-up history of that. Starting off with worshipping the planet, then working with it and respecting it. Then wanting to possess it and fighting over it. Then exploiting it, and finally destroying it. We could end with how we need to save it.' I was talking quickly. 'And you know the South African Theatre I saw with

Grant and how I told you they used giant paper puppets? We could make a giant model of the earth out of paper-mâché or something and that could be like the character of the planet, like a third dancer.'

Freida didn't say anything. I wanted to keep talking to convince her but I knew I needed to give her time to take in what I'd already said. We kept walking slowly beneath a row of willow trees. Their trailing branches flickered as the tiny lime green bumps of leaf buds caught the light.

'I like the globe idea.' Freida stared into the distance as if she were imagining it. 'I could make that in Art. Mum would help.' She speeded up again and strode ahead so I had to jog to keep up with her. 'We'd need to get some real violence in there. We could throw the globe about, punch it, destroy it even, to demonstrate how we're killing the planet.' Freida did a flying Thai boxing kick.

'Yep. We can build to a frenzy of destruction and despair.'

'Cool.' Freida double-punched the air. Two gardeners stopped raking leaves to stare at her. She smiled at them and did a cartwheel.

'So, you think it could work?' I skipped after her staying upright but catching her high spirits.

'We can give it a go – why not.'

We'd reached the bandstand and Freida took the steps in one bound. Standing in the centre of the wooden floor she stomped out the dance we'd choreographed for *The Crucible* giving her full menu of buttock moves.

'Yeah, dance for the planet. I like the idea.' She said.

''Dance for the Planet' – that's what we should call it.' I joined her on the bandstand, doing my best to shake my butt as she did.

'And,' I started to speak.

'Enough for now, no more talking.' Freida put her

hands over her head and doubled at the waist making swaying elephant trunk movements and moaning loudly.

'Look at this.' I passed Frieda the leaflet for the Extinction Rebellion protest that the tree hugger student had given me. 'Isn't your Mum involved with them?'

'Yeah, she helps out with the costumes and the art design.'

'What about if we performed our dance at their protest? Stood up for what we believe in. Made it into a real protest dance?'

Frieda burst out laughing.

'Pen Flowers – I've turned you into an activist. I'll talk to Mum.'

I wanted to hug Frieda. With her on side, we could do this. We began improvising some 'Dance for the Planet' moves. Imagining a giant globe hanging from the ceiling of the bandstand like a disco ball, Frieda and I circled like whirling dervishes. We were going to dance up a tornado that would force governments to act.

23

I stood in front of the full-length mirror in Mum and Dad's room - or what used to be theirs and was now Mum's - and contemplated my appearance.

Dance training was changing my body shape. I had muscle definition in my arms and legs, and I could even see my abs without flexing. I was starting to look like a dancer. Melody had chosen a deep red silk slip dress for me to wear. A simple close-fitting sheath that slid over my body in a sensuous glide. I couldn't wear any underwear, just the dress and my DMs. She'd also taken me to have my hair done. Whatever Mel's failings as a friend, there was no doubt that she had style. I was happy for her to take control. Her hairdresser, Gary, kept most of my hair long but gave me an undercut. Tied up in a ponytail, as it was today, revealed a band of shaved hair running around my head at ear level. The short hair felt soft and furry. I stroked myself and hoped that Grant would feel compelled to do the same.

Mum hadn't been happy about me going to Mel's wedding. But I'd insisted and she'd given in.

'You look lovely, darling,' she managed to say when I came downstairs. 'But not like a bridesmaid.'

'Mel's wearing a gold mini dress.'

'Oh well, just take care. I hope Grant looks after you.'

'I can look after myself!' Sometimes Mum was so dated in her thinking.

'That girl is trouble. You'll freeze to death in that dress – have you got a coat?'

I nodded and made for the door. Mel had lent me a vintage 70s Afghan which was total rock 'n roll. If Mum saw me wearing it, she'd assume I was taking heroin.

'Pen,' Mum called after me. 'Try and understand, I want you to have fun, I want you to lead a brave, bold life and do everything that I've been too scared to do. But I don't want you to get hurt. That music world is dangerous. Promise me you'll be sensible.'

I came back into the kitchen and gave her a quick hug.

'I won't take any drugs,' I promised. 'Nor get drunk or anything like that so don't worry. I won't even stay late - I've got dance training tomorrow morning.'

Grant rang the doorbell and I managed to slip away without Mum spotting the Afghan. Grant didn't say anything when he saw me, but I felt as if he was stroking me with his eyes. My heart was doing a Chachacha at the sight of him. Even in school uniform, Grant was handsome. But in a charcoal suit with a pink shirt and his quiff newly washed and springing down over his eyes, he looked like a film star. This beautiful man was my boyfriend. Desire ran through me like lava, melting every muscle in its path. Thank goodness for skin and bone otherwise I'd have been a puddle on the concrete.

'New hair?' Grant started the engine with one hand and leaned over and ran his other hand down the shaved part of my head, 'like a furry animal.'

'I'm channelling my inner wild cat,' I said growling in what I hoped was a sexy way.

'I was thinking more squirrel,' Grant said grinning at me.

Outside the Registry Office a small crowd was gathered. At its centre stood Melody. She looked spectacular in her shining gold mini dress and ridiculously high gold platform boots. Her long skinny legs were bare. Her hair was shaved into a sort of Mohican with the central strip of auburn hair backcombed and braided and standing high like a show horse's mane. She carried two bunches of white daisies and as we approached, she tossed me the smaller posy. I caught them and Grant and I joined the bridal party.

Marlon, at Melody's side, was dressed in a black and gold brocade jacket. He seemed to be the one directing proceedings. With them were the rest of The Night Angels, Mel's friends Dog and Gary the hairdresser. I appeared to be the only other girl. There was no sign of any family members. Marlon led the way inside through the glass doors. I was glad Grant was with me and kept hold of his hand. He grinned at me and squeezed my palm. I could tell he was loving the showbiz atmosphere.

Once inside the Registry Office Marlon disappeared and Melody came over, her ankles rocking as she struggled to balance on her crazy high heels. Wearing them she towered over me.

'Who's this then?' Melody honed straight in on Grant.

'This is Grant,' I said then added, 'my boyfriend,' feeling ridiculously proud.

'Well done, Pen,' she said and leaned forward to kiss him on the cheek. 'Welcome to my wedding Grant.' Grant kissed her on the other cheek.

'Delighted to be here, though obviously devastated.' Grant pretended to clutch at his heart. 'I'm a big fan.'

Melody laughed. 'I like this one,' she told me.

Marlon appeared by her side. 'They're ready for us.'

'Marlon, you know Pen – this is Grant.' Mel introduced us.

'Hi,' he said, 'thanks for coming. We need to move through now.'

He took hold of Mel's arm and guided her towards the

doors leading out of the waiting room. Grant and I followed them and everyone else came in behind.

I'd never been to a wedding before, but I'd seen them in films. I kept looking at Grant's profile. But the soft swelling feelings inside me didn't seem in evidence anywhere else in the bland beige room. There were no readings, no specially written vows. We were party to a legal transaction. The wedding took just fifteen minutes. The only personal touch was a Night Angels track playing as we walked out of the exit door into the gardens. Before we'd left the room the next group was entering noisily.

Outside there were several photographers waiting with cameras pointed. I heard Marlon whisper to Mel, '*The Post* are here'. He swooped Melody up in his arms and carried her toward the cameras. She flung her arms around his neck, and they kissed as the photographers clicked away. The romance lacking inside was now vividly displayed. The couple answered questions thrown out to them by a young woman in a trouser suit.

'Aren't you too young to get married, Melody?' The woman asked.

'I'm an old soul in a young body,' she said. 'Ask Marlon.'

'She's wise enough to choose me.' Marlon looked at Mel tenderly.

'How will the marriage affect the band?' The journalist seemed to be looking for an angle.

'I wanted to marry them all,' Melody said. 'But I had to choose one.' Everyone laughed, even Marlon.

'What about the *Great British Talent Show?*' A young man behind one of the cameras asked. 'New Music Brum readers have been asking: have the Night Angels entered?'

'You betcha,' Marlon exchanged glances with Melody.

'We intend to go all the way.'

'The Winners.' They both said together lifting their joined hands in a victory salute.

Beside me, I felt Grant's hand on my back tense. The challenge for him and Vivienne just got harder. I still hadn't confessed that Frieda and I had also entered.

The encounter with the press lasted way longer than the marriage ceremony. Melody and Marlon were happy to do anything for the cameras. Grant was watching them as if he were studying for an exam, throwing himself forward into any group shots and trailing Melody with his eyes. He seemed to be enjoying himself, whereas my smile felt fake. Marlon invited us to join them at a local pub and Grant was keen to go along.

Once we were away from the press the mood settled into something that felt more genuine. We took the steps down to Gas Street and made our way beside the canal. Channels of greeny-grey water reflected the surrounding redbrick warehouses. Even though they'd been converted into restaurants and pubs they still retained a sense of history, of working people moving slowly before the invention of planet-destroying cars.

The wedding party paraded along the towpath, laughing, and messing about. The bride and grooms' golden outfits sparked in the sunlight and Melody's friend Dog, who looked like a feral dog, jumped onto one of the parked narrow boats, then ran leaping from deck to deck alongside the path. Grant held my hand as we walked behind them. Stopping he put his arm around my shoulder and kissed me. The rippling water was like a twinkling sheet of diamonds, and the sky was sapphire. I was hanging out with a semi-famous rock group, and a super fit boy was holding me close. The cameras had gone but I felt like I was in a Hollywood movie.

*

We piled into one of the pubs that overlooked the canal. A converted warehouse with high ceilings, red brick walls and giant arched windows through which flooded quivering watery light. Marlon appeared to know the manager. There was a mezzanine level reached by wrought iron stairs. A large circular table in front of a huge central arched window had been reserved for us.

Melody and Marlon sat together in front of the window.

'Hey Pen,' Melody called over, 'come and sit by me and...'

'Grant,' I helped.

'Yeah, Grant too.'

We moved round to the right side of Melody. She had Marlon on her left.

'We should go boy girl,' Melody said so Grant and I switched places and Al, the drummer in The Night Angels sat down next to me. As there were only two girls the boy-girl arrangement ended there.

A waiter brought up a wine bucket with a bottle of champagne chilling and started laying out fluted glasses for everyone.

'Compliments of the manager,' he said.

Marlon started to speak, saying 'No thanks,' but Melody put her hand on his arm, and whispered, 'it's my wedding day, for the others,' in a desperate child's voice.

Marlon gave way.

'Thanks,' he said nodding at the waiter to start pouring.

'We'll need a couple more of these,' Melody said. 'To go round,' her voice insistent as Marlon frowned.

'One more champagne and two large bottles of sparkling water.' Marlon gave the order. I bet he was the oldest in a big family. He had that automatic responsibility.

The waiter poured out the champagne and Marlon put his hand over his and Melody's glasses, filling them with sparkling water when it arrived. Melody smiled at him, but I'd seen that hard blank look in her eyes before.

'A toast. We should have a toast. I'm making a speech.' She climbed up onto her chair wobbling dangerously in her platform boots. She looked otherworldly, backlit by the green rippling light from the giant window.

'To my gorgeous husband Marlon, and The Night Angels. Here's to fame and fortune.' She swayed back and leaned against the glass. I imagined her crashing through. Both Marlon and Grant reached up to hold her.

'Come down,' Marlon ordered her, pulling at her arm.

'I haven't finished,' she pulled away from him. Grant had his hand on her waist steadying her.

'Thank you, darling,' she smiled down at him. 'This is my wedding day and it's just the start. Here's to the music and to getting super freakin' rich.'

'To the music,' Marlon said, and everyone drank. 'Come down Mel, I don't want you falling through the window. Let's make our millions before we start wrecking places.'

Melody allowed Marlon to help her down. He refilled her glass with sparkling water. She glared at him, and he held her stare. The afternoon didn't seem destined to be a perfect start to married life. My stomach tightened.

Waiters arrived with trays of food: mini hamburgers, chicken drumsticks, bowls of fries, grilled halloumi, and red onion tarts were laid out on the table. I sipped at my champagne. I'd never had champagne before. It was sharp and itchy on my tongue. Melody was loading food onto Grant's plate. She was focusing her attention on him and ignoring Marlon.

Al sitting next to me was talking.

'Try this it's delicious.' He put a piece of halloumi on my plate. But the dry rubbery texture was difficult to swallow. I helped myself to water.

Melody was whispering in Grant's ear, and he was laughing. She had a hand on his leg. I had trouble concentrating on what Al was saying.

'I like that dance film you did to 'Night Angel'. It was tense, like intimate but threatening. I watched it a few times.

'Thanks, it was just a piece we did for class.'

'You should have gone in for the BBC talent show.'

'We have.' I admitted, hoping Grant hadn't overheard.

I didn't need to worry. Grant was totally focused on Melody. Already he was at the centre of the party. He and Melody were the beautiful people. They didn't need to do anything, just the way they looked guaranteed them attention. Marlon was talking to Yogi but keeping an eye on Melody. I could sense he wasn't happy.

Grant asked Melody about her song writing. She told him about their first album. It was like he brought his own spotlight with him. If he was focusing on you, you felt bathed in sunshine. Melody was constantly touching him. I understood why. My whole body felt hungry for him. I wanted to rip off my dress and tear open his shirt and press myself skin to skin. I was sucked towards him, like he was the sun, and I was too small a planet to resist the gravitational pull.

Melody kept looking at the champagne in Grant's glass.

'I'm driving,' he whispered and switched his glass for hers. I clutched at his leg. He shouldn't have done that. Mel saluted him and lifted the glass.

Marlon swung round, 'No!' He wrestled for the glass

in Melody's hand. 'That's it, show over.' He spoke quietly but firmly. He was keeping his tone light, but he was serious. Conversation stopped around the table. Everyone was waiting for Melody to explode. Marlon had hold of her hand, forcing her to let go of the glass. He was keeping eye contact. He wasn't afraid of her. Marlon was controlling her, but was this abusive or supportive? I wasn't sure.

'Come on baby,' he said quietly. 'Don't give in now.'

She flung her arms around his neck.

'Take me home. I want to go home.' She sounded like a tired four-year-old. Marlon held her close whispering in her ear. She rested her head on his shoulder, eyes closed. He seemed to have some trick of calming her down.

'Thank you for coming. We're off now. I've paid the bill so please stay and enjoy the food and drink.' Marlon said.

Melody had vanished before our eyes. She clung to Marlon limp, boneless. As they left the table Marlon squeezed Yogi's shoulder, nodded at the rest of us, and disappeared down the stairs with a 'see ya next week.' Melody, her head down, didn't say a word.

'Let's go,' Grant said as they left. I was glad to get away.

Out in the cold February air I shivered inside my Afghan coat.

'That was weird,' Grant said.

'It's always tense around Melody,' I said.

'Marlon's a total control freak. What's he got over her?'

'The whole wedding was strange.' I agreed.

'I'm surprised they've entered the talent show. It's supposed to be for new acts. The Night Angels are already established.' Grant was frowning. We were crossing over the canal. Now was the time to tell him about Frieda and me. Surely, he must realise that every performer in Birmingham would be giving it a go. His sulky expression made me want to laugh. He was adorable like a cute puppy. I couldn't spoil the moment.

'Let's get a photo.' I said. Grant with his longer arms held out my phone and clicked. We got lucky. The sun was setting, and the low-angled light turned the green water golden, while the sky was a blazing salmon pink. We were looking at each other and smiling, backlit by shimmering water and framed by glowing red buildings. Even I looked beautiful with my fancy hair and Afghan coat. I felt a shift in the universe. Time juddered to a stop, the pavements buckled, and the air turned viscous. I was moving in slow motion. A message printed in giant black capitals dropped into my brain: I'M IN LOVE.

Love was huge, so much deeper than lust. Love was expanding me, opening inner worlds, galaxies multiplying to infinity. Love had turned me into a giant space balloon and was flying me out of my ordinary life. Love was everything I'd dreamed it would be.

Part 3

Dance for the Planet

24

Once exams were over Grant and I were going to stay in a log cabin owned by his grandparents. The cabin, complete with hot tub, was in a forest near Cannock Chase about an hour's drive away.

Ever since I'd realised that I was in love with Grant I'd been desperate to have sex. Grant was the one holding back, wanting me to wait. The weekend in the cabin was his idea. For him my virginity was a big deal. Sweet how romantic he was. Two nights and a whole weekend alone together, no parents or siblings to negotiate. I couldn't wait.

Mum had agreed to my going. Without directly lying I'd managed to give the impression that Grant's grandparents would be there. By the time I returned, and she discovered the truth there'd be nothing she could do.

We weren't telling anyone. Planning a private shared sex adventure was super erotic. I kept having to break into dance moves between lessons because the jiggling, writhing, snakes inside my guts were driving me wild.

'What is the matter with you?' Viv said during the afternoon break before double English. 'Stop wriggling about – you're driving me crazy.'

Nothing Viv could say was going to bring me down. The moment the final bell rang I exploded down the drive parting the dawdling crowds of Year 7 and 8s like I was Moses slicing through the Red Sea. Clear the way, supercharged sex rocket coming through. My Mission, not to save the people of Israel from slavery, but to give myself entirely to carnal pleasure.

Grant was waiting for me in his Mum's car. I threw my rucksack with my weekend stuff into the back and leaned over to kiss him.

'Let the party begin,' I said and shrugged off my blazer as he pulled away.

We wanted to get to the cabin while it was still light. Grant put his foot down and dodged between lanes. We had The Night Angels playing and the car was filled with Melody's throaty voice. This felt like the most adult thing I'd ever done.

'You know what's going to be special?' Grant said.

Well having sex obviously! But I didn't say that I just shook my head.

'Sleeping together, waking up together. That's the best bit.' He said this with such certainty that I wondered if he'd brought other girlfriends up here for the weekend. I pushed away the idea of Grant having sex with other girls. I was glad he was more experienced than I was.

He was singing along to the music, tapping out a rhythm with his fingers on the steering wheel. I gorged my eyes on his face. I loved his mouth. Those full soft lips contrasted with his long angular face. His mouth never stopped moving. He was always pulling faces, pouting, grimacing, but mainly smiling.

He turned and caught me gazing at him and stretched his luscious lips into a huge wide grin. Moving his hand onto my thigh he pushed up my school skirt. I opened my legs and then laughed.

'What?' Grant asked.

'I've just realised why people call alcohol a leg opener.'

He moved his hand further up and did the eyebrow thing.

'We need to stop for supplies. There's a supermarket in a few miles.'

*

At the supermarket we raced the trolley down the aisles, jumping on the back and riding as fast as we could along the lines of shelves. When you were in love the most ordinary everyday things were lit up. In the readymade section we stocked up on pizzas and pasta. We added breakfast cereal and milk and biscuits and a bottle of Prosecco that Grant said I'd like.

Grant liked pepperoni pizza and chocolate Hobnobs. He hated Weetabix and only drank oat milk. Who knew that such everyday details could be sexy, could make me love him more than I already did? We bought two big bags of food, more than we could ever eat. If we got snowed into the cabin for a fortnight we'd survive. I wished we could be.

The sun was starting to set when we turned off the main road onto a narrow country lane. The low angle made the sunlight blaze straight into our eyes.

'Pass me my shades, babe.' I handed Grant his sunglasses and when he put them on my insides did a loop the loop. I put my glasses on too. Sunnies turned real life into a movie.

About a mile down the road on the left-hand side was a sign saying Chase Forest Cabins beside an open gate. We followed the rough gravel track through a thickly planted forest of evergreens and deciduous trees. Branching off on either side were drives marked with names saying Oak Cabin, Sycamore Cabin, Beach Cabin.

'We're in Silver Birch, on the left any minute.'

'There.' I pointed to a turning on my side of the track and Grant braked and did a swerving skid on the gravel then slowed down and bumped us carefully along the uneven narrow driveway between the trees.

We pulled up in front of a large wood-panelled cabin that stood high off the ground. Steps led up to a wooden veranda. The place was surrounded by tall trees. If there were other cabins nearby I couldn't see them. The plot was completely private and a bit spooky as the sun dropped lower in the sky.

'Wow,' I said. 'It's beautiful. But talk about remote, you could get away with murder here.'

'Or other evil deeds,' Grant grinned. Then reaching over he bit my lip and placed his hand on my left breast. 'You need to get naked if you want to go inside.'

The sun was sinking fast, creating a luscious raspberry pink sky. The sun was a giant orange ball floating behind the black tree branches.

'Gentlemen first,' I said.

Grant leapt out of the car and walked towards the cabin pulling his shirt over his head. On the bottom step of the stairs up to the front doors he kicked off his trainers. I followed stepping out of my skirt and undoing the buttons on my shirt. By the time we were both on the veranda, Grant was down to his boxers and I was left with only my underwear to go.

'Ladies first,' Grant said undoing my bra. I stepped out of my knickers and stood naked in front of him.

He ran his eyes up and down and gave a low whistle.

'You've got a fantastic body,' he said.

'Your turn,' I said, and he obliged. I started to shiver. Desire or the freezing temperature, I wasn't sure.

Grant entered the code into a key box and let us inside the cabin. Giant glass double doors opened into a kitchen and living room with a high-beamed ceiling, a wood-burner and two squishy sofas. The whole place smelt of wood.

'This is amazing, I love it.' I threw myself against Grant and expressed my appreciation. We toppled over onto one of the sofas, exploring the novelty of total nakedness, skin to skin.

'Come on,' Grant leapt up and his erect dick pointed at me. It looked alarmingly huge. He pulled me through a door that led deeper into the cabin.

'Bathroom, spare room,' he gave a guided tour. I was having difficulty noticing anything but his obvious arousal. 'And master bedroom.' He announced dramatically propelling me into a square room with more glass doors opening onto a balcony that looked out at the forest. Most of the room was filled with a king-sized double bed. The last of the sun's rays blazed through the glass doors making a wedge of glowing orange light across the white puffy duvet.

Grant dived onto the bed and lay there grinning at me. Sunlight striped his body highlighting his mid-section. I really didn't need the stage lighting. Grant patted the bed beside him.

Was this it, the moment? Already? I climbed onto the bed next to him and Grant put his arms around me and kissed me.

'It's okay,' he said, understanding. 'We've got the whole weekend.'

We lay there watching the sun go down and the room go dark, stroking each other's skin. I calmed down.

'The hot tub's on the veranda, you'll love it. I'll get our stuff from the car.' Grant got up and I stretched out making snow angels in the super thick duvet. My duvet at home was so old there was only a trickle of filling left inside.

'This is a great bed,' I said.

'Oh God, I might just have to fuck you now,' Grant said standing at the bottom of the bed between my open thighs. His eyes were like searchlights over my body. I was enjoying the effect my nakedness had on him. Here was a new power.

'I can do the splits you know?' I told him.

'I might need to see that,' Grant knelt on the bed.

'Are you impressed?' I asked.

'So impressed,' Grant was working his fingers up the inside of my thighs, 'so impressed I'm coming in for a closer look.' He dipped his head, and I discovered a whole new reason to love his full mobile mouth. Sensations on a scale formerly unknown to human experience pulsed through my body. I clutched at the duvet and tried not to scream.

'Hello,' a man's voice called from inside the cabin. I did scream, a yelp of panic. Grant leapt up. Our clothes were scattered over the veranda. Grant discovered a dressing gown on the back of the bedroom door and put it on. His erection pushed the striped cotton into a tent below the waist. I giggled and he frowned at me.

'Cover yourself up,' he whispered and went out of the room.

I could hear the conversation in the living room.

'Hi there, I saw the car. Came to check everything's okay.'

'Thanks. I'm Grant, Alan's grandson. Just having a shower.'

'Right, okay, sorry to disturb you. I'm Cyril, the manager. Alan said you were here this weekend, so I put the hot tub on earlier. Should be ready now. You know how everything works? I can show you – it's no trouble.'

'No thanks, I've been here before.'

'You know where I am if you need anything. The Manager's Office first turning on the left and if I'm not there then my mobile's on the site map.'

'Thanks.' Grant was politely nonresponsive.

'You want to do anything I can sort you out bikes, kayaks, there's fishing.'

'No thanks, we're alright.'

'Well, well good. As I say, call if you need anything at all. You sure you don't need me to show you how the cooker works?'

'I'm okay, thanks.' Grant was using thanks as a way of saying get lost. I wanted to giggle. The voices faded but I could still hear Cyril talking outside on the veranda, explaining how the hot tub worked. I didn't dare move from the bed.

Eventually, Grant came back into the bedroom still wearing the old man's striped dressing gown. I burst into laughter.

'That was crazy.'

'He's a pain in the arse, poking his nose in. I bet he just came to find out who was here.' Grant didn't come back to bed. His mood had shifted. I wondered if he was worried about gossip getting back to his grandparents.

'Our clothes must have been everywhere.' I said.

Grant smiled. 'Your bra was over the handrail. I kicked my boxers under the boots stand, don't let me forget. I'm going to get the stuff from the car and then let's get in the hot tub.' He walked out.

I rolled over and leaning on my elbow looked out of the window. It was almost dark outside now. I felt like a cat, sleek and purring. Even Cyril interrupting us was perfect somehow, making a shared story.

I found an old lady's silk scarf hanging in the wardrobe and tied it around me. It was the sort of thing Melody would do. The scarf felt soft and slippery over my body but didn't achieve much as a cover-up.

In the kitchen, Grant was putting our food supplies in the fridge.

'That's Grandma's,' he said looking me over.

'Should I take it off?'

'No, I like it. Sort of pervy,' he said.

'Talking of pervy, you in that dressing gown!'

Grant waggled his eyebrows and leered.

'Come 'ere darlin'.' Hands out in front of him in grab mode he chased me round the room, dressing gown flapping open. I nearly wet myself. Total perv.

The hot tub was a new experience. Grant had poured Prosecco into two plastic glasses. He climbed in first and settled in a corner putting the glasses on a special tray-shaped section on the lip of the tub. I stepped down carefully into the water. I didn't want to fall over and make a tit of myself. It was like getting into a giant hot bath. I sat opposite Grant on a seat-shaped dip in the plastic moulding. The water came over my chin. Grant pressed a button and the surface started to seethe and bubble ferociously. I thought I might drown. I kept my mouth closed but the bubbles went up my nose.

Grant laughed. 'You're so tiny I forgot. Try this seat it's higher.'

I moved to the seat next to him and my shoulders nudged out of the water.

'Listen,' Grant said touching my arm under the water. We sat and the silence of the night settled around us. The sky was proper black with no city light pollution.

My body was submerged in hot swirling water but there was cool evening air on my face, neck, and shoulders. The piney smell of the forest seemed stronger in the darkness like the trees were breathing out perfume. Into the thick stillness of the forest came the call of an owl – woo woo terwit woo. Next to me, his thigh pressed against mine, was the most gorgeous man I'd ever met. This moment – the most perfect in my whole life.

Grant passed me a glass and I drank. I wasn't sure about the taste but drinking bubbles felt right for the setting, so I gulped it down.

'Feel the jets,' Grant said. 'There's some at the front of the seats.'

I nodded I could feel my thighs being pummelled by a water jet.

'Try sitting on that,' he said grinning. 'Girls like them.'

I shifted forward on the seat and angled my body into the pressure stream.

'Wow,' I said grinning back at him my eyebrows lifting, 'that-is-a-maze-balls'

The thought of him bringing other girls up here intruded again.

Before long the deed was done. Penetration was achieved with some difficulty and some pain. Two glasses of Prosecco probably helped. I wasn't riding on waves of pleasure. That wasn't too awful was what I mainly thought. The best bit was after, Grant holding me, my head on his shoulder, the smell of the wooden bedroom and our sweaty bodies. The throbbing inside my vagina reminded me of Grant inside my body, more intimate than anything I'd ever experienced. We fell asleep curled up together and I'm sure I smiled all night.

In the morning we tried again. Grant said it would get better and it did. The pain went away, and I stopped worrying about whether I was getting it right and just sank into my body. When I closed my eyes, we became two beings moving as one. Sex was just like dancing.

'You're a natural,' Grant told me and having nothing to compare I believed him.

25

Saturday was a beautiful morning with light slicing through the trees in space rays. I could see the bumps of new leaves on the bare branches waiting to unfurl. Everywhere I looked life was poised to burst out. Grant and I walked hand in hand through the forest. There were drifts of snowdrops beneath the trees. Snowdrops made my heart almost stop beating I loved them so much. The humility of their hanging heads, so understated and fragile, and yet so much tougher than they looked. The first flowers to force their way through the frozen winter earth. They were symbols of courage and persistence. I felt like I had finally broken through my years of loneliness to the sunshine of being loved.

We avoided the site office and the tracks leading back to the other cabins. Heading deeper into the forest we left behind the noise of cars and human voices and were surrounded by bird song. I couldn't see any actual birds, but their presence was everywhere like a heavenly chorus cheering us on. The forest floor was springy as the layers of fallen leaves had mulched into a soft mattress that made each step bounce. I was feeling bouncy anyway, so I double-bounced my way through the trees. My fingers curled into Grant's and a bubbly, hot chocolate with marshmallows, sensation filled up the whole of my insides.

We tried not very successfully to have sex against a tree trunk. We ended up rolling on the ground, clothes soaked and covered in leaf litter. Grant had mud on his nose and my knees were pitted with red marks from bits of stone. Obviously, this meant running back to the cabin and warming up in the hot tub before a return to the bedroom.

The moment we'd finished Grant checked his phone. The BBC had said they'd let people know today who'd been selected for the auditions. Even in the woods where there was no signal he kept checking.. I tried to push my irritation away. Why couldn't he just leave the rest of the world alone and be here with me?

We had cheese on toast for lunch which we ate sitting outside on the veranda. I wanted this weekend to go on forever. I didn't want to go back home. Grant and I could live here in the forest foraging for berries.

Inside the cabin, Grant's phone pinged, and he hurried to reach it. He came back out to the veranda.

'Shit Pen, it's from the BBC,' his face was white, focused on the screen. There was a pause while he opened and read the email. I waited, knowing that the continued happiness of our weekend was under threat.

'We're in, Viv and I, we've been selected for the auditions.' He fist-pumped the air. 'Next Saturday in Digbeth. Yes.' He pulled me out of my seat, lifted me up and swung me around.

'I love you Pen Flowers,' he said kissing me. I could hardly believe he'd said the words first.

'I love you too,' I said, glad to be able to finally give voice to the volcano erupting inside me. But alongside my elation at Grant's declaration was a stab of anxiety. Somehow, I'd never managed to tell Grant that Frieda and I had also entered. I made a silent prayer for us to be rejected so that he need never know.

My phone pinged from the bedroom.

'I bet that's Viv telling you,' Grant called through the door as I went to look.

But it was a message from Frieda.

We're in – she'd written with a strong-arm emoji. I gulped. Now I really did have to tell Grant. I wished I'd done it earlier. This was going to be awkward.

I went back into the living room. Grant was still on his phone.

'They've posted a list of everyone who's auditioning. Jeez there's loads!'

I hoped my news wouldn't put a damper on his euphoria.

'Grant,' I tried to interrupt him.

'The Night Angels, no brainer, I guessed they'd be there.'

'Grant there's something I need to tell you.'

'Hold on Pen I'm reading this. There's another band, never heard of them, a couple of dance groups, stand-up comics, acrobats, poets ffs! Total mishmash. Looks like we're the only actors. Loads of singers.'

Grant looked up from his phone and stared at me.

'Dance duet by Frieda Santos and Pen Flowers.' He read out.

'I was trying to tell you.'

'Why didn't you tell me before?' Grant was looking at me like he'd discovered I was venomous.

'I was…'

'All the time I've been going on about the show you didn't say a word.'

'Sorry, Frieda insisted, I….'

'Did Vivienne know you'd entered?'

I nodded, feeling dreadful.

'What was it – let's all laugh at Grant?'

'I didn't think we'd get in.'

'So, your pride was more important than making a complete twat out of me.'

'No I, I just thought you wouldn't like me entering, I don't know, I didn't think.'

Grant walked back into the bedroom, and I followed him.

'I should have told you before. But it's great news that we've both got an audition.'

Grant had his back to me. He took his jacket out of the wardrobe. When he turned round his face was white, unsmiling. He wouldn't look at me and pushed past me out of the bedroom. Walked out of the cabin, onto the veranda and down the steps.

'Grant what's going on? Where are you going?' I called after him. But he didn't reply. I ran down the steps as he got in the car and reversed on the gravel drive.

'Grant this is crazy.' My feet were bare and running after him on gravel was painful. I hopped after the car, shouting at him. 'Where are you going? Stop. You can't leave me here. I'm sorry, okay.'

Having swung the car around he drove down the track leaving me standing in the middle of the parking space.

How dare he go off like that? What was I supposed to do? Just wait for him to sort himself out. I hadn't made him look like an idiot. He'd done that himself by overreacting.

I limped back up the stairs to the veranda and sat down to pick the gravel out of my feet. One moment he says he loves me and then he throws a wobbly and abandons me. So much for our perfect weekend. I should have told him, I knew that. I couldn't think why I hadn't. There just never seemed to be the right moment. I'd felt awkward, so I'd avoided it – that was the truth. I'd thought Grant might be upset and his reaction today showed me I was right. But I should have had the courage to face up to him and be honest. It was my fault.

But why had he run off like that? What was I supposed to do here on my own?

I started clearing up our lunch stuff and tidying the mess in the cabin. He'd have to come back. There was no way he could just leave me here.

I sent him a text – where r u? what's going on?

No reply.

I texted Grant again – sorry. I messed up. come back.

No reply.

The silent treatment - he must be furious. Why did the BBC have to let us know today? Why couldn't they have waited until Monday? Blame the BBC. I didn't know what to do with myself. I felt disconnected to my body. The big warm cavern that had been filled with love was now like a wind tunnel. There was an arctic gale blowing through me. I wandered aimlessly around the cabin.

I texted Frieda - yeah superstar.

No need to take my problems out on her. She wanted this much more than me.

Frieda forwarded the BBC email to me. It was the same one Grant had received. We had to arrive half an hour before our time slot at 3.15 pm bringing an adult guardian if we were under eighteen. Hopefully, Anna would come with us. I didn't want to have to ask Dad – and obviously my Mum couldn't do it.

I wished we hadn't got in. I was desperate to talk to Grant. Somehow, we had to sort this out. But how could we when he wasn't here? I didn't want to be like Mum crazy texting Mike, but this was different I was stranded in a forest.

I texted him again – when r u coming back?

No reply. I tried calling, but he didn't answer. I kicked the back of the sofa in frustration.

Feeling trapped I went outside and walked down the

steps to the edge of the forest. I couldn't even go for a walk because Grant had the key, and I couldn't leave the cabin unlocked. I was like Mum stuck at home. Serve Grant right if I left it open and everything got stolen.

There was a lone snowdrop, head hanging, bobbing in the breeze by the side of the gravel drive. The tiny flower looked so crushed and insignificant cut off from the large drifts inside the forest. I stroked its sweet petals. You and me, both lonesome. Just this morning I'd believed I'd never be lonely again. How wrong could a girl be?

An hour later, an hour which seemed to last several centuries, Grant still hadn't returned, hadn't answered my texts or my calls. I'd cleaned the cabin, had a shower, and washed my hair. I'd run out of anything to do with myself. What if he didn't come back? How would I get home? I'd have to call Dad and ask him to collect me. I'd have to get Cyril, the weird nosey manager to lock up the cabin. Why was Grant doing this? Surely all that love couldn't just disappear in one second. He couldn't walk out on me without saying a word. Was everything over between us?

My heart was being stretched and stretched so that the muscle fibres would surely snap at any moment. I had to do something, or I'd run into the kitchen and stab myself with the carving knife just to stop the agony.

I pushed the furniture to the side of the room and cleared a space in the centre of the living room. At least I could dance. The wooden floor was perfect. On my mobile I had some tracks we were considering for our 'Dance for the Planet'. I played through them as I warmed up. Exploring the music with my body was the best way to choose. Even if my life was in ruins I could still try and do something for the environment. I turned the music up loud and threw myself into the path of the beat.

*

'That's typical.' Grant was standing in front of the glass doors glaring at me. I hadn't heard the car. I didn't know how long I'd been dancing because I'd gotten absorbed in the music. 'All you care about is dancing.'

'What else was I supposed to do? You've been gone ages. You didn't answer my calls.'

Grant ignored me and walked past into the kitchen area.

'Grant please talk to me.' I followed him.

He looked around the room and then at me as if I'd trashed the place.

'I'll put the furniture back where it was.' I moved the sofa forward.

Grant pushed back an armchair and sat down. He put the telly on.

'This is silly, we've got to talk,' I knelt in front of him, and put my hand on his knee.

He didn't move.

'I'm sorry okay, really sorry.' I was looking up into his face, but he kept watching the telly. 'I should have told you and I don't know why I didn't. It was stupid of me. Frieda wanted to enter not me, she did the application, and I really didn't think we stood a chance. Please don't be angry, I don't want this to spoil our weekend. I'm so pleased that you and Viv got through. We should celebrate and not fight each other.'

Grant finally looked at me.

'You pretend you're not ambitious, but you are. You're ruthless like Melody,' he said.

'I'm not,' he had me so wrong.

'Yeah well, I don't want to talk about it okay. Forget it.'

The football results came on and Grant turned up the sound. Outside the sun was going down. Twenty-four hours ago, we'd just arrived and been so happy together. Now I felt worse than I'd ever imagined I could feel. The thought of losing Grant, of him dumping me after last night, after letting him inside my body, was unbearable. All I wanted was to make him love me again. I got up off my knees. I had no idea how to fix this.

'I could make us some pasta,' I said.

We ate, watched TV, I washed up and gradually Grant thawed. Not the best evening of my life but I wasn't banished to the spare room. Where there was flesh there was hope. To start with Grant kept away from me in the big double bed but in the soft forgiving dark he reached over, and I rolled gratefully into his arms. The sex felt different. We were coming together to heal a rift. Heat and hurt mixed together, with fewer words, but greater intensity. We clung to each other. I cried hot tears into his shoulder.

In the morning Grant was back to his usual self. We messed about in the hot tub, had breakfast, and walked in the woods but left earlier than we'd planned. Grant said he and Vivienne had a meeting with Mrs Mulligan. Whenever anything to do with the *Great British Talent Show* was mentioned there was a tenderness in the conversation, as if we were both moving with bruised muscles. Grant had stopped sharing his excitement with me and I felt excluded. I knew how important the show was for him and I was sad that we couldn't be thrilled about it together. But I didn't push it.

As we drove away from the cabin through the towering trees I felt as if our relationship had grown roots. We'd had sex, Grant had said he loved me, and we'd survived our first row.

26

The auditions were being held in an outdoor stadium in Digbeth. I'd arranged to meet Frieda outside the Arts Centre on the main road. Anna was coming as our legal guardian, but I was a bit unnerved when Tamasin arrived with them. I shouldn't have been surprised. Their relationship had gone from secret to serious overnight. They appeared to spend every non-school hour sewn together. I could have done without Tamasin being there.

We walked through the brick railway arches and along the streets by the industrial units. The stadium was near The Midnight Bell Club. I'd only been here at night before. In daylight, the clubs, bars, and restaurants were locked shut and there was a spooky echoing silence in the empty streets. I could hear our footsteps on the pavement even though we were wearing trainers. Not another person in sight.

Until we turned the corner. Outside the stadium hundreds of people were standing in a queue that stretched down the side of a high brick wall. From inside came the noise of electric feedback and the chatter of many voices. We joined the back of the queue.

'Didn't they give you a time slot?' Tamasin asked.

Frieda nodded. 'So?' She fired back.

'I'm surprised you have to queue, that's all. Jeez look at the state of some of the other contestants. Freak show!.'

Frieda turned away from Tamasin and moved closer to Anna. She kept cracking her knuckles, her nervous tell. The queue moved forward at a steady pace. In front of us, a team of jugglers was dressed in bright pink body suits. Not the most flattering of outfits. Behind us a group of acapella singers was warming up.

The auditions were organised alphabetically, so Grant and Vivienne had already had theirs and left in the morning.

'Grant says you only get five minutes and then they give you a red or green ticket. If it's red you're out. If it's green you're a possible.'

Frieda gulped. 'Oh God, I wish I didn't know that.'

'What did Viv and Grant get?' Tamasin asked.

'They got green.'

The queue shunted forward. Usually, I was the nervous one but I didn't really care about getting through, so I felt quite relaxed. Seeing so many entrants, I was sure we didn't stand a chance. I was glad things had gone well for Grant and Viv.

We were standing in front of the giant face of a girl smoking a cigarette painted onto the wall behind, when music blared out from the stadium.

'Listen,' I said.

'The Night Angels,' Frieda recognised them from the intro. Melody's soulful husky voice floated through the brick wall. 'She's singing 'Night Angel'. I hope that won't be a problem for us?'

I shrugged. Nothing we could do about it now. When the song finished, there was applause.

'They'll get through.' Tamasin said and no one contradicted her.

We were almost at the entrance when a young woman with a clipboard and earphones approached us.

'Name?' She didn't even bother to smile. Frieda stepped forward.

'Frieda Santos and Pen Flowers. Dance duet.'

The girl ticked us off her list. 'You're Number 154.' She handed Frieda a printed number. 'One of you needs to pin this to your costume so the judges can see it. Did you send us your music?'

'Yes,' Frieda gave her a huge smile trying to engage. 'I was wondering...'

The girl had already moved on down the line.

When we got to the door two big security guys checked our number and waved us through. There was a covered stage and a vast open auditorium packed with people. Another young woman with a mass of curly hair and a round smiley face approached us.

'Hi there. You're 154, Frieda and Pen?

'Yeah.' We said together.

'Okay, so you're sixteen? Do you have a legal guardian with you?'

Anna stepped forward. 'Anna Santos.'

'Great, Anna, can you fill in these forms? I'll collect them later.' She turned to Frieda and me. 'Welcome to the *Great British Talent Show* auditions. Please follow the line there in front of you into the Blue Zone. Wait there for your number to be called. You've got five minutes on stage so make sure you're ready to go. We'll cue your music and you just start. Don't take any notice of anything going on around. As you can see,' she laughed, 'it's a bit chaotic. Afterward, you'll be given a card – red or green - and take that with you to the Red or Green Zone. Is that clear?' She smiled at us but didn't wait for questions. 'Good Luck,' she added, already moving onto the group behind us and repeating the same spiel.

We followed a roped-off path toward a blue sign. There were hundreds of people with numbers pinned to their backs crammed into the penned-off areas. Tamasin burst out laughing.

'Oh my God, this is like a cattle market. It's like you're prize pigs being auctioned off.'

Frieda swooped around and looked down on her. I'd never seen her so angry.

'Enough. Just go now.'

'I was only joking,' Tamasin looked and sounded scared as Frieda towered over her.

'I'm fed up with your sarky comments. Please go.' Frieda turned her back towards Tamasin and crossed her arms.

Tamasin looked first at Anna and then at me, trying to get support. I became fascinated by a crack in the concrete floor where a weed was pushing through. She made a sound halfway between a sob and a cough and ran out of the stadium. And I'd thought that Tamasin might break Frieda's heart!

'Savage!' I said to Frieda, but I was glad to see Tamasin go.

'She hasn't got a clue.' Frieda said, not unkindly, shaking her head.

I was totally impressed by the way Frieda had stood up for herself.

I was glad we'd worn the tracksuits we were dancing in. Some people were having to change out in the open. There were port-a-loos lined up at the back and a few bins for rubbish but otherwise the facilities were non-existent. At least it wasn't raining. When our number was called, we rushed up onto the stage. There was a row of judges sitting at the far side of the stage. One of the men was older, balding, and looked familiar but I couldn't think where I'd seen him. Maybe he was semi-famous. A stage manager told us to get into position. The judges weren't even looking at us they were talking to each other.

Three minutes later it was over. Two hours queueing for that! The stage manager ushered us down the steps on the other side of the stage and told us to wait. Anna came and joined us.

'You were great,' she said squeezing Frieda's arm. Both Frieda and I felt disappointed. What a waste of time.

The acapella group began singing on the stage above us as the curly-haired friendly young woman reappeared and gave us a green ticket.

'Well done,' she said. 'Have you got your forms? Anna handed them over. 'Thanks. Make your way to the Green Zone and someone will come and talk to you.'

Frieda led the way. The tension had gone from her body, and she bounded over the rough concrete.

The light was starting to go and the stadium was emptying. There were only a few people left in the green zone. The girl with the clipboard was talking to an older woman with grey hair down to her waist. I wondered what her act was. We sat down on the floor to wait and before long the balding man from the judging panel walked over.

I remembered where I'd seen him. At Mrs Mulligan's party. He was her husband, the BBC director who'd helped Grant and Viv with their video. Surely, he couldn't be a judge? That wouldn't be fair.

'Hi, Pen, is it?' He put out his hand for me to shake and I scrambled up to my feet and introduced Frieda and Anna. We all shook hands like we were professionals.

'We loved your dance,' he said. 'But we've got a problem. We've already selected The Night Angels and we can't have you both using the same song. Have you got another piece you can do? We're filming in two weeks?'

'Sure,' Frieda piped up without consulting me, 'we've

got this great duet called 'Dance for the Planet', an environmental piece about saving the earth.'

'Love it - sounds perfect. If you're happy to do that instead – you're in. We'll be in touch.'

As he walked away Frieda was lifting Anna off the ground.

'Yeah, yeah, yeah! We're in! Five hundred quid. We're going to Portugal to see Avo.'

How could I make a fuss when this meant so much to Frieda? But I didn't see how we could possibly get ready in time. We hadn't even decided on our music. All we had was a concept and now a very tight deadline. We'd have to spend every spare hour working on it and I'd wanted to be there to support Grant. I didn't think he'd be thrilled that we were also through to the filming.

27

'Sweet,' said Frieda, 'the planet looks awesome, Mum, Ed, youse two are genius.'

We were in the dance studio at college watching a video playback of 'Dance for the Planet'. Our support team was a tight little unit of Joe Thorne, Anna, and Ed.

Ed had been Vivienne's suggestion. Because we were so short of time Anna had taken over making the model of the earth. She'd used a new flexible plastic that she could mould and print onto. It was semi-transparent and very light, but she didn't know how to hang it. We wanted the globe suspended at head height, stable but able to move when we danced with it.

'You should ask Ed,' Vivienne said. 'He was brilliant with the staging on *The Crucible*. He's a total techy nerd. I bet he'd help.'

Between them, he and Anna had created this amazing facsimile planet that revolved on a chain like a giant mobile. There were lights inside that started off white and gradually through the dance turned red and then finally went out, so the globe went dark.

'Yeh, brilliant planet,' I agreed. 'Shame about the dance.' The dance wasn't working. It was all globe and no action.

Everyone shouted at once. 'No!'

'What's with the negative vibe Pen?' Frieda challenged me. 'We look fab.'

'Yes, wonderful, powerful, full of heart,' Anna said.

Ed said evenly, 'I think it works, got an important message.'

'Come on Pen, you gotta believe.' Frieda put her arm around my shoulder. I loved her confidence and wished I could get a transfusion. Whatever gene made you doubt yourself was missing from Frieda's DNA. I seemed to have got her share. I was basically a double helix of doubt with brown hair.

I looked at Joe. If anyone was going to tell the truth, he would.

'Joe?' I asked.

'Given how little time you've had, you've done pretty well,' he said. 'Working with props is difficult. If you make the next round, we can improve the relationship between you and the globe.'

'If you're worried Pen we can run through it again.' Frieda wanted me to be happy. She didn't like anyone being upset. I looked at my phone to check the time. Something was badly wrong with the final sequence. I couldn't think how to fix it. Maybe we should keep working? But I'd promised Grant I'd watch their final run-through. I stared at the blank screen of the monitor as if some ghost in the black depths was going to answer my dilemma.

Anna and Joe started to pack up the globe. Ed and Frieda were looking at me.

'No, we're fine,' I said. 'Sorry to be negative, just nerves.'

Frieda gave me one of her bear hugs. 'I'm meeting Tamasin in Moseley. Why don't you and Ed come too?' Frieda and Tamasin had made up, but Tamasin hadn't been invited to any of our rehearsals since. I was glad. My confidence couldn't handle one of Tamasin's brutal critiques.

'Thanks, but I'm going to watch Viv and Grant run through their scene.'

'Checking out the competition?' Frieda narrowed her eyes. 'Make sure they're not as good as us.'

I laughed. 'How am I supposed to do that?'

'I don't know, sabotage. Tell Grant he's rubbish, dump him for someone else.' She grinned. 'Give them my love.'

By the time I'd showered and changed the sun had set and the streetlamps were on. I ran most of the way even though my legs were tired and heavy. A shortcut through the back streets took me past the community gardens where Viv's Dad had his allotment. I jogged up the hill past her house. I wished I was meeting Viv here and having one of her Mum's homemade lasagne.

I was in defeat mode. My head drooped, and my shoulders hunched forward. Our dance wasn't ready, and I needed time to think. As I reached the end of Viv's street, a number eleven bus pulled up at the stop opposite the school gates. I wanted to get on and sit with my eyes closed, playing through the dance in my head.

But I couldn't let Grant down. I pulled my shoulders back, lifted my chin and did a fast sprint across the road and up the school drive.

With Mr Mulligan on the selection panel, it was no surprise that Viv and Grant had got through. I said to Frieda that this didn't seem fair, but she pointed out that the same could be said about us. Mrs Mulligan could have told him we were entering.

'It's always about who you know.' Frieda told me. 'We just got lucky.'

They were rehearsing in the drama studio with Mrs Mulligan and some fancy London director. There were more directors than actors on their team. I liked to work my own way through problems and found too many different points of view confusing. Grant was the opposite; he couldn't get enough input. He was always wanting to know what I thought. We'd been over and over his performance until I knew both his and Vivienne's lines.

'What if I did this? Is this better?' By the end of an evening with him, I felt drained of any opinion.

I opened the drama studio door quietly so as not to interrupt but everyone was sitting on chairs chatting. Vivienne and Grant were in costume. I was surprised to see Louis sitting next to Vivienne.

'Sorry I'm late,' I said joining them and taking a chair next to Grant.

'Too late,' he said, 'we've finished.'

'Oh sorry, our rehearsal took longer than I expected. We had some problems. How did yours go?'

'How did it go, Pen wants to know,' Grant made our conversation public.

'Excellent,' Mrs Mulligan said.

The London director nodded. She had a sharp blond bob, and a long narrow face as if someone had squeezed the sides in. Her bad skin, a sort of yellowy grey colour, was made worse by red lipstick.

'What did you think, Louis?' Grant asked. 'You were seeing the scene for the first time?'

Grant had a way of making me feel guilty. He was drawing attention to Louis being there for Vivienne when I hadn't been there for him.

Louis looked at Vivienne lovingly. I was behind on the gossip. Seemed like the win Louis back campaign was going well.

'You did good baby! Made me wanna see more.'

Vivienne reached over and they squeezed hands. She caught me looking at her with my eyebrows lifted and pulled a face.

The director took Grant aside to give him notes. He was like a puppy dog pawing at her knee for attention. Vivienne wanted to get out of her costume, so I followed her into the changing rooms.

'Is Louis here in a directorial or boyfriend capacity?' I asked.

'Both,' she said from inside the dress she was wriggling out of. 'Can you pull?' I gave the dress a good yank and she emerged. 'Thanks.'

'And Harriet?' I asked.

'No longer a problem.' Vivienne allowed herself a triumphant smirk.

'Told you,' I said.

'And the best thing is that Louis feels so guilty he'll do anything for me. I'm getting all the lurve baby.'

'Yeah, you two look loved up.' Vivienne was struggling into skin-tight jeans. I missed her. What time I had left over from school and dancing I spent with Grant.

'And what about you?' she asked. 'How are things with Grant? How did your rehearsal go? You know what, once tomorrow's over, we should have like a massive catch up – just the two of us. I've been obsessed with this Louis – Harriet craziness.'

I needed to see Viv badly. There was so much I wanted to talk over.

'That'd be so very good. I'd like that muchly.' Being with Grant wasn't like being with Vivienne. The intimacy with Grant was physical. He liked to hear my ideas but only about his stuff. He never asked me about dancing. 'I'm not sure about our dance. I don't think it's working.'

'You always think that and you're always brilliant.' She put an arm around my shoulder in a warm embrace. 'You seem a bit down?'

I sighed, letting go for a moment. 'Just tired, worried about tomorrow, nervous. You know how I get.'

'Tomorrow'll be fun. Try and enjoy it, Pen. Frieda will, Grant will, I will. We're going to be on telly.' Vivienne had her coat on and was heading for the changing room door. I stopped her.

'This won't happen but just in case. If Frieda and I win a place in the finals and you and Grant don't, will you hate me?'

Vivienne came back in the room and hugged me.

'Oh, Pen you are such an idiot! Of course I won't hate you. What about the other way round? You gonna dump me if I win and you don't?'

'Course not.'

'There you go – you sayin' I'm a crap friend then?'

'You're the best. Sorry just stupid tonight.'

'You need to sleep. Is Grant driving you home? He's got his car here.'

When we got back to the drama studio Grant was back in his school uniform talking to Louis. He looked relaxed and happy and when we walked over, he put his arm round my waist and kissed me.

'You okay to get the bus home Pen? It's just I've got a load of notes that I want to work on before tomorrow.'

'Sure, no problem. I'll get off then.'

'Okay I'll finish up here,' he said.

'Sorry I missed your run-through. I ran all the way from college.'

'On your little legs. Don't worry squirrel, see you tomorrow.'

Grant leaned forward and bit my nose gently. I felt reassured. Maybe everything would be okay.

When the bus arrived, I dragged my aching body up the stairs. There was no one else on the top deck. I took my usual seat at the front of the bus and sank into the silence. Just to be alone and still and have time with my thoughts was such a relief. I was glad not to be in the car with Grant. Even though he seemed more confident than me, in some ways he was like Mum, needing constant attention. I loved being with Grant, but I never felt totally relaxed. There was always some bit of me checking to see if he was okay. Having a boyfriend was exhausting.

I leant my head against the cold glass of the window and breathed out fogging the pane, then drew a heart in the mist and wrote mine and Grant's initials. Soothed by the rhythm of the rolling bus, I let my mind drift.

If only the filming wasn't tomorrow. I wasn't happy with our dance, and I hated that. Grant kept saying I was ambitious but I wasn't worried about winning like he was. I didn't care. I wished we weren't doing the show. I don't know how Vivienne expected me to enjoy it. Everyone, particularly me, would be wound up and nervous.

But maybe I was ambitious because I was upset about our dance not being ready. This was a chance to express how passionately I cared about the destruction of our planet. The idea that had started that night out dancing by the Westfield Grove oak tree had morphed into a love poem. Only it wasn't powerful enough. I wanted to make a mighty statement, worthy of the Mighty Oak. Give shape to my grief for the pain of the planet. I knew the dance wasn't right. I was letting down the Earth.

28

The moment I achieved consciousness the nervous snakes started wriggling in my stomach. My heart felt so heavy I had difficulty rising from the horizontal. I lay weighted to the bed running through our dance in my head. The start was good as we circled the globe bowing and adoring, scared and amazed. I was pleased with the way a growing intimacy developed as we touched and moved the planet. And I liked how this built into a whirling frenzy and then burst into violence. But the final section where we rocked and soothed the globe like a hurt child didn't work. It left me with a bad feeling. I'd hoped the night would bring me inspiration, but it hadn't.

Mum and Thomas were already up and about when I got downstairs. They were going to pick up the puppy this morning. They'd set up a bed for Bouncer in the corner of the kitchen. I wished I was going with them. Our first ever dog deserved to be welcomed by everyone in the family. Instead, I was going to be filmed doing a rubbish dance and my shame would be broadcast to an audience of millions.

Filming was at the BBC Pebble Mill Studios on the Bristol Road and Dad was dropping me off. He obviously disapproved of the venture, and we drove in silence. His lack of interest was almost soothing. At least one person would be happy when we didn't make it to the next round.

I sighed loudly wishing I could snap out of my negative mindset.

Dad flicked a quick glance at me and then back to the road ahead. Unlike Mum he was a safe driver. He could look at the road and talk at the same time.

'I know you think I'm a monster for not supporting your ambitions as a dancer,'

'No, I don't,' I protested but he ignored me.

'At your age, you think you're going to be rich and famous but very few people are you know.'

'Yeah, yeah, I know. Van Gogh never sold a painting, died poor and mad.'

Dad laughed but carried on speaking like he'd been planning this speech and had to get it out.

'You clearly have a gift for dancing. People with special talents should use them. The musicians I love had terrible lives, but they've given me hours of pleasure. I'd be a hypocrite if I told you to ignore what you're passionate about. And I see how hard you're prepared to work. But don't chase fame and fortune. These TV shows are exploitative of young people's fantasies. I'm not suggesting you stop dancing. I'm just asking you to think about what really matters. This showbusiness world - it's an illusion. You can spend your life pursuing something that doesn't exist.'

Wow, Dad had said I'd got talent and he was talking to me like I was an adult for like the first time ever.

'Thanks, Dad, for being honest. You're right about this stupid show. And I don't want to be famous. I don't even like people looking at me. But dancing's how I express myself. Like the dance we're doing today – it's called 'Dance for the Planet' and it's about how much Frieda and I care about what's happening with the climate emergency and how we want to inspire people to do something about it.'

He nodded. 'That sounds good.'

Dad had actually managed to make me feel better.

'I do miss you, Dad.'

'And I miss you, both of you. More than I'd imagined possible.' Dad sounded sad. I stared at him. Maybe he really did love us. We drove in silence again and suddenly as the traffic lights switched from red to green, I realised what was wrong with our dance. We needed to be more challenging and confront the audience. We needed to end not with tenderness but outrage.

Dad turned off the Bristol Road and pulled up in front of Pebble Mill Studios. There was a pile-up of cars waiting to get into the car park.

'I'll just drop you here,' Dad said. 'I don't want to get trapped.'

'Okay,' I reached for my bag from the back seat.

'Hope it goes well,' he managed to say.

'Thanks.' I was on the pavement closing the door. Dad stopped me.

'And Penny, when you and Thomas come tomorrow, I've got something important to tell you.'

He sounded awkward, embarrassed. Was he coming out as gay? Planning to transition?

'What?' I immediately asked.

'I'll tell you tomorrow.'

I slammed the door. Typical – we have a great conversation and then he spoils it. Giving me something to worry about just before I perform. He was so selfish. I stomped up the path to the front entrance grinding Dad's face into the paving stones with my boots. Why say something dramatic like that? Did he have cancer? Had he lost his job? Hideous alternatives competed in my brain.

Pebble Mill reception was full of people. I didn't know how many acts had been chosen for filming, but it seemed like loads. People were standing in small gaggles chatting. There didn't seem to be anyone in charge. The noise in the room was high-pitched, waspish. I could feel my body push out armour and lock into fortress mode.

I texted Frieda – where r u?

My phone rang. 'We're in the car park. It's chaos here. I've just seen Melody and The Night Angels unloading. I haven't seen Vivienne or Grant yet. Where are you?' Frieda's voice bubbled with excitement.

'I'm in reception; chaos here too. No one seems to know what's going on. I'll come and find you.'

I was glad to be outside again away from a room full of bodies spitting out nervous tension like bullets. I walked across the strip of neatly edged lawn, so green and tidy it could have been fake, to the driveway with barriers where the man in the control hut was talking to the driver of a white van. I squeezed behind the barrier and walked along the side of the studio buildings until the drive widened into the car park.

A man in a neon safety vest was trying to sort out a snarl-up. On the open loading bay, a huge roll-up door was lifted three-quarters high revealing a cavernous studio space inside. A woman in jeans and funnel neck jumper was consulting a tablet. Marlon was standing next to her, and Al was unloading his drum kit from the back of a van. I couldn't see Melody.

There was a queue behind The Night Angels and I saw Frieda hanging out of the window of a battered blue VW van. She waved at me, and I gave her a thumbs up and ran over. Anna was driving and Frieda was sitting on Ed's knee in the front. The Night Angels' van pulled away from the loading bay and the queue shunted forward.

Frieda opened the van door and jumped out.

'So, this is lit,' she shook her ass in a display of high spirits and threw a few shapes. 'We're gonna be on TV!'

The van crawled forward. We skipped along beside it.

'Hi Ed, Anna,' I said through the window. Now that I was part of a team I cheered up. Perhaps I could enjoy this.

Once Anna's van had reached the loading bay and she'd manouvered into position Ed got out and hobbled towards the back doors.

'Don't think I'll ever walk again,' he said to Frieda.

'Poor Ed - me on his lap all the way from Kings Heath.' They both laughed.

Our globe was covered in layers of bubble wrap and wedged inside a wooden box frame. The four of us took a corner each and lifted it onto a metal trolley. The woman in the jeans with the tablet came over.

'Which act are you?' She asked Ed.

Frieda stepped in. "Dance for the Planet' – Frieda Santos and Pen Flowers.'

'Okay you're in Studio 3 – what equipment have you brought?'

'We've got a globe that needs to be hung and a film to project.'

'Okay take that with you and report in with the floor manager when you get there – it's the last studio at the far end.'

We loaded everything onto the giant flatbed trolley. Ed pushed with Frieda walking ahead and me by the side to hold the globe steady. Anna went to park the van. Down a long corridor, we passed signs for dressing rooms and toilets, double doors into Studio 1, then Studio 2, until we reached the far end where a sign with a red-light box above it said Studio 3.

Inside was a large bare space with a grey-painted floor and an elaborate metal lighting grid above. In one corner was the set for the Pebble Mill lunchtime news. It looked tiny, made of thin painted plywood with cheap furniture. Yet on the telly, it looked smart. The floor manager came over and held open the door so we could wheel our trolley through.

'Okay guys, which act are you?'

Frieda did the talking.

'You're last.' He was checking his phone for details, 'I presume this is the globe you want us to hang? And you've got a video for projection?'

Unlike the bustle outside, the studio was still and silent. Peaceful even. This man gave off a sense of order. He seemed to know exactly what was going on.

'You're scheduled to set at 11.00 am. At 11.40 the judges will arrive to watch your camera rehearsal. This afternoon you'll film the dance as live at 3.00 pm, and then move straight through to Studio 1 to film the results. There'll also be two crews doing vox pop interviews who'll catch you at some point this morning. Is that clear?'

'Defo,' Frieda nodded. She was smiling but I could see that she'd been hit by nerves. The timetable was a reality bomb. My stomach had a herd of wild horses galloping through it.

'If I were you,' the floor manager said. 'I'd go and wait in the canteen. Get yourself a cup of coffee and relax.'

Relax! Like telling a man on a rack to enjoy the stretch.

'Good idea,' Ed answered as both Frieda and I had gone quiet. 'I am starving. I didn't get any breakfast.'

The canteen had big rectangular windows along one side and was filled with spring morning sunlight. The room was almost empty, just one young woman sitting with someone who could be her Mum and a table of middle-aged men who looked as if they belonged there. Maybe they were the crew.

Ed got us coffee and himself a bacon sandwich. Neither Frieda nor I felt capable of eating. I couldn't believe I was passing up on a bacon butty. Anna called to find out where we were, and Frieda went off to find her.

I closed my eyes and felt the sun on my eyelids, imagining the warmth entering the cells of my body and filling them full of energy. I opened my eyes and saw Ed tucking into his butty. He smiled and I smiled back. He never got flustered. Whatever madness was going on around him he kept his own steady pace. Sitting next to him the horses in my belly slowed to a trot. If I stayed close to Ed, I could get through this. He put his hand on my arm.

'You'll be fine Pen. It's going to be good,' he said, and I believed him.

He had soft dark brown eyes and a big nose that was slightly off centre. His mouth didn't smile evenly but went up more on one side. I felt an impulse to throw myself onto his chest. He was holding my gaze. I had a disturbing thought.

'You're not going to leave, are you? Once the globe's hung?'

Ed paused as if deciding. There was no reason for him to stay for the afternoon. He'd already given us loads of his time. I was being selfish wanting him to stay.

'No, I'll be here for the filming. Just in case there're any issues.'

I felt ridiculously relieved. We both went quiet. I reached for my empty coffee cup not knowing what to do with my hands.

There was a commotion by the door as Frieda and Anna, Grant and Vivienne, plus Louis, and Mr Cooper came through. The gentle quiet was drowned by a tsunami of noise.

'Look who I found,' Frieda called out.

Grant sat down on the other side of me to Ed and Vivienne sat opposite us. Mr Cooper was beaming.

'Hello, Pen, haven't seen you for ages. You're in the show as well as these two? This is exciting, isn't it?' He was looking around. 'Well, I've never been in here before. What it is to have famous young friends. The BBC canteen, I wonder if we'll see anyone I recognise.'

'We're in Studio 1,' Vivienne said, 'where are you?'

'It's the biggest studio, where they're filming the judges' decisions,' Grant said as if it was a competition. 'The Night Angels are on first and then us.'

Mr Cooper and Louis were sorting out drinks for everyone. Ed got up to help.

'What's Ed doing here?' Grant asked.

'He's helping us with the set,' I said and felt guilty as if I'd been keeping Ed's involvement secret. Grant never asked anything about our dance, so I'd never had a chance to tell him.

'We're on last so hopefully I can come and see your camera rehearsal.' I said.

'Sure.' Grant turned to talk to Louis.

He was a bit off with me. My body locked back into tense mode.

The table of middle-aged men got up to go and a Tannoy announcement asked for the first acts to return to the studios. Leaving Frieda and the others in the canteen I went with Vivienne and Grant to see their dressing room.

'Wow this feels so professional,' I said. 'Your names on the door, costumes waiting on the rail.'

'Your name will be on one too. We're sharing with The Night Angels.' Vivienne pulled a grumpy face. 'Luckily they're already setting up.'

Grant sat down in front of the make-up mirror tugging at his hair. He'd been growing it long for the part.

'I love your hair like that,' I said moving to stand behind him. 'You should keep it long.'

He looked up at me and I bent down to kiss him.

'If you two are going to start snogging I'm going to the studio to watch them rehearse.' Viv opened the door.

'You go, Pen,' Grant said. 'I want to get changed and run through my lines.' Grant went over to the clothes rail.

'You don't need me to go through your lines with you?' I asked.

'No, I'm all right.'

'I'll get there to watch your run-through, I promise.' I wanted to make up for missing his rehearsal last night.

'Okay,' Grant didn't appear bothered. I hoped he was being cold because he was nervous.

'You're sure?'

'Just go Pen!' Grant closed the door on me. I ran down the corridor to catch up with Vivienne.

Studio 1 was three times the size of our studio. The Night Angels were doing a sound check on a raised stage in the centre of the room. Off to one side was a smaller bare set where I guessed Vivienne and Grant would be performing and there was a third set of a studio panel, presumably where the judges would be filmed giving their decisions.

Viv and I stood in a dark corner watching the sound check. I felt her hand reach for mine. We both squeezed.

'How ya doing?' Viv asked.

The horses were making a mess of my guts with their hooves.

'I want to run and run and never stop running.'

Vivienne snorted.

'I want to eat a giant bag of Maltesers.'

29

Melody started singing. She was wearing her wedding dress outfit. With a football stadium's worth of lights pointed at her she blazed, a pure gold baby. The way she sucked in attention was remarkable. The floor cameras were manoeuvring positions, shifting to get in closer, and two electricians moving a trolley of cables stopped to listen.

'It's super annoying how good she is,' Vivienne said in a low voice.

'They're gonna win aren't they?' I said.

'Yep.' Vivienne didn't sound that bothered.

'Grant will be devastated if you don't get through.' I voiced my biggest fear.

'He'll get over it.' Viv wasn't wasting any sympathy on Grant.

By the time the Night Angels were ready for their camera rehearsal, the studio was full. Frieda, Ed, Anna, Mr Cooper, and Louis had joined Viv and me. Grant, now in costume, had come through. Seemed as if every person in the building had come to watch. Even the Midlands Today weather woman was there. Mr Cooper was thrilled. I hoped we wouldn't get an audience. I'd much prefer it if our studio stayed empty.

At exactly 9.30 am the three judges arrived. They were well-known TV celebrities, a singer, actor, and dancer. They made their way through the crowd to a row of empty chairs set up in front of the stage. All but the safety lights in the studio went out. I watched the floor manager counting down seconds on his fingers. The guitars screamed and the stage was bombarded with the full force of the lighting rig. Melody was a bar of gold, forty-eight carats of gleaming brightness, like a hammer between the eyeballs.

Playing at The Midnight Bell to a crowded room had prepared The Night Angels for this moment. Slick, professional, and compelling, Melody mesmerised the audience. The applause when they finished was genuine, even denting the vacuum of the soundproofed studio.

The judges filed out moving on to Studio 2 and most of the audience followed them.

'I'd better go and get changed,' Vivienne said. She and Grant were next on in Studio 1. Grant walked over to the smaller stage. I followed him.

'You'll be fantastic.' I reached over to kiss him, but he held me away.

'Can't you see I'm made up?' He snapped. I wasn't going to get upset or fight back. Nerves made everyone super sensitive. He didn't seem to want me around, so I took the hint.

'Okay see you later. And good luck.'

Back in Studio 3, Ed and Anna were supervising the hanging of the globe on our stage. The judges arrived to watch the stand-up comedian we were sharing a dressing room with. He tried hard but wasn't very funny. I felt sorry for him, but at least we wouldn't be the worst act. Then I felt like a bad person for thinking like that.

Frieda insisted we took photos of our names on the dressing room door. Inside were our bags and costumes. On the dressing table was a card addressed to Frieda and me and a plant pot full of snowdrops.

'Oh, I love snowdrops, are these from Anna?' I asked Frieda. She shook her head.

'Don't think so, open the card.'

Grant must have done this. Remembering the snowdrops at the cabin. Even though he was performing himself. Such a thoughtful boyfriend.

Inside the card was a message written in biro: Picked this morning. Dance for the Planet. Love Ed.

I read the words to Frieda.

'That man is sooo sweet I could eat him up,' she said.

'How did he know I love snowdrops?'

'No idea. Where's my card from Tamasin – I want to know?'

'This is to both of us.'

'If you say so.' Frieda gave me a superior knowing look.

'I need to get back to Studio 1. Grant will kill me if I miss their run-through again.'

Frieda came with me. We joined the people gathered behind the judges' chairs by the small stage. Vivienne and Grant's scene began with a clap of thunder and a flash of lightning. Dramatic moody photographs of the Yorkshire Moors were projected onto a screen behind the bare stage. The soundtrack was a low eerie drone like the noise of a fierce wind through leaves. The scene was passionate, physical, and violent as Cathy and Heathcliff loved and hated each other from life into death.

Grant with his long curly dark brown hair made a stunningly handsome Heathcliff. He hadn't captured the underlying ruthlessness of the character, but he was believable. Even loving Grant as I did, I couldn't help knowing that Vivienne was ten times better as an actor. She gave full expression to her talent as Cathy. She really went for it; wild, wilful, enchanting, brimming with sexuality, a forceful woman.

How could the judges decide between such different

acts? Vivienne and Grant were just as good as The Night Angels. I'd vote for them. The applause in the studio was loud. I tried to see the reactions on the judges' faces.

'We need to get back now,' Frieda said.

I wanted to say well done to Grant. But he and Viv were being interviewed by a roving camerawoman.

'We have to go.' Frieda tugged my arm.

We ran back down the corridor. I'd hardly thought about our dance, I'd been so worried about Grant's performance. Now I could concentrate on what I was doing.

The globe hung in the centre of our stage as if it were floating in the darkness of outer space. With the lights shining on it you couldn't see the chain it was hung on. I whooped for joy and hugged Ed.

'This is just how I imagined it,' I said.

Ed went pink and looked pleased.

'Watch the internal lighting,' he pointed and ran through the different lighting states inside the globe.

'The globe's going to be a winner even if Frieda and I suck,' I said feeling ridiculously happy for some reason. 'Oh, and Ed, the snowdrops are lovely. Did you know they were my favourite flowers?'

He shook his head. 'Just saw them this morning.'

'Well, I love them.' I hugged him again. He held onto me for a moment. He was a solid wall of muscle, not fat, but substantial, so different from Grant's slender, hip-jutting frame. I let myself breathe in his woody smell.

'Positions please,' called the floor manager. Frieda and I climbed onto the stage. We did a technical check walking through the moves to fit them onto the stage. The director in the gallery worked out the camera angles and the cues for the projections and lights. I enjoyed the process. The floor manager, camera operators, and sound guys made suggestions on how to make the dance work for the screen.

Frieda and I kept looking at each other and smiling.

The pure love of dancing whooshed through my body and took over. I remembered that this, just this, was what I wanted to do with the rest of my life. I remembered the idea I'd had with Dad in the car. I knew how to solve the problem with the final sequence.

'Stop a moment please,' I called up to the studio gallery. I demonstrated the new move to Frieda. 'At the end when we turn and cradle the globe – that's not right, we should move forward face into the camera, and do this.' I showed her the move that had dropped into my head. 'We finish like this standing on either side of the globe making a direct confrontation to the audience. What do you think?'

Frieda copied me, 'I like it.'

'This is our end sequence,' I called to the gallery. 'Can the cameras move in close.'

We ran through the dance again to the music with the new ending.

'That's better,' Anna agreed. 'Stronger.'

'Okay, five minutes to the rehearsal. Clear the set.' The floor manager announced.

He was putting out the chairs for the three judges. The crazy wild horses in my belly bucked, striking out with their hooves. Ed gave us a big thumbs up from the floor. People were gathering to watch. Vivienne, Louis, and Mr Cooper came in. No sign of Grant.

There was a commotion by the studio doors as the judges made their way through the room. Grant, Melody, and Marlon were with them. Grant was chatting to the actor, and Melody and Marlon were laughing with the singer as if they were old friends. The judges took their seats and Melody standing behind them gave me a wave and a power salute. Grant blew me a kiss.

The studio lights went out. A single beam was focused

on the globe and an African drumbeat started. Energy blazed inside me. My friends were here; my boyfriend, my best friend, my wild crazy friend, and Ed, my new friend, they were all rooting for me. I was like our globe: floating but supported, lit up and loved.

The stage lights faded up like dawn rising on the horizon. Frieda and I began to move. My nerves disappeared. I wanted this dance to reach out to others. The choreography was intended to carry meaning and purpose. I'd poured my passion for nature into the dance. We were showing how as human beings we had begun by worshiping the earth as sacred and ended by destroying it. I wanted the audience to feel the earth's pain. This was a love dance and a death dance, with Frieda and I as guardians of the planet challenging everyone to help us to turn back the earth from the brink of extinction.

Dancing with Frieda was a joy. She moved with such ease, everything she did with her body spoke of strength, grace, and a mighty heart. The routine was physically demanding. The globe was light to lift but I had to raise Frieda off the ground as she lifted it high above her. Not for nothing had I been training every morning with Joe Thorne. There was nothing 'girly' in either of our performances. There was tenderness and fragility but also ugliness and brutality.

The new ending worked, and I felt elated. My fears about the dance evaporated. We finished with a fierce confrontational stare that demanded attention for the plight of our planet.

The applause we received sounded thunderous. Frieda and I hugged. A camera was pointing in our faces and a young woman holding a microphone on a boom was asking questions.

'Is this a political dance?'

'Why do you want to win today?'

I let Frieda do most of the talking. She'd pushed for this. Any credit should go to her.

When the camera crew had finished with us, one of the judges, the dance expert, Anthony Wyn-Jones was waiting to speak to us. He was well known as a former dancer on *Strictly Come Dancing*. I didn't think he'd like our kind of campaigning dance.

'Frieda and Pen, is it?' He asked. 'Which is which?'

'I'm Frieda,' said Frieda.

'Which makes you Pen,' he said shaking our hands in a formal manner. 'You're the pair that Jock Briggs sponsored?'

'Yeah, Pen's worked with him.' Frieda spoke before I could.

'That was powerful and original. Who did the choreography?'

'Pen,' Frieda jumped in again. 'She's an amazing choreographer.'

'We come up with the moves together,' I corrected Frieda.

'In these sorts of competitions, it's not easy for contemporary dance to get through. But I think you stand a chance. A ten from me anyway.' He grinned and put his hand on my shoulder. 'I'll look forward to your performance this afternoon.'

As he walked away Frieda and I couldn't help doing a spontaneous victory dance spinning each other around like kids. Ed came over grinning like a corn on the cob, two rows of even teeth on display.

'I'm guessing he liked it.'

'He bloody LOVED it.' Frieda grabbed hold of Ed and spun him around.

'I just need to check the lights inside the globe.' Ed

kept his feet solidly on the ground. 'Africa didn't go red, need to fix that before this afternoon. The others have gone up to the canteen. Evidently, there's a slap-up buffet.'

The canteen was packed. No longer a haven of peace, the noise level was at maximum with post-performance adrenalin-fuelled shouting. As we were the last act to rehearse the buffet had been decimated. We foraged amongst the remnants, and I saved a plate for Ed in case he didn't get back in time.

Marlon and Yogi were standing at the bar talking to the judges. Marlon was obviously on a charm offensive to make sure they made it to the finals.

Anna and Mr Cooper had grabbed a table on the far side of the room by the windows. Vivienne was with them. We pushed our way through the milling people to join them. Anna leapt up to cuddle her daughter, tears down her face.

'You were wonderful, wonderful,' she said between sobs.

'Oh Mum, don't be silly.' Frieda said squeezing her until she struggled to breathe. They were so cute together, big Frieda and tiny Anna, both powerhouses.

'Another triumph.' Mr Cooper beamed at me. 'You're all so talented.'

'Where's everyone else?' I asked.

'Louis had to leave. He said to say you were brilliant. Which you were.' Viv said.

'Where's Grant?' I was desperate to know what he thought of our dance.

'He wanted to get changed out of his Heathcliff gear.'

I wasn't really feeling hungry. I had a bite of a cheese sandwich and ate a couple of crisps.

'I'm going to find Grant.' I got up, 'I'll catch you later.'

On my way out I passed Ed coming in.

'Lights are fixed, one of the bulbs had gone. Should be perfect for this afternoon.'

'Thanks so much, Ed, for everything you've done. We couldn't have managed without you.'

I loved the way Ed lit up like one of his red bulbs when you complimented him.

'Aren't you eating?' he asked. I shook my head.

'I saved a plate for you. I'll be back in a minute.'

'Okay,' Ed made his way over to the table. Maybe I should stay and not worry about Grant? I hesitated at the door. But I wanted a private moment with him, to tell him how wonderful he'd been and see if he liked our dance.

I galloped down the stairs, three at a time, still elated by Anthony Wyn-Jones' comments. The dance had felt good. I was so pleased we'd sorted out the ending. The studio corridor was deserted with everyone up in the canteen. Grant and Vivienne's dressing room was right at the far end. As I was passing the doors to Studio 1, Al, the drummer with The Night Angels, came out.

'Hi Al,' I stopped him. 'I'm looking for Grant, have you seen him?'

Al shook his head. 'Try the dressing room.' He pushed open a fire exit and bright daylight striped the floor. 'I'm going out to vape,' he said, 'which is forbidden on BBC premises.'

'Vaping's terrible for the planet.' I told him. 'At least with smoking, you're only killing yourself.'

Al laughed, shaking his head.

There were voices coming from their dressing room. I recognised Grant's.

'Found you,' I said pushing open the door and stepping inside.

Melody was sitting on the make-up bench in front of the mirror. Her gold dress pulled up to her waist. Grant was standing between her thighs thrusting his hips forward.

30

Shock hit me like an invisible wall. I was clutching at air trying to hold on to nothing. Falling back. No ground anywhere.

'Whoops!', said Melody. 'Embarrassing.'

I couldn't accept what I was seeing. I swiped my hand in front of my face as if I could wipe away the sight.

Grant stepped back from Melody and turned away from me.

The thaw came fast like a zip of lightning. A blade of agony split me apart. I turned and ran.

'Pen,' Grant called after me.

I crashed out of the fire exit into the cold air. A narrow path ran between a thick privet hedge and the side of the building. Al was leaning against the wall breathing out a cloud of moisture. I fled past him to the front of the building then onto the street and turned right and kept running. I came to a junction and didn't stop. A car blared its horn at me. I still didn't stop. On and on I ran. The pain in my heart was so immense the only thing to do was run. If I could run far enough and fast enough, I'd leave behind the scene in the dressing room.

When my breath finally collapsed and called a halt to my flight, everything inside my body hurt. Lungs, thighs, belly, arms, throat, and heart. I was a pumping, screeching, tearing, twisting, living lump of unbearable pain.

There was a bench on the pavement looking out over four lanes of traffic. Why put a bench there? Who would want to sit and look at an ugly, concrete office block through a prism of passing cars? I slumped down and put my head in my hands, palms over my eyes. I could still see Grant thrusting into Melody. I wanted to tear myself open so that the pain inside me could fly out. I wanted to run into the traffic and be mown down by a bus. The impulse to run into the road was intense.

'No,' a voice inside my head shouted, sounding like a cross between Vivienne and my Mum. I gripped the wooden bench. No, I wouldn't do that. They were not worth dying for.

Melody had betrayed me before. I should have known she could hurt me again. She had no sense of morality, no boundary between right and wrong. But Grant, he said he loved me. I'd lost my virginity to him only a few weeks ago. How could he?

How could they do this to me? I didn't deserve to be treated like this. My hands were trembling, my whole body was quivering. How was I going to get back enough control of my muscles to dance? I couldn't go back to the studios. I couldn't be in the same building as Grant and Melody.

The image of Melody with her dress pulled up and Grant plugged into her body was frozen on the screen of my mind. I was traumatising myself by focusing on the details: her legs curled around his waist, her platform heels in the air, one of her hands on the back of his neck, her wide smile. How could he do this to me?

I wanted to hate him, but as I sat on the bench watching a double-decker stop and pour out passengers, the feeling that dominated, that clutched and twisted at my belly, that made me fold over and want to vomit on the pavement, was jealousy. Terrible, terrible, sexual jealousy.

The thought of Grant with Melody was unbearable. Her hands on his body, his hands on her. Melody was more experienced than me, and way more beautiful. How could I compete?

I'd never felt anything like this before. I wanted to

push him away. He didn't deserve my love, but I was overwhelmed with desire for him. This horrible sick poisonous feeling was like super glue sticking me to him, not letting me get away. I wanted him between my legs, thrusting into me, not Melody. He was my boyfriend, my lover, not hers. I wanted, with an overwhelming force, to hold him to me, to ease my pain with the comfort of his body. It didn't make any sense. My head said he was a bad person and to get him out of my life, but my heart was wailing like an abandoned child. My groin was on fire with lust for him. I was at war with my own body.

I'd always trusted my body to guide me, save me, keep me strong. But now that I'd let Grant inside me, I couldn't get him out. He'd stolen my most precious possession, the place I lived, my home. How could I be a dancer when I wasn't in control of my body anymore?

These thoughts were buzzing endlessly as if my head was trapped inside a wasp nest and every idea was a poisonous sting. I stood up and faced the wind letting the force tug at my hair and stretch the skin of my face tight over my bones. I opened my mouth and ate air. If only the wind could blow me clean of these emotions. I wanted to be completely empty.

I couldn't let Frieda down. Nor Ed, nor Anna. Not after the work they'd done. I needed to get a grip. I had to do the filming, I had to find a way to dance. I couldn't tell anyone what had happened. I was going to have to pretend I was okay. I had to freeze my feelings, squeeze them into a tight inner corner and lock them up. Like carbon under pressure, I would make a razor-sharp diamond of pain in the centre of my heart. I'd manage somehow. As long as I didn't see Grant with Melody, I'd get through.

*

I retraced my steps back to Pebble Mill and used the back door from the car park. I took the long way round avoiding the studio corridor by going up a floor. A similar corridor one level up passed through deserted production offices. Rows of desks had laptops and computers with blank black screens. If only I could shut down the screen in my head, frozen on that hideous picture.

I managed to get into our dressing room without meeting anyone. If I stayed here until we had to perform then hopefully the only people I'd meet would be Frieda, Ed and Anna and possibly the bad comedian. I looked at Ed's snowdrops, their heads drooping and stroked their petals. Poor little flowers, uprooted from their home, wilting under the forensic light of the make-up mirror.

'She's here.' Frieda called down the corridor. 'We've been worried about you. You disappeared and didn't answer your phone. We didn't know where you'd got to.'

Ed came through the door.

'Sorry I was feeling a bit sick, so I went for a walk to get some fresh air. I forgot to take my phone.'

Both Frieda and Ed were staring at me.

'Are you alright? You look dead pale?' Frieda asked.

'I'm fine. Sorry to worry you.'

'You didn't have anything to eat, let me get you something,' Ed said.

'No, no. I'm fine, I've got water here. I'm just going to sit here until it's time for the filming.'

'You're not going to watch Viv and Grant?'

I shook my head. Just the mention of his name was a knife in my side. 'But you go.'

'We watched The Night Angels. They rocked. I mean seriously good.' Frieda said.

I didn't say anything.

'If you're okay Pen, I'll go. Mum and Mr Cooper are already in there. Coming Ed?'

'Nah, I'll stay here.'

Frieda left. I had no idea how I was going to get through the next hour. I had never felt less like performing. I found my phone in my coat pocket. There were several messages. Mum wishing me luck. Frieda trying to find me. Viv trying to find me. Nothing from Grant. The locked-up feelings were starting to squeeze out. I am hard and cold as a diamond. I am hard and cold as a diamond.

Ed gave a loud bark of laughter. He was on his phone.

'Sorry,' he said.

'What are you watching?' I asked.

'Just stupid clips.'

'Let me see,' I sat next to him, and we watched the screen. It was a clip of a madly excited dog jumping backwards to catch a ball and falling into a swimming pool. The dog looked so surprised it was hilarious.

'There's loads,' Ed said. 'I love dogs, they're such idiots.' Sitting next to Ed, our bodies touching as we huddled over his phone, some of his oak-like calmness spread through me. I could sense my pulse slowing .

'We're getting a puppy,' I told him. 'My Mum and brother are picking him up today.'

'What sort?'

'Labradoodle.'

'Labradors are the best. We've got a black lab called Bella but she's old now.' Ed showed me photos of her.

Looking at dog videos provided some healing ointment to my broken heart.

By the time Frieda came back and the Tannoy called for us I'd recovered sufficiently to believe I could do the dance. For Frieda, for Ed, for the planet. My hero, Jock Briggs had said I was tough, now was the time to prove it. I wasn't going to let Grant and Melody defeat me. I was the mighty Pen Flowers with her cold diamond heart. If there was one thing in the world I could do – I could dance.

The strange thing was I didn't feel nervous anymore. I didn't have enough emotional bandwidth left to feel nervous.

The floor manager waved us through to our starting positions. A few people had gathered to watch but not as many as this morning. Mr Cooper and Viv arrived to stand by Ed and Anna. The judges trooped in and took their places. Anthony Wyn-Jones nodded and smiled. He was clearly rooting for us. Frieda and I faced each other on the stage.

'Here goes,' she said.

'Dance for the Planet,' I said.

We stood on stage in darkness with only the globe lit up from inside. The floor manager was counting down on his fingers. Just before the house lights went off the studio door opened, and I looked up and saw Grant and Melody slip into the room together.

My body reacted as if an invisible surgeon had extracted my backbone in one swift slice. I collapsed inside. Everything fell; my knees sagged, my head dropped, my belly hit the floor. I missed the opening music cue hardly able to move my limbs.

Frieda looked at me in panic. I forced myself to move.

Frieda carried me. She knew there was something wrong and doubled her efforts. I fought to clear my head, to sink into the dance, but I was in turmoil. My mind was filled with the image of Grant and Melody standing together watching me. Only muscle memory kept me going. I was on autopilot. I was doing the moves, but I wasn't dancing them.

The longest two minutes of my life. A form of slow-motion torture. I couldn't engage with the moves; my body and mind were disconnected. I was a rag doll, a puppet, and without passion I was miming. Every time I looked at Frieda's face, I saw concern. I was letting her down, letting everyone down. Somehow, I staggered through. Until the final sequence when, as Frieda turned to make her fierce strong stance facing into the camera, I forgot the new ending and cradled the globe instead. I realised my mistake and panicked standing arms by my side looking freaked out. We were entirely out of sync with each other.

There was nothing I could do. I'd gone wrong in a way that would be obvious to everyone in the studio and anyone who ever watched the show. My humiliation was now complete.

The lights went down, and I burst into tears. All the squeezed-down emotions burst out of the frozen diamond.

'I'm sorry, so sorry, Frieda.'

She strode across the stage, pushing aside the globe and putting her arms around me.

'What happened Pen, what's up?' she asked.

Before I could answer her there was a camera pointing in my face. I heard the young female producer whisper, 'quick get in there, this is TV gold.'

'How did that go?' she asked us, her face crumpled in mock concern.

Frieda was magnificent.

'Could have gone better. But overall, we're happy. I hope we got our message across that we need to fight for this planet.'

But that wasn't what the evil producer wanted. The camera swung back to me. I could smell peppermint and tobacco on the cameraman's breath.

The woman insisted. 'So, Pen how did you feel it went?'

Tears were pouring down my cheeks.

'I messed up. I've let everyone down.' And I pushed the camera away and ran from the stage. I was contractually obliged to do the interview, but I couldn't.

I ran through the studio to our dressing room and bolted the door behind me.

31

'Pen, let me in!' Frieda was pulling on the handle trying to open the door. But I wasn't going to unlock it. There might be cameras out there.

'Pen please let me help.' Frieda sounded upset. She'd put so much work into this show. It was one thing ruining my own life, but I couldn't bear that I'd let her down so badly.

Anna's voice, 'Pen we're worried about you.'

A female voice, probably that awful television producer said,

'What's going on here?'

'Excuse me, we need a moment of privacy.' Anna said firmly.

'Everyone has to go to Studio 1 for the judges' decisions,' the bossy woman insisted.

'We'll be there in a minute,' Frieda said. There was a pause then she whispered, 'Pen you have to come out. We've got to be filmed. We signed the contract.'

I heard Ed say quietly, 'I'm getting Vivienne.'

'I can't,' I mouthed to myself in the mirror. My face was blotchy and red from crying, and tears were still leaking out. I couldn't be in the same room as Grant and Melody.

'You lot go to the studio – we'll join you soon.' Vivienne's voice.

There was a loud banging on the door.

'Pen, open the door or I'll get Ed to kick it down and you'll have to pay damages. Everyone has gone away — it's just me and Ed.' Vivienne's voice.

I went and stood by the door.

'Just you.'

'Ed's going now. Just me.'

'Promise?'

'I promise.'

I slowly pulled back the bolt and opened the door. Vivienne slipped inside and I bolted it behind her.

'Oh Pen,' she looked at me and then pulled me into a bear hug. 'These things happen I'm sorry, but it's not the end of the world.'

'It is,' I whispered not looking at her.

'I promise,' Viv was at her most insistent, 'you'll dance again, and you'll dance better, as if this little blip is going to stop you, Pen. You were born to dance.'

'It's not the dancing. It's Grant.' I managed to admit. I turned away so that I didn't have to look at her face. I felt so ashamed.

'Oh,' there was a long pause. 'You found out about Coco?' she sighed.

'Coco?' My head came up and I glared at Vivienne, 'what about Coco?'

Vivienne looked flustered. 'Sorry nothing, I didn't mean.'

'I found him and Melody shagging in their dressing room.'

Another pause.

'He really is a little shit!' Vivienne spat out. 'I bet he did that on purpose because your dance this morning was so good. The little wanker! He's pathetic, ambitious, spoilt.'

Vivienne wasn't holding back. I had no idea this was what she thought of Grant.

'But I love him,' I told her. 'I thought you liked him.'

'That was before I realised he was still seeing Coco while he was going out with you. He's not worth it Pen.'

'He's been seeing Coco?' Was Viv really saying that?

'Louis said not to say anything because I didn't know for certain, but I'd heard him talking to her on the phone and last night when you got the bus home, I saw her getting into his car. He doesn't deserve you Pen. You're out of his league.'

'Don't you mean I'm out of his league. Only beautiful girls like Coco or Melody need apply.' I was crying again.

'No, I do not mean that!' Vivienne was getting loud and stomping about the dressing room. 'You're a kind, loving, funny, incredibly creative person and he's nothing, nothing but a pretty face.'

There was a knock on the door. Ed's voice. 'Sorry but they're calling for you. They're about to start filming.'

'We're coming,' Vivienne said.

'I can't,' I said.

'You've got to,' she told me. 'And you can. Where's your backbone?'

'I don't have one,' I said but I turned on the tap and ran cold water into my hands and held them to my face.

'You've got it easy.' Viv snorted. 'I've got to stand next to him and smile when I want to punch him in the face. I tell you having to be madly in love with Grant Barker has tested my acting skills to the max.'

'And I, stupid idiot, really am in love with him.' I blew my nose and wiped up the worst damage to my face.

'You're not, you just think you are.'

'Tell my heart that. You know it does actually ache, heart ache.' I held my hand to the centre of my chest. 'I've never felt this before, this terrible pain right here.'

'Oh God, I know that pain – when I thought Louis was leaving me for Harriet: arghh. You ready?'

I nodded.

'Shoulders back, chin up. Pen Flowers, dancer extraordinaire. You can do this.'

She unbolted and opened the door.

I hesitated. 'I don't think I can.' I said in a pathetic child's voice.

Vivienne pushed me through the door.

'You're tough remember?'

'I've let Frieda down.'

'Stop. Don't talk, walk. You're not going to let Grant or Melody see that you're upset. Even if you've got no pride, I have pride. I won't let you give that pair the satisfaction.' She marched me down the corridor and into Studio 1.

'And the first act going through to the London Palladium is ...' How they loved to draw the tension out. At least I didn't need to worry about our name being called. 'The Night Angels.'

Huge cheers in the studio, spotlights up on Melody and the band. All the acts were standing on the main stage in darkness. If you were selected a spotlight would come up, otherwise you would just be a vague shadowy outline. That suited me fine. Frieda had her arm around my shoulders. She was being incredibly kind. Luckily Vivienne and Grant were on the opposite side of the stage to us. Vivienne was standing so that she blocked Grant from my sight.

'And the second act going through to the final is.... Christabelle.' She was the young singer we'd seen sitting with her Mum at breakfast time. I hadn't heard her sing but someone, Anna or Mr Cooper, had said she had a great voice.

'And the final act selected from Birmingham for The Great British Talent Show is ..... Ashley Stiles.'

The unfunny comedian. Even in my vulnerable state I wondered on what basis he'd been chosen. His father must be the Head of the BBC or something. I really didn't care. I just wanted this grim experience to be over as quickly as possible.

'I'm sorry,' I whispered to Frieda.

She smiled and shrugged. 'Look we won five hundred quid. Mum and I are still going to Portugal. I'm happy.'

She seemed genuinely okay. Grant would be devastated. But at least I didn't have to deal with that anymore.

32

Mr Cooper kindly drove me home in his van. Mum heard the door and came into the hall while I was taking off my coat.

'Oh dear,' she said, seeing my face. 'Not good?'

I shook my head. 'Terrible. I went wrong, and we didn't get through.'

'Oh darling, I'm sorry. But there's someone here who'll cheer you up.' She beckoned me through to the living room.

In the middle of the carpet sat Bouncer, his paw on a white furry toy that might once have been a rabbit but was already earless. He'd grown bigger since we'd seen him. He was now the size of a small rabbit himself, but his ears were firmly attached and flopped down on either side of his head in a cute bob. He bounded over to greet me, his whole body involved in wagging his tail. He was pleased to see me, yelping, and jumping. I knelt and swooped him into my arms. His little pink tongue came out and he licked my face.

'Hello Bouncer, you beautiful boy.' I snuggled him to my neck and felt tears at the corner of my eyes. He was so soft and warm and happy.

'You sit down with him, and I'll bring your tea in – I bet you're starving.' Mum said.

Thomas was on his PlayStation, but he turned to me.

'Careful he doesn't wee on you. He does if he gets excited.'

I didn't care. I needed all the love Bouncer had to give. I sat on the sofa holding him on my chest, stroking his silky fur and he went very still.

'Has he gone to sleep?' I asked Thomas.

'Yeah, he sleeps a lot. Wakes up has a crazy ten minutes, then sleeps again. We're not supposed to wake him.'

I watched his little ribs move in and out with each breath. He'd settled between my breasts in the centre of my chest where the pain from my heart was worst. I felt as if he was loving me better.

Mum thought I was sad about the show. I didn't tell her anything about Grant. I just said that Melody had gotten through to the next round, but we hadn't. I honestly didn't care about the show - apart from letting Frieda down. I was pleased not to have to worry about it anymore. That the comic got through showed how phoney it was. Dad was right, the TV world was full of fakes.

I went to bed early. My body was in a weird state. Every drop of energy had drained away, but I couldn't relax. My muscles seemed made of steel wool, tight and scratchy. At the core of me was an empty crater surrounded by barbed wire. The moment I lay down and closed my eyes the image of Grant and Melody in the dressing room filled my head.

I hadn't expected to enjoy today but I hadn't imagined it would be the worst day of my life. Worse even than the night I'd spent on the streets in London. Seeing Grant and Melody entwined was like being stabbed in the belly again and again.

Why had I trusted him? How had I imagined that he loved me? I tried to work it out. The Christmas tree kiss felt like fate ringing a bell. He'd been the one who'd pursued me. He'd done so many lovely things: taken me to

Stratford, bought me presents. He hadn't pressurised me to have sex but wanted to wait until I was ready. And he'd said he loved me. Yet all the time he'd been secretly seeing Coco.

My overwhelming sensation was one of terrible shame. As if I were naked on the main stage of Studio 1 with a spotlight on me and the audience laughing. I was another of Grant Barker's besotted cast-offs. Everyone at school would pity me. I couldn't bear it.

I'd fallen in love with a fraud. I'd believed this was the real deal, that we'd spend the rest of our lives together. I was such a stupid, stupid, naive idiot.

Maybe Vivienne was right, maybe he'd even shagged Melody deliberately – to upset me and ruin our dance. I believed he was capable of that now. So why was I blaming myself? I'd been faithful and loyal to him, genuine in my feelings. Why was I feeling ashamed? He was the liar and the cheat.

Hate that matched the love I'd felt erupted inside me. He was a horrid little twisted worm and I wanted to crush him beneath my feet. Stamp on his wriggling deceitful two-timing body until I'd mashed him into a pulp.

My empty crater became a boiling cauldron of rage. I must have increased the temperature in the bedroom by at least ten degrees. This was not global but local warming. A lethal fire storm inside my body.

Vivienne was right. There was no way I was going to let despicable people like Grant and Melody defeat me. I had pride. I was tough and I was mad. Mad as fire. Lying in bed was torture. I'd explode if I didn't get up and move.

Moonlight seeped through my thin curtains silvering the end of my bed. I took my anger out into the street. The night was cold and clear with an almost full moon huge and low in the sky.

I didn't know which was worse, the agony of heartbreak or this overwhelming rage. Skin stretched over flame. I punched and kicked the air. Imagined myself kneeing Grant in the groin, swinging Melody by her braid. As I stormed up and down Knightlow Road I danced a dance of violent revenge. I wanted to hurt them as much as they'd hurt me. Stab for stab. These feelings were ugly. I didn't like being full of hate, but I couldn't stop myself.

I wanted to break things. I kicked out at walls hurting my feet, and punched brick walls scraping the skin off my knuckles. I wanted to plunge from the sky all beak and claws, swoop down on Grant and tear him into pieces. I pictured myself flying through the sky to his house and attacking him in bed, stabbing him repeatedly through the heart, blood spurting everywhere.

This must be how murderers felt. Where did this uncontrollable rage come from? How could I have such huge aggression inside me? How could I contain it?

The night was light blue with the moon so large I could see every flaw on her pockmarked face. I stretched my arms to the moon begging her to fill me with ice.

The moon had seen betrayal and worse. Had seen muggings and burglaries and murder. In the back alleys, in deserted corners, what acts of human cruelty had the moon not witnessed? The knife to my heart. The axe to my brain. Thrusts that felt fatal. To the moon they were nettle stings. From her distance, she wouldn't even register the heat of my rage. I wouldn't raise her temperature by a zillionth of a degree. She'd watched continents burn, and glaciers melt. She watched missiles exploding and bodies flying, humans killing humans in massive numbers. She watched millions fleeing from their homes, villages dying of starvation, and rainforests razed to the ground. The pain of one small, lonely dancer wasn't going to make her bleed.

I needed to drink in her icy powers because I was

burning. I danced a prayer for help, but she refused my request.

So, I danced black vengeance instead, with clawed fingers and a snapping, biting mouth. I stopped resisting the rage, stopped thinking that I shouldn't feel like this and gave in to the emotion. I became one hundred percent anger. I was living rage. Rage on legs. Rage on wings. I was vengeance in bodily form. I was dragon, burning inside, speaking fire. Pen Dragon Flowers.

Rage was supercharging my muscles. I was jumping higher than I'd ever reached before, running faster, my power was immense. I was pure dragon and if I roared, I could burn down the street. Grant and Melody's betrayal had released some power inside me that I hadn't known was there. I felt as if I could lift the parked cars from their gravel drives and hurl them down the street. With a single bound, I could vault over rooftops and tear up lamp posts like I was uprooting daffodils.

Maybe it was the weeks of training with Joe or compensation for messing up the talent show. Or maybe the best revenge I could ever have on Grant and Melody, but I began to dance as I'd never danced before. I felt my abilities shift up a gear.

I stopped thinking about Grant and started using the power.

I let the rage dance through me. I remembered the photograph of Jock Briggs doing that amazing, impossible jump. How I'd sworn that one day I too would jump like that. Tonight, I could. Tonight, fuelled by rage, I could touch the stars.

I was burning, the planet was burning. Forget about Grant and Melody, they didn't matter. Nor was this about winning or losing some stupid talent competition. I was vibrating at the level of the planet. Feeling the earth's rage.

If I could plug this energy into our dance, we'd become the voice of the planet. I'd harness this power for something important.

33

Dragon power, it turned out, was predominantly nocturnal. My rage and the sense of purpose it had given me faded with the light of day. When I woke late the next morning, I felt broken in body and spirit. I had messages from Vivienne, Frieda and Ed but not a word from Grant. What a snivelling little coward he was. My loneliness, the overwhelming sense of being unlovable, was back with a vengeance.

Bouncer was making short, high-pitched barks downstairs in the kitchen. I hauled my hurting body out of bed and went to see him. At least there was one good thing in my life. Breakfast was the cause of his excitement. He was noisily and messily attacking his bowl and spraying biscuits everywhere in his hurry to eat. He seemed completely at home.

'Did he cry in the night?' I asked Mum.

'Not that I heard,' she said.

'No, me neither. What a brave boy.' I knelt beside him and patted his head. He was so small and perfect and silky soft. I wanted to cry.

'Shouldn't you get dressed; your father will be here any minute?'

I'd forgotten that Thomas and I were going to Dad's for lunch. I remembered that Dad had something to tell us. I didn't think I could cope with more bad news.

*

Dad's flat was on the top floor of a big Victorian house in the old part of Harborne. The place came fully furnished and Dad hadn't done anything to make it personal. Visiting him was like being in a stranger's house. The sofa smelt like stale biscuits, sweet with an underlying whiff of mould.

In the large high-ceilinged living room, Dad's CDs and vinyl collection were stacked in boxes in one corner next to his music system. A television screen was mounted on the wall over the fireplace. Dad had the rugby on and as we came into the room a team of men dressed in black was doing the most extraordinary dance. Shunting forward in a low squat with their huge thigh muscles straining, they slapped their chests in rhythm and made a complex pattern of arm movements.

'What's this, Dad?' I called. He was in the tiny kitchen at the back of the house finishing the roast dinner. He came through into the living room dressed in a flowery apron.

'That's the haka. The All Blacks, New Zealand's rugby team, perform it before every match. It's a Māori tradition.'

'I love it.'

Their dance was raw and fierce reminding me of the power that I'd felt out on the street last night.

Following the smell of roast chicken, I wandered into the kitchen. The window looked out over the back garden onto an overgrown lawn. Either rewilding or neglect. Dad was putting food onto plates. I was pleased to see that his roast potatoes were crispy, and he'd done sausages and stuffing and gravy. He was a much better cook than Mum.

'Take this through to Thomas,' he handed me a plate. 'And this one's yours.' Dad wasn't perfect. He annoyed me a lot, but he was capable. I wished he still lived with us. Coming to Dad's flat made the separation feel real. I always felt sad here.

Mum made us eat at the kitchen table but with Dad we

sat on the sofa. His table was covered in piles of books and papers. His World War Two in Birmingham research for the local history society. I wondered when he'd get round to his big announcement. I wasn't going to ask him.

We ate in silence while Dad watched the rugby. I tried to follow what was going on. Huge, bearded men chased a melon-shaped ball around a field, bashing into each other before embracing in a muddy group cuddle. Didn't make any sense.

'How's school?' Dad asked Thomas. This was his stock question. He'd not mentioned the talent competition, no inquiry as to how I'd done. Either Mum had already told him and he was being tactful, or he was so uninterested he'd forgotten. Either way suited me.

'Can we bring Bouncer with us next time? Once he's allowed out of the house?' Thomas asked.

'Yes well,' Dad coughed as if he'd got a lump of chicken stuck in his throat. Then he muted the telly. 'Next time I see you, won't be here. I'm moving.'

If this was his announcement, why was he making such a big deal about it? Behind his glasses, his eyes were making nervous darting movements from me to the TV and back to Thomas. It made him look shifty. He coughed again.

'I'm moving in with Susan, my friend from the local history society. You've both met her.'

Thomas looked up from his plate, his mouth open so I could see a horrible mess of mushed-up dinner inside. I turned back to Dad whose eyes were now fixed on the TV screen even though it was halftime and there were only commentators mouthing words we couldn't hear. He was avoiding looking at me.

What exactly did he mean? Was he going to be her lodger or her boyfriend? Would he be sleeping in the spare room or with her?

'I know your mother has been seeing other men. Well, Susan and I are...' Dad's voice faltered then faded out.

'Is this why you left us? For Susan?' I couldn't believe it – all men were two-timing, deceiving liars. Even my own Dad.

'Of course not!' Dad said, but I didn't believe him. He still wouldn't look at me.

'Have you told Mum?' I asked.

'I wanted to tell you both first.'

'So that we'd tell Mum.'

'Of course not,' Dad said. But I didn't believe that either. He was a coward like Grant.

I said to Thomas, 'Dad should tell Mum not us, okay?'

Thomas wasn't understanding the full implications. Dad cleared away the plates and brought out a shop-bought Victoria sponge cake. Bribing us with sugar. I refused a slice. Thomas tucked in demonstrating that no conflict of loyalties should get in the way of cake.

When Dad dropped us back home, he refused to come in and see Bouncer which proved he was avoiding telling Mum. At the front door, I held Thomas back.

'Mum won't be happy about Dad living with Susan.'

'Why not?'

'She'll feel betrayed. He should tell her not us, okay?'

Thomas agreed but I hadn't much faith in him being able to keep quiet. Mum always interrogated him about everything Dad had said and done.

I had an essay to do for History. The Great Pretenders – James and Charles Stuart – for whom I couldn't pretend any enthusiasm. The words of the textbook rolled through my brain but left no tracks. Sentences marched from ear to ear but carried no meaning. My mental capacities were preoccupied by The Great Betrayers – Grant and Dad.

The pain I felt over Grant's betrayal was like a bleeding gash in my heart, jagged, stinging, making me want to scream. But Dad, Dad leaving us, that was deep down in my bowels, a constant ache like a worm was chewing its way through my intestines. I didn't think about it most of the time, but it was always there underneath everything. Dad moving in with Susan made me realise he was never coming back. What if he and Susan had children and he stopped paying maintenance for us? Why didn't he love us enough to stay? Thinking of Dad leaving made me want to run into Grant's arms. I wanted sex so that oozy feel-good sensations would stop this deep, desperate, ache. I knew that Grant wasn't the right person to hold onto, but my body craved the physical comfort of being with him.

My thumbs itched to send him a message. One moment I was writing him an angry text – telling him what I thought of him and then the next I'd want to beg him to come round. But I refused to humiliate myself. As my hand started to crawl against my will towards the phone I leapt up and started doing an anti-men war dance to distract myself.

I stamped and snarled. Facing my bedroom mirror, I enjoyed becoming scarier and more aggressive with each new version. Jock had told me to use my fierceness. This was the moment. I googled war dance and amongst the videos of martial artists and African and Native American dancers was a haka performed by the New Zealand women's rugby team. Even though I couldn't understand what they were saying the dance was beautiful in a fierce but also tender way. Tears came into my eyes. I found a translation of their chant online.

'Life force from above. Life force from below (earth)
The gathering clouds
The mountains that pierce the sky

Let us proceed
To the seas
From the corners of the island
To the neighbouring islands
And around the world
You stand tall and proud.
Women of strength.
Who will bear the future.
The Black Ferns of New Zealand.
Rise and press on
When the challenge arrives.
We will gather and unite together.
Strength together. It will be done.'

You stand tall and proud. Women of strength. Strength together. The words matched their movements. No wonder I'd cried watching them. And they honoured the earth. We should learn from the Māori how to respect the earth as sacred.

I needed a dance that would make me strong and powerful. I should create one for myself. Why not? I started with the stamping moves I'd choreographed for *The Crucible*, toning down the sex and increasing the aggression. I used my dragon power and added in leaps and open-mouthed fire-breathing exhalations.

'What the hell's going on up there?' Mum called up the stairs. 'Sounds like a herd of elephants.'

'Dance practice,' I shouted back.

'Well don't bring the ceiling down. You've woken Bouncer up.'

Ha! Good! I was making the house shake. I'd bring the walls of paternalism crumbling down.

I heard shouting downstairs, then louder shouting, then screaming. I guessed immediately what had happened and ran down the stairs. Thomas was alone in the living room.

'You told her,' I said.

'She kept asking me questions. It just came out. She's on the phone to Dad.' He looked guilty but I couldn't blame him. From the moment Dad had told us this was inevitable.

'I warned you she wouldn't be happy.'

Thomas shrugged and went back to his PlayStation.

'Can't get any worse, can it? I mean they've already split up.'

He had a point.

Mum flung open the living room door. Eyes narrowed, jaw thrusting, you could almost see flames shooting from her mouth and nose, easily more frightening than any of the New Zealand rugby players.

'He claims that nothing happened before he left, but I don't believe him.' She walked over to the window. 'What about him going off to Leicester earlier and earlier on Sundays? I bet he was seeing her.' Mum pressed her face against the glass as if she could see the truth out in the garden. She was probably right.

'Remember he used to take me with him on his local history research trips,' I said, 'and then he started going with Susan and leaving me at home.' Mum marched back towards me.

'I'd forgotten that. Yes, this has been going on for ages. When he stopped being interested in us as a family, I knew something was wrong. He made me feel as if I was going mad when he was just looking for an excuse to leave.'

I agreed with Mum which was unusual.

'I could kill him,' she said.

Thomas looked up, worried.

'She doesn't mean that,' I reassured him.

'I do. I bloody do.' Mum shouted.

Bouncer, disturbed by the shouting, ran underneath the sofa and whimpered. I was concerned that Mum would lose it big time and hurt Bouncer, or us or herself. I tried to calm her down.

'I'm not surprised you're angry.' I said.

Mum picked up a vase from the mantelpiece above the fireplace and hurled it across the room. Pottery shards flew everywhere pinging against the window. Bouncer started barking.

'Mum don't,' I grabbed her hand as she reached for a vintage teapot that I knew she loved. 'Do my power dance instead – look.'

I demonstrated.

'This is to make you stand strong and proud.' I started dancing and she watched, putting down the teapot. 'Come and do it – you'll feel better, I promise.' I kept repeating the dance and Mum came over and stood next to me. 'It's easy,' I pulled her arm. 'Just bend your knees.'

Mum joined in. She picked up the moves quickly.

'Brilliant Mum, and you Thomas. Join in, come on.'

Thomas put down his controller and got up. In the centre of the living room, I taught them both the Pen Flowers power dance. We used to dance a lot as a family when we were happy. Mum and Dad had met doing rock and roll dancing. Before Dad went weird, we often put on one of his old-time rhythm and blues records and danced around the room. I knew how to jive before I learned to ride a bike.

Today was different. This was the three of us united against Dad who had abandoned us. I was in the middle with Mum and Thomas on either side. The dance felt even more powerful as a group. The atmosphere in the room flipped into fun. We made loud war cries and laughed at each other's fierce expressions.

'I wish I could see us doing this,' I said.

'We could video it,' Thomas suggested.

'Awesome,' I ran upstairs to get my phone. Thomas set a timer and we balanced the phone on the table so that we fitted full length in the frame. The phone flashed, we sprang into action and Bouncer decided to join in.

The video was a triumph. I knew Mum had been a good ballroom dancer, but I was still surprised at how well she moved, and Thomas was great too. Bouncer ran around our feet, barking. We looked fierce and proud but also funny and sweet dancing together.

'Forget about Dad, we don't need him.' I put my arms around them both.

The dance had prevented Mum from spiralling off into hysterics and stopped me thinking about Grant. This was powerful magic.

I called Frieda.

'Pen are you okay? Mum and I have been worried.'

'I'm surviving. Look I'm sorry about yesterday. I need to explain.'

I told her about Grant and Melody.

'I don't friggin' believe it. Oh Pen, I'm not surprised you freaked. What a shit! You poor darling.'

I didn't want to be pitied. Sympathy made me start crying and feeling sorry for myself.

'I'm okay, good riddance.' I said hoping my heart would listen.

'Changing the subject then - Mum wants to know if you still want to do 'Dance for the Planet' at the Extinction Rebellion event. Don't feel you've got to.'

I felt a moment of tension. What if I went wrong again? But it was an easy decision.

'Of course we should do it. That's why we made the dance. I've got an idea for a new finish. Have a look at this.'

I sent her our family power dance. We waited a few minutes for it to download.

'Is that your Mum and your brother? And the puppy? They're cool. I LOVE this!' Frieda shouted down the phone.

'I thought we could do this right at the end of our dance instead of the bit I messed up.'

'Babe you're a genius.'

I laughed. 'Just full of rage is all.'

'The rage of Pen Flowers – a mighty force.'

'The only thing is – I got the idea from the New Zealand women's rugby team – I'll send you the link. Is this cultural appropriation do you think?'

I waited while Frieda watched their video.

'Wow, talk about mighty. They're incredible. I don't think we need to worry - your moves are totally different. You've tried to capture the same spirit, but I think that's okay. Theirs is the kind of spirit we all need.'

'Strength together. That's what their haka says and that's the idea I want for the end of our dance. I thought we could maybe shout out 'Strength Together' like a war cry?'

'Let's do it, sister.'

34

Frieda came to my early morning training session with Joe. He was annoyed with me for losing it at the talent show.

'I don't care what was happening in your personal life, you should never let that interfere with your professionalism. I've been too soft on you.'

Frieda and I exchanged glances. No one could accuse Joe of erring through softness.

'It won't happen again,' I said. I didn't need to be told off. I felt bad enough already. Frieda changed the subject.

'Show Joe the video of your Mum and bro,' she said. I passed my phone to Joe. Frieda carried on. 'This is going to be the final sequence of our dance now. We want to put a film of me and Pen doing this up on the college YouTube site and ask others to copy and film themselves. Call it Strength Together and get a reel going.'

'Then we could project them on the stage at the protest like everyone was dancing together.' We were sure it could work.

'You can't force a YouTube sensation.' Joe was a cold wet fish. If we listened to him, we'd never make anything happen.

'We don't need loads,' I insisted.

'The other students will do one for sure.' Frieda wasn't going to be defeated by Joe's gloom either.

'What you need is a celebrity to back you,' Joe said. 'What about The Night Angels? They're getting loads of publicity now. You know them, don't you? Will they do one?'

'No,' I shouted before I could stop myself. Joe reared back as if I'd slapped him. Frieda jumped in.

'Dancing's not really their style,' she said. 'But there must be someone famous we could get.'

'Jock Briggs might do one,' I said.

Joe let his face crack into a smile. 'He'd be perfect. He's got international reach.'

'My Mum will do one,' Frieda said.

'We've already got my Mum and brother. I'm sure we can get a few more.'

I was glad to have a new project to focus on. Grant and I hadn't had any contact since that moment in the dressing room. I didn't know what I'd do if we bumped into each other at school. Would I blank him? Would he blank me?

I decided to stay in the girl's school and not spend any time in the sixth form extension – that way I wouldn't stumble across him unprepared. This wouldn't prevent me from coming face-to-face with Coco. My main concern was that my private life remained private. If my humiliation became school gossip, I'd, I'd… Best not to go there, too hideous a prospect. Focus on dancing, focus on the protest, and doing something worthwhile.

I stuck close to Vivienne who was the only one who knew what had happened. Unless Frieda had told Tamasin. Tamasin was being super sweet to me so maybe she had. Ever since the row at the auditions, Tamasin had been less sarcastic. Frieda was obviously giving her empathy training. Walking the school corridors between lessons, I had Vivienne on one shoulder and Tamasin on the other as if they were my bodyguards. I was grateful. At least I had loyal friends.

I kept my movements to a minimum, concentrating on schoolwork, eating my packed lunch in the classroom, and using my free periods to get my essay done. No encounters with Coco. No sightings of Grant. Day One post-Great British Betrayal survived.

I sent Jock the video of my family doing the 'Strength Together' dance and asked if he and any of the Tartan Fling dancers would film a version for us. I explained about 'Dance for the Planet' and the Extinction Rebellion protest on Saturday.

When the landline rang that evening I assumed it was Dad. Mum answered and I waited for the shouting to begin. But I heard Mum laughing. She called me and smiling passed me the phone 'Jock Briggs, he likes our reel.'

'I can see where you get your talent.' Jock sounded amused. 'Your Mum and brother are great. Though the puppy steals the show. Of course, we'll do you a video. Great that you're using dance to campaign for the environment. How are you?'

'That would be brill, thanks so much Jock. I'm fine, college is good.'

'I saw Anthony Wyn-Jones on Sunday at a gala show. He told me that you'd done a superb dance and were the judges' first choice, but you'd fallen apart during the filming. He thought you couldn't handle the pressure. But that didn't sound like the Pen Flowers I know.'

Oh Jeez! Did everyone in the whole dance world know what I'd done? I hadn't even got to the London School of Contemporary Dance and already I had a reputation for being unreliable.

'It wasn't that. Something happened, something personal. I got freaked and I messed up.' I remembered Joe's lecture, 'I know I shouldn't have let my personal life affect my professional life. I don't know why I couldn't hold it together. I was...'

Jock interrupted me, laughing down the phone.

'Stop, stop, enough with the self-flagellation. You're only sixteen. Everyone messes up but I can see you've bounced back. I hope you'll keep messing up and bouncing back for the rest of your life Pen.'

Jock always made me feel like everything happened for a reason.

'So, you'll help me with the bounce back then?'

'Proud to.'

By mid-morning break the next day Jock had sent through a video of the Tartan Fling company doing our 'Strength Together' dance. I forwarded it to Frieda at college and she phoned me back.

'Pen, this is – no words.' Then she discovered one, 'immense.' She went on, 'I'm here with Craig. We've set up a YouTube account, we've put up our video and yours with your family and my Mum's done one and I got a load of the students here to do one and now we've got Tartan Fling's – it looks amazing. We're going to start a call out for more. This is genius because we can promote the protest at the same time.'

I was so elated after Frieda's call that I risked going to the sixth form extension for my free period without the protection of Tamasin and Vivienne who'd gone to drama. The Gods were shining down on me because Ed was there with his books spread across one of the big central tables. He was completely absorbed in a complex algebraic equation. He was frowning and twisting his mouth into odd shapes. He'd been so kind to me on Saturday. A warm buttery feeling spread through my body watching him.

'Room for me?' I asked.

He looked up and grinned.

'Sure,' he shuffled some papers.

'Don't worry I don't need much space.'

I sat down and got out my history books. I'd nearly finished my essay on The Great Pretenders. Ed stopped working and smiled at me, the tips of his ears turning pink.

'Thanks for helping on Saturday,' I said.

'No problem. This Saturday will be better.'

'You know about that?'

'Yeah, Anna and I have been sorting out how to hang the globe. She reckons there'll be thousands of people.'

Ed was right. Performing at the protest would be much better because we were dancing for a reason. He went back to his equations, and I got on with my essay. Sitting next to Ed it was easy to concentrate.

When I felt a hand on my shoulder I jumped.

'Pen, can we talk?'

Grant was standing behind me.

Anything remotely resembling calmness drained from my body and was replaced by a snake pit of anxiety. I looked over at Ed who was glaring at Grant as if he wanted to hit him. I wasn't sure what to do. Ed shifted in his chair and looked at me like he was waiting for a signal.

'Pen,' Grant repeated turning his back on Ed.

'Okay,' I decided and got up. I had to sort this out myself.

Grant led the way to one of the small study rooms. I couldn't stop my body's response. I wanted to clutch hold of him, press myself against him. I followed behind watching his hips and shoulder blades move, thinking about us writhing naked together at the cabin. The vision of him with Melody in the dressing room returned.

The study window looked out over the park next door. Beneath the trees a blanket of snowdrops nodded their heads in the wind. Grant closed the door and turned to face me.

'So, Saturday, bad timing,' he laughed. Was he really

going to try and laugh this off? Unbelievable! 'Look, we were sharing that dressing room and Melody was coming on to me all day. The moment Marlon was out of the way she pounced. I shouldn't have given in but with the adrenalin of the show and everything. I'm only human. I'm into you Pen, but we don't have to be exclusive. Melody says that she and Marlon have an open relationship.'

I don't know what I thought Grant would say but nothing had prepared me for this bullshit.

'That way you can keep sleeping with Coco too?'

'Where did you get that from? You're crazy, we're just friends.' His immediate instinct was denial but then he remembered his earlier position. 'I've never said I wanted an exclusive relationship.'

'You didn't mention 'non-exclusive' before we had sex. I trusted you. You said what we had was precious.'

'It was. It is. But no one's into monogamy anymore.' Like he was talking about a brand of trainers.

'Yeah well, I'm obviously not cool enough because when I love someone it's with my whole heart. I loved you, Grant, with everything I had. But that wasn't enough for you. So thanks, but no thanks.'

I turned away and walked calmly out of the room. I was pleased to see Ed still working. I sat down and pretended to read. I could feel the heat in my cheeks, and I knew my whole face would be ketchup red. I put my palms to my cheeks as if I could cool them down. My heart was dancing at two hundred and fifty beats a minute, fast, fast, fast.

I took a deep breath.

'You okay?' Ed asked.

'I just broke up with Grant,' I told him. 'My choice.'

I felt sad, terribly sad. But strong. I'd stood up for myself.

35

Mum and Thomas were coming with me to the Extinction Rebellion Protest. Their video had started the whole Strength Together idea, so I wanted them to be part of this. I didn't know if Mum would be able to handle being outside with so many people. She'd been doing better now she could drive. Frieda and Anna knew about Mum's agoraphobia and Anna said she'd look after Mum while I was dancing.

I expected Mum to pull out at the last minute, to make an excuse and say she couldn't leave Bouncer. Instead, she'd organised for Mrs Bell to come round and look after the puppy. Mum was dressed and ready to go early, nagging Thomas to get a move on.

I'd been worried that Dad's affair with Susan would lead to a deterioration in her mental health. But after her initial fury, the news made her stronger because her suspicions had been justified. She hadn't been paranoid, she'd been right. Fired up by the magic of our power dance she'd kept up with her well-being classes and was doing her exercises. She drove us into the city even managing to change gear and talk at the same time.

'There're more videos on your YouTube site this morning. One from Russia.' Mum was our number one fan.

'Yeah, we've had a few from other dance groups. But I like the ones of ordinary people best. Did you see Frieda's old primary school has done one? So cute, those tiny ones being strong and fierce.' I said.

'As long as no one at my school sees ours.' Thomas wasn't sharing the love. He'd been fine dancing in our living room but was grumpy about going public. We were inviting people to come on stage and join us for the Strength Together sequence, but Thomas was refusing. He didn't even want to come to the protest, but Mum had insisted.

Melody and The Night Angels were filming today in the finals at The London Palladium. Vivienne was in London too. She and Grant may not have gotten through, but Viv had been asked to audition for a BBC series. I had no idea what Grant was doing.

We were lucky with the weather. The sun was out and the sky cloudless. Daffodils were blazing in the flower beds around the fountain in Centenary Square, a bouncing yellow frame to the green semi-circle of grass. The stage was set up in front of Symphony Hall, the same as at the Black Lives Matter protest. We were early but already groups of young people were setting up camps, laying down ground sheets, putting up chairs, and erecting banners. The atmosphere was noisy but well-mannered. Uniformed police stood in groups of two or three watching from the pavements.

Mum was walking next to me without holding my hand. Her left arm wasn't even jerking. She was smiling and looking about her as if walking through crowds in the city centre was something she did all the time. Even Thomas had stopped being sulky and was taking in the pumped-up atmosphere. I led them towards the stage where Frieda and Ed were unloading the globe from the back of Anna's blue van.

I introduced everyone and we helped carry the globe to the stage. There was a framework of metal scaffolding.

Ed was talking to one of the organisers. He came over to tell us the plan.

'They're happy to keep the globe there throughout the speeches. They love it,' he reported back to us. 'They want you to come on at the end as a finale. They've put your reel on their website, so I bet you get more. They've got millions of followers worldwide.'

Frieda was on her phone. 'That was Craig, he's at college. He's got so many videos coming in he's overwhelmed. We're going viral.' She danced around.

Once Ed had hung the globe, we were allowed a quick rehearsal to adapt the dance to the smaller space of this makeshift stage. From the stage, we had a great view out over the square. The grass was disappearing as more people arrived. Lots of folks had rainbow-coloured face paints and carried banners with slogans. 'Everyone can change.' 'This is not a drill.' 'Deeds not words.' 'This is change.' I found the energy inspiring. Instead of feeling miserable about the state of the world, I felt part of a determination to change things.

Today was so different from last Saturday at the talent show. We were outside in the open air, part of something important, something bigger than our egos. We were doing what we could to bring about change, not trying to be famous.

Frieda and I marked out the dance and then we practiced getting the others to join us on stage for the Strength Together finale. Mum and Anna were so keen that Frieda and I would have to watch our backs, or they'd be taking over. Thomas was refusing to join in despite Frieda and Anna making a huge fuss of him.

'Come on Thomas, we've got this,' Ed suddenly announced. 'I'll do it if you will.' Reluctantly Thomas stood next to Ed on the stage. Frieda and I turned and watched them. Ed was great. He'd learnt the moves and fully committed to performing them.

'Ed, you dark horse,' Frieda hugged him. Ed's face switched into red mode. He couldn't handle any attention and remain normal coloured.

When we came down off the stage some of the organisers from Extinction Rebellion asked if they could learn the dance and a small crowd gathered in front of the stage. Freida and I led an impromptu class. There was a charge in the air, a sense of momentum building. Frieda and I kept looking at each other and laughing. Mum and Thomas being there felt special. For once I wasn't on my own. I even wished that Dad could be there.

Tamasin arrived with her mother. I was surprised because Mrs Fox was a lawyer and I'd have thought she'd disapprove of Extinction Rebellion. But she was enthusiastic and instead of her usual couture outfit she was dressed in jeans and trainers.

'Tamasin's taught me the moves but I'm not very good I'm afraid.' She laughed. I stared at Tamasin who shrugged. 'We're here to fight for the planet,' she said. I was touched that she'd learnt the dance and taught her Mum.

'Thanks, Tam, for being here.' I squeezed her arm.

'Blame Frieda,' she said.

By the official start time, the square was packed with people and there was a huge police presence lined around the edges. They were in full riot gear and looked threatening. I hoped that everything would remain peaceful. The television cameras were on one side of the stage and there were a few journalists. The media could do something constructive for a change like spread the need for climate action and film any police violence.

The speeches were alarming and inspiring. A Professor

argued that we were already too late to stop the climate emergency but that the impact of environmental disasters might provide the motivation for governments to change. A *Guardian* journalist said that capitalism was a gun pointed at the heart of the planet. When he finished there were deafening cheers and stamping. Then Frieda and I were on.

One of the leaders of Extinction Rebellion introduced us as a global dance phenomenon - bit of exaggeration there - but the crowd cheered so loudly that he had to call for quiet so we could start.

In front of the stage waiting to join us were our supporters. Mum was standing between Anna and Thomas and looked as happy as I'd ever seen her. Ed was next to Thomas. Tamasin was with her Mum. Joe was there with a group of our classmates from college. I felt surrounded by people I loved. It was a shame that Vivienne couldn't be with us. If Frieda and I had won a place in the Talent Show finals, we wouldn't have been here. We'd be stuck in some dark studio being treated like performing monkeys. I should be glad that Grant had shagged Melody. He'd done me a favour.

If the dance judge Anthony Wyn-Jones had thought our rehearsal at the talent show was good, then he should have seen us at Extinction Rebellion. We were flying. This was dragon power. This was pure flame. This was the molten lava at the earth's core. This was dancing with your whole heart. Frieda and I poured every litre of blood flowing through our bodies into the moves. We were so in tune with each other that it was as if we were one body with four legs and four arms. When I lifted her holding the globe, I had such strength I felt like I could support the earth and every living creature on my shoulders.

We did our Strength Together challenge at the end of the dance and maybe because of the projected videos on the wall of Symphony Hall or because people had seen it on the website, there was a cheer of recognition. Anna and Mum led people up onto the stage. I turned round to grin at them and blinked. Was I dreaming? Between Mum and Anna were some of the Tartan Fling dancers with Jock Briggs. Jock grinned at me. Behind them, more people lined up around and beneath the globe. The stage was packed.

Frieda and I were so overwhelmed we didn't know what to do. One of the Extinction Rebellion leaders called out 'Dance for the Planet' and Jock gave a mighty war cry and leapt up into the air, landing in the opening stance. Frieda and I took a position on either side of him and facing the audience we started. In the crowd below us, people joined in. Even if they didn't know the moves, they were copying them as best they could.

'Again,' Jock shouted when we'd finished. Frieda and I led everyone through the dance three times. The energy was enough to replace fossil fuels forever. Tears were leaking down my face. To be part of this eruption, surrounded by my favourite people. I felt proud and strong, loved, and loving. This was how to love like your heart's on fire.

Romantic love was a minefield, but this was universal love. I was panting, blood pumped into every muscle fibre. I felt like a horse that had run long and hard, not to win a race but for sheer joy. I couldn't stop smiling and hugging people.

The cameras and journalists came rushing in. I let Frieda do the talking and when she told them that Jock was a famous dancer, they moved on to him.

Mum was at my shoulder. She seemed quite relaxed.

'That was wonderful Pen. So proud of you,' she said.

'Having you and Thomas there made it brilliant.'

'Thomas wants to go now and I'm worrying about

Bouncer. Can you get the bus back?' She asked. I nodded.

'But what about you? Will you be okay – getting home with just Thomas, on your own?' I said staring at the same mother who couldn't walk to the end of the road without having a panic attack.

'Let's hope so,' she laughed making a joke at herself. Change could happen – here was proof.

'Thanks, Thomas you were brave.' He was risking ridicule if the kids at his school saw him on the telly dancing. I watched Mum and Thomas follow the crowds of people drifting out of the square. They were tough, strong people. I'd been used to thinking of my family as a swamp of insecurities.

When the journalists had finished with him, Jock came over to talk to Frieda and me.

'You came from London just for this?' I was amazed.

'Group decision. The company wanted to support 'Dance for the Planet'. I want to introduce you to a friend of mine. This is Clara.'

A slim older woman with pure white hair and dark lipstick was dressed in a plum-coloured trouser suit. She held out her hand. I was embarrassed as I placed my sweaty palm against her soft smooth skin.

'I loved 'Dance for the Planet'. Congratulations on a genuine initiative. There's real integrity here.'

Frieda and I thanked her, wondering who she was.

'I'm Head of Choreography at the London School of Contemporary Dance. I'd like to invite you to come down and talk to our students. Is it okay if Jock gives me your email?'

Frieda was silenced.

'Wow,' I said. 'Thanks, yes of course. It's my dream to study at your school.'

'Well, we're always interested in students with exceptional talent. We should talk further.'

She left with Jock and the Tartan Fling dancers. They had to race to catch a train back to London as they were performing that night.

Once they'd gone Frieda demonstrated her war cry.

'London School of Contemporary Dance - Yes!'

Tamasin rushed over and Frieda treated her to a long slow, too-much-for-public-consumption, kiss. Ed and I exchanged embarrassed glances. Frieda had no inhibitions.

When we'd packed everything up Anna took the van home and Frieda, Tamasin, Ed, and I went for a pizza in the city. Mrs Fox was treating us as her contribution. After we'd finished eating, I felt exhausted as the adrenalin drained from my body. I wanted to go home. Ed said he'd walk with me to the bus stop.

Broad Street was almost empty, just a few people waiting at the bus stops. It was that in-between time of day when the shoppers had gone home, and the pub goers and clubbers hadn't come out. The street lamps had come on but there was still light in the sky. A soft pink glow edged the rooftops.

'What I like about March,' Ed said, 'is the way the light comes back. Have you noticed? Still cold, but every day there's more light.'

He'd read my mind. 'Yeh, I like that too,' I said.

We were both looking up at the sky and a skein of geese passed high overhead. We walked along in silence. I was thinking about how different today had been from last Saturday.

'Thanks for everything you've done for us. We couldn't have managed without you. This is my stop.' I said.

'Today was good,' he said.

'Yeah, really good. You don't have to stay with me if

you need to get home.' There weren't any buses in sight.

'You're all right I'm in no hurry.'

'That was kind - what you did with Thomas this afternoon.'

Ed smiled. 'I've got younger brothers, so I know what they're like.'

'When did you learn the routine?' I asked.

'I watched the video last night. The moves aren't complicated.'

'You're a natural.'

'I don't think so,' he blushed. 'Just happy to make a fool of myself.'

We were standing opposite each other close enough so I could smell the mix of soap and wood that I associated with him. Ed smell. I liked it. Clean and earthy. He stepped in closer and before I realised what he was doing he kissed me gently on the mouth.

I wasn't expecting this, and my eyes opened wide in surprise, but I didn't back off. I was deciding in my head what I thought about this development, when my body acted by itself, moving forward, and pressing against his chest. Ed's arms reached around me, and I snuggled closer in and put my face up to be kissed some more. Being in Ed's arms felt safe and, well, lovely. For some reason, I thought of drifts of snowdrops. A sweet, tender warmth spread through my body.

I felt weirdly, deeply, happy. Relaxed in a way I'd never felt before.

Ed pulled away.

'Your bus is here,' he said. He kissed me again. 'See you on Monday.'

I got on the bus and climbed up to the top deck and looked out of the window. Ed was watching for me and waved. He had such a lovely kind face.

36

Vivienne had redecorated her bedroom while she was going through her break with Louis. I was curled up on her bed clutching one of her new fake fur cushions. I found myself missing the old bilberry boudoir. The room was now new model Vivienne – grown up and stylish, with white walls, framed black and white photographs, and velvet curtains in forest green. It had a slightly bohemian, vintage feel. I was reminded quite forcefully of Mrs Mulligan's house. Vivienne sat on a crimson velvet armchair that looked like it had come from the props department of the youth theatre, in full-on regal mode.

'I have BIG news,' she proclaimed. 'That's why you had to come over.'

'You got the part?' Was this the beginning of Viv's inevitable rise to fame?

'Nah, the audition was awful. Hundreds of other girls. I was only in there for five minutes.'

'So, what's the big news then?'

'Louis came to London with me and – we're engaged.'

'Wow, congratulations.' I was shocked. 'Aren't you a bit young to get married? What do your parents say?'

'Oh, we're not getting married for ages, not until after I've been to Drama School. But since the Harriet business, we wanted to make a commitment to each other.'

'I get that. Well, I'm thrilled for you.' And I was happy for her, but I felt myself slip down a rung on the loneliness ladder.

As if she was reading my thoughts Viv changed the subject. 'How was Extinction Rebellion?'

'Brilliant. So inspiring. Everyone was super fired up.' I told her how the dance had gone, with Jock turning up with Tartan Fling and the woman from the London School of Contemporary Dance.

'Wow, Pen that's like totally exciting.' She sat forward in her chair.

'And Ed kissed me.'

'Oh my God! And??' Vivienne was leaning so far forward any moment she'd nosedive into the carpet.

'And – I don't know – lovely. Different to Grant. But sort of wonderful.'

'Ed doesn't give much away but I'd say he was crazy about you.'

'But you know I was passionately in love with Grant, maybe I still am, even though he's an arsehole. Ed, I like him, I mean I really like him. And the more I get to know him the more I like him. But I don't know.'

'You're always in such a rush Pen. Just see what happens, go step by step.'

On Thursday when I had my free period, I headed over to the sixth form extension and set myself up at our usual table. I didn't know what I was hoping would happen. The common room door opened, and Ed came in with his heavy backpack on his shoulder. He saw me and smiled, his ears going maroon and a flush spreading up his neck. I smiled back and he came over.

'Okay if I sit down?' He asked.

'Course,' I moved some of my books to make more room.

'You made it onto the local news,' he said.

'So I heard.' I hadn't watched but Mum had been

glued to the telly. I hated watching myself dance. It never looked as good as it felt inside.

'Mum thought you were great.' Ed said.

'Oh, thanks.'

We both sat not saying anything. Ed got his books out. Then he looked up.

'Ballet Rambert are at the Birmingham Rep this week? I wondered if you'd like to go tomorrow evening?'

'I didn't know you liked contemporary dance.'

'I like watching you and Frieda.'

'Are you asking me out on a date?' I played with him a bit.

Ed mumbled something that could have been yes and his face notched a further rung up the red scale. I wondered if I could get his entire head to turn purple. I waited like I was considering.

'I'd love that,' I said after I'd made him squirm in his chair. We both laughed and I felt a warm happy feeling inside, not snakes going wild, just happy that there were possibilities waiting to be explored.

The common room door opened, and a bunch of boys burst into the room shouting and laughing. One of them was Grant. My treacherous stomach lurched at the sight of him. He saw me and came straight over.

'Dad said he saw you on TV, and you're in the paper too.'

'The Extinction Rebellion protest is.'

'They say you're a YouTube phenomenon.'

'The press exaggerates.' Why was I underplaying what we'd done? I should stop. He seemed so defeated I felt sorry for him.

'Look can we talk?' He asked, glancing at Ed who was staring at me. I didn't know what to do. Grant was standing next to Ed. Both looking straight at me. I couldn't help comparing them. Ed had a square open face and a strong sturdy body. He looked the way he felt, reliable, steady, kind. He couldn't compete with Grant's looks.

Grant focused his slanting green eyes on me. His tall lean body seemed to ooze sexuality. He gave me a rueful smile. I thought about his lips, where they'd been on my body.

'I messed up Pen,' Grant said. 'I'm an idiot. I didn't mean to hurt you.'

Ed started to pack up his books. His head had gone down, no longer looking at me. I didn't know what to do. But then my body did that thing again, acted of its own accord. My hand reached out and grasped Ed's arm to stop him from leaving.

'Don't go,' I said. Then I looked up at Grant.

'You're okay, don't worry about it. I'm fine.' I said. Because I was.

Grant stared at me for a moment then turned and walked out of the room. Ed and I went back to work. Under the table, my foot decided to stretch out until it rubbed against Ed's.

Coming Soon

Dance Like Your Soul's On Fire

the final part in the On Fire trilogy.

Pen Flowers is living the dream. She's moved to London to study Contemporary Dance. When she's offered a life-changing opportunity she leaps in with her usual enthusiasm and courage.

What can possibly go wrong?

In the final part of the On Fire trilogy Pen is confronted by impossible choices. How much can she sacrifice for her art? Battling despair, she's forced to confront her own failings and wrestle with what living and dancing with integrity demands of her.

Acknowledgements

Writing a novel is always an adventure. Research for Love Like Your Heart's On Fire took me to Birmingham the summer after the Commonwealth Games where I found a city boisterous with energy and confidence. I spent an exciting night out in Digbeth exploring a world I wouldn't otherwise have seen.

I'm grateful to the staff and pupils at Caister Academy, particularly the members of Write Club, for answering my questions and sharing their experiences. Thanks to the Sixth form class at Norwich School who made me welcome and challenged me with their opinions.

To the worldwide community of Lindy hop and Balboa dancers, particularly my friends at Fine City Swing, thank you for reawakening my love of dance and for the many delightful hours spent in your company. Thanks for all the dances, guys.

Thank you to Professor Rupert Read for access and information on climate justice activism.

Heartfelt gratitude to two organisations who have done so much to support me as a writer and who do fantastic work for the wider writing community. I could not have got here without the National Centre for Writing and The Literary Consultancy.

I would like to acknowledge All Blacks Experience for the contextual information about Ko Uhia Mai, the Black Ferns Haka, and for the translation from the Māori to English.

Every writer needs a team of supporters. Thank you to my first readers Mia Sharrock and Hannah Edwards for their invaluable insights and suggestions.

Thank you to Sara Willett, Rebecca Stirrup, Rachel Higgs, Cath Sharrock, Ella Sharrock, Paula Morris, Cory Pohley, Elizabeth Jolly, Sarah-Jane Pearce, Alice Noon, Michael Gamlen, Andrea Cornes, Johnny Fincham, Sarah Passingham, Amanda Addison, Richard Lambert, Els Beerten, and Agnes Lillis who have been lavish in their enthusiasm.

Thank you to the readers of my Substack blog who have followed the journey of this novel and cheered me on. Sallyannelomas.substack.com – please join us.

To Mum, Robin, and Rod, thank you for being my biggest fans, your regular encouragement on family zoom kept me going.

Thank you to my friend and mentor, Yvvette Edwards, for being my writing buddy. When I close my eyes and think of writing this novel, I see you sitting at the table opposite me tapping away.

Thank you to the team at Story Machine for their talent and hard work on behalf of this story. Most gratitude to my editor and publisher, Sam Ruddock, whose creative vision and generous heart are forging new pathways in fiction.

Finally, to Blue, the best dog ever, for teaching me how to love. And Tony, for, well, everything.

Thank you for supporting planet-positive publishing

Story Machine seeks to have a net positive social and environmental impact. That means the environment and people's lives are actually better off for every book we print. Story Machine offsets our entire carbon footprint plus 10% through a www.ClimateCare.org programme. We are now investing in converting to use only 100% renewable energies and seeking out the most planet-positive means of shipping books to our readers.

The printing industry is a huge polluter, requiring the use of huge amounts of water, toxic chemicals, and energy. Even FSC certified mix paper sources drive deforestation. That's why we are proud to be working with www.Seacort.net, a global leader in planet positive printing. Not only have they developed a waterless and chemical-free process, they use only 100% renewable energies, FSC certified recycled paper, and direct absolutely no waste to landfill. That's why they were crowned Europe's most sustainable SME in 2017, and have been recognised as one of the top three environmental printers in the world.

Planet-positive printing costs us a little more. But we think this is a small price to pay for a better world, today and in the future. If you agree, please share our message, and encourage other publishers and authors to commit to planet-positive printing. Stories can change the world. They deserve publishers that want to make sure they do.

Together, we can make publishing more sustainable.